Praise for N.J. Walters'
Alexandra's Legacy

"N. J. Walters offers heat, passion, and intrigue with Alexandra's Legacy..."
~ *TwoLips Reviews*

"This book, from the beginning, is intense. It has what every top notch paranormal should have: action, passion, and wolfies, to die for. I, for one, cannot wait to see what the next book in the Legacy series holds."
~ *Dark Diva Reviews*

"The action-packed plot kept me hanging on the edge of my seat with exciting anticipation eager to discover just how the breathtaking story would unfold. I can't wait to get my hands on the next thrilling novel in this series!"
~ *Fallen Angel Reviews*

"N. J. Walters writes with such passion and gives so much to all of these characters. This is one to read more than once and enjoy every time. But don't be surprised if your fingers blister just a bit; I promise it is worth it in the end."
~ *Long and Short Reviews*

"I highly recommend this to paranormal romance lovers. You might want to get a fan - this story isn't just good - it's HOT!"
~ *Paranormal Romance Reviews*

Look for these titles by
N.J. Walters

Now Available:

The Jamesville Series:

Discovering Dani (Book 1)

The Way Home (Book 2)

The Return of Patrick O'Rourke (Book 3)

The Seduction of Shamus O'Rourke (Book 4)

A Legal Affair (Book 5)

By the Book (Book 6)

Past Promises (Book 7)

The Legacy Series

Alexandra's Legacy (Book 1)

Alexandra's Legacy

N.J. Walters

A Samhain publishing, Ltd. publication.

Samhain Publishing, Ltd.
577 Mulberry Street, Suite 1520
Macon, GA 31201
www.samhainpublishing.com

Alexandra's Legacy
Copyright © 2010 by N.J. Walters
Print ISBN: 978-1-60504-778-2
Digital ISBN: 978-1-60504-803-1

Editing by Heidi Moore
Cover by Tuesday Dube

First Samhain Publishing, Ltd. electronic publication: October 2009
First Samhain Publishing, Ltd. print publication: August 2010

Dedication

This book is for Gerard. Thank you for always believing.

Thank you to my amazing editor, Heidi Moore. Your sharp eye and timely suggestions always make my books better. I promise to strike certain words from my vocabulary...or at least to use them more sparingly.

Chapter One

She could feel the eyes watching her as she ambled down the sidewalk. The street looked deserted, but Alexandra Riley wasn't fooled by appearances. She'd grown up in Chicago, and although this was a working-class neighborhood, she knew the walls and alleys had eyes and ears.

The night dwellers were beginning to slink back into their daytime hideaways until the sun set again. A new day was just breaking, and the streetlights were beginning to wink out as the dawn brightened the sky. The people of the South Side were just beginning to roll out of bed, getting ready to start another working day.

Juggling two large, hot steaming coffees and a bag of freshly baked blueberry muffins, Alex headed for the large building at the end of the street. Although she was very aware of her surroundings, she wasn't afraid. This was her home and, for better or worse, these were her people. They all knew her, but more than that, they knew her father. And James Riley would cheerfully rip the head off anyone who so much as stared at her the wrong way.

A whisper of movement caught her eye and she tensed only to relax a moment later.

"Hi, Divine."

The aging prostitute was on her way home after a hard night's work. Alex didn't know how Divine could do what she did, but she didn't look down on the other woman. Everyone made their own choices and did what they had to in order to survive.

"Morning, Alex." Divine tottered over on her high-heeled,

black leather boots. The tops of her boots came to her knees, leaving a large expanse of bare leg between it and the bottom of her skirt. Her voice was raspy, her eyes bloodshot. Too many years of smoking, drinking and whoring had left their mark. Her bleached blonde hair was mussed, her make-up all but disappeared, showing the age of the woman beneath the façade.

"Hard night?" Alex stopped as Divine came alongside her.

"Strange night." She paused, glancing nervously over her shoulder. "There's some weird shit going on."

Alex could feel the hair on the nape of her neck rise. Someone was watching them. "What kind of shit?" For the past couple of days, feelings of unease had been her constant companion.

Divine shrugged, eyeing the coffee in Alex's hand. "Everyone is tense. Jumpy. There seems to be a lot of *them* prowling around."

Alex shifted her weight from one foot to the other, not quite sure what to say. She knew Divine believed that vampires, werewolves, witches and demons populated the city, living alongside the rest of the population. Personally, Alex thought that Divine had done too much drugs before she'd finally kicked the habit a year ago.

Thankfully, Divine didn't seem to need a reply. She pulled her tattered sweater tighter around her shoulders and shivered. "It's safe enough in the daytime. Those creatures like the night."

The city didn't need vampires or demons to make it unsafe. There were enough weirdoes and criminals for that. But Divine was right about one thing, most of them usually only came out after the sun went down. "You be careful." Alex knew it was no good to tell Divine to stay home. If she didn't work, she didn't eat.

"I will." She stared at the coffee, licking her lips.

Alex sighed inwardly even as she handed over one of the steaming beverages. "Here. You look like you could use this." Coffee was one of Alex's weaknesses, and one she indulged on a regular basis. Otto Bykowski, over at the bakery, kept a supply of her favorite roast on hand for her daily visits.

"You sure?" she asked even as she reached for the recycled paper cup, wrapping her red-tipped fingernails around it.

"Yeah. I'm sure."

"Thanks, Alex. Say hi to your dad for me." Divine raised the cup to her lips, gulping the beverage as she stumbled off toward home.

"Sure," Alex mumbled as she watched her coffee disappear. Turning her head slowly, she scanned the buildings that surrounded her. Some were more derelict than others, covered in graffiti, but others were clean and well kept, the gang slogans and racial slurs rigorously scrubbed off the walls each time they appeared.

There was a core of decent, hardworking people in her neighborhood who fought the never-ending battle to keep their homes and businesses from falling into disrepair. Urban renewal was happening all over the city, but it hadn't quite reached every corner of their little section of it. But it was only a matter of time. The large garage at the end of the street was in better repair than most. Sensing all was right, for the moment, Alex strode toward her destination.

This was the only world that Alex had ever known. She smiled as she stepped up onto the sidewalk, ignoring the cracks and crevices that split it. The faded red brick building in front of her might not be everyone's idea of home, but it was hers. She'd grown up in the large apartment above the garage.

As quietly as possible, she twisted the handle on the door and eased it open. It wasn't locked. Her father was always up early and unlocked it for her. Grinning, she slid through the small opening, keeping her back against the wall. Her booted feet made no sound on the concrete floor. The sun was just beginning to break over the city as the door slid silently shut behind her.

"About time you got here." The gruff voice came from down low to the ground. She could see her father's legs sticking out from beneath a vintage Mustang.

Alex shook her head and puffed out a huge sigh as she strode across the room, depositing the lone coffee and the muffins on the long, tool-lined workbench. "What gave me away?" She'd never been able to sneak up on her father, no matter how hard she tried. No one could.

He rolled out from beneath the car and stood, slowly

unfolding his large, lithe body. "Coffee."

Alex grinned. Her father was a man of few words. "Oh." She feigned surprise. "Did you want coffee?"

He stalked toward her, his gait loose and limber. Reaching out, he snagged the paper cup even as he leaned down to nuzzle the top of her head in a familiar, affectionate caress. "Brat."

Alex laughed as he pried off the lid and downed half the brew in one swallow. Her father did love his coffee. And she was her father's daughter. The smell of the rich coffee blend made her groan.

He lowered the cup and licked his lips. "Who'd you give yours to?" He knew her so well.

"Divine. She looked as if she could use it worse than me. She said to say hi." Alex rubbed her hands over her arms, her fleece sweatshirt doing little to warm her as a chill shot down her spine. "She said that there's some strange shit going on at night, as well as strangers prowling around the neighborhood."

Slowly, he lowered the cup back to the workbench, his golden brown eyes burning with some inner fire. "Did she say who?"

"No. I don't think she knew. You know Divine. She sees vampires, demons and werewolves everywhere." Alex hesitated, wondering if she should tell her father about her unusual feelings the past few days. She immediately decided against it. He was already overprotective enough over her. She'd had to fight with him for a year before he'd agreed to let her move to her own place just down the road. And even then his acceptance had been grudgingly given. She was twenty-two years old for crying out loud. She didn't want to be living with her father, no matter how much she loved him.

"What's wrong?" As always, he'd sensed her disquiet and responded immediately, ready to handle whatever problem was bothering her. He'd been that way since she was a child.

Some kids in the neighborhood might have been neglected or abused, but not Alex. Her earliest memory was of her father caring for her, loving her. She'd even been home-schooled, learning how to read and write in this very room. There had been field trips to the Art Institute of Chicago, the Harold

Washington Library and the Lincoln Park Zoo. He'd taken her to the theatre and to hear opera and blues music. And since the ballpark was close by, they'd spent many an afternoon cheering on the White Sox.

As she'd grown older, he'd taught her how to fix cars and how to survive. She knew how to defend herself, how to handle a knife and how to shoot a gun. It was the two of them against the world.

And now he was waiting for a response from her. He'd wait all day if he had to. He was nothing if not patient. Not to mention stubborn. She knew because she was just like him. She shrugged. "Nothing."

His eyes narrowed and his lips pursed into a thin line. She sighed and shook her head. She was a grown woman, but she still couldn't manage to hide anything from her father. "Okay, it's just a feeling."

"What kind of feeling?" He picked up his coffee and handed it to her when she shivered again.

Taking it gratefully, she gulped down the warm brew, needing the heat as well as the caffeine kick. "Just uneasiness." She hesitated briefly, but in the end, told him the truth. "This morning, I felt like someone was watching me."

"You'll move back in with me for a few weeks." It was a pronouncement, not a suggestion.

As much as Alex loved her small apartment and her privacy, she wasn't stupid. The feeling of apprehension, coupled with the sense of being watched this morning, had really creeped her out. If there were strangers skulking around the neighborhood like Divine said, then maybe it wouldn't hurt to stay with her dad for a while. Gang violence didn't often spill over into their neighborhood, but it did happen.

"Okay, I'll stay tonight. Just until things settle down again." If she weren't careful, her father would have her moved back in with him permanently. She loved him dearly, but she needed her own space, and he tended to be overprotective.

Taking the empty cup from her hand, he chucked it in the garbage bin and drew her into his strong arms. She snuggled close, breathing in his familiar smell of engine oil and sandalwood soap. That smell meant home to her. His lips brushed the top of her hair. "I won't let anyone hurt you."

"I know," she whispered. And she did know. Her father would protect her with his life. "I'm sure it's nothing."

"Maybe." He released her and stepped back. "But I'm not taking any chances. I've been feeling a bit uneasy myself the past few days. I'll go back to your place with you after work so that you can pick up a few things."

If her father was on edge she needed to pay attention, even if it meant curtailing her independence for a short while. James Riley had an uncanny way of being able to read the vibes of the city, knowing when violence was about to erupt. Illegal drugs and liquor often mixed with anger and despair, and sometimes the combination was lethal.

Her father jerked his head toward the back room. "I've got a small bag of coffee out back if you want some."

"Do I ever. You're a lifesaver." Alex licked her lips. The taste she'd had was just enough to make her crave more. She watched as her father opened the brown paper bag and withdrew the muffins she'd picked up. "I'd better start a pot of coffee. Those few mouthfuls won't hold either one of us for long."

Leaving his watchful eyes behind, she hurried into the office area and grabbed the empty carafe. Stepping into the small bathroom, she thrust it beneath the water tap, allowing her thoughts to wander as it filled.

Alex was still no closer to knowing exactly why she was so edgy. The hair on the back of her neck seemed to be standing permanently on end, and on occasion she experienced a rippling beneath her skin that raised goose bumps on her flesh.

She hadn't felt like herself for a few weeks now. The changes had been so gradual she hadn't really noticed them at first. It was as if her senses were heightened. Her skin felt too tight and at night it itched, not enough to make her scratch, but just enough to make her squirm.

The worst of it was the heat.

Lying alone in her single bed at night, a warm tingling would start between her thighs, little more than a flutter at first. Gradually the tingle became a deep, pulsing throb that made her writhe on top of her sheets, unable to bear even the light touch of the fabric against her skin.

The warmth grew within her, building rapidly until her skin felt as if it was on fire. Like a living creature, the heat slid over her belly, climbing up her ribs one at a time, until it enveloped her breasts. Her nipples puckered and tightened painfully. The only way to relieve the ache was for her to touch herself.

Only it never really helped, instead it drove the heat and need to higher levels. After the first few times it had happened, she'd learned to hold on tight to the sheets and ride out the painful desires that splintered through her, finally ending her nights sweat-soaked and completely exhausted.

The familiar heat washed over her now. Her nipples stiffened, pressing against the fabric of her cheap cotton bra. Low in her belly, her inner muscles spasmed and her panties grew damp. She jerked her hand back as the water spilled over the side of the carafe. Swearing, she hauled it back and gave the tap a twist, stopping the water flow.

Pouring out the excess, she strode back into the office. She dumped the water into the coffeemaker and slammed the carafe down onto the burner, wincing at the loud crack. She was damned lucky she hadn't broken it. Grabbing the small bag of coffee, she opened it. The rich smell of coffee wafted up and she breathed deeply, inhaling the fragrant aroma. She found a spoon and loaded ground coffee into the filter. Flicking on the machine, she prayed it would be quick.

Stepping back to the doorway separating the garage from the office, she leaned against the doorframe and studied her father. He was about six-foot-two. She'd gotten her height from him. At five-foot-ten, she was tall for a woman. She'd also inherited his strong, lithe build. Her father was deceptively strong. Many larger men had made the mistake of challenging him to a fight, assuming he'd be an easy mark. They quickly figured out their mistake.

They had the same colored hair too—brown, but with just about every shade or variation of that color from amber to mahogany. Her father's shoulder-length hair was tied back in a thong, but it was tinged with silver at the temples, making his appearance even fiercer. Alex kept her hair cut short on the back and sides, longer on the top. Made it easier to take care of.

She wasn't the type of woman to waste money on expensive beauty products or to primp in front of a mirror. Strictly a wash-and-go girl, the style suited her just fine.

Their eyes were very different. Her father's eyes were a piercing golden brown while hers were a pale, silvery gray. James Riley's eyes were always searching, always aware of his surroundings, but when they settled on you it was as if he could see into your very soul.

For about the thousandth time, she wondered why he'd never married. Heck, he'd never even had a steady girlfriend. She wasn't stupid. She knew that he went out prowling some nights and enjoyed female company, but he never brought any of them home. Did he ever get lonely?

Her mother had been a prostitute who'd tried to go straight and had gotten pregnant. When James Riley had discovered he was the father, he'd taken her into his home and looked after her until she'd had the baby. She'd run off just two days after Alex was born, unable to cope with motherhood. She'd never met the woman, didn't know if she was even still alive and, truthfully, didn't care. Having a kid to raise certainly hadn't helped her father find a woman. Yet, he never once made her feel as though he'd have it any other way.

Raising her hand, she rubbed it over her breastbone. Maybe it was loneliness she was feeling at night as she lay in her bed. God only knows, she'd felt like a freak growing up. While other girls her age had been boy crazy, all she'd wanted to do was tinker in the garage with her father. She plain just wasn't interested. She'd been kissed more than once, even engaged in some heavy petting in her teens, but she'd never had sex with a guy. It just hadn't seemed worth the effort. Now, she wondered.

"You want to bring me a cup of that coffee?" Her father's voice yanked her from her thoughts. What was wrong with her? She was never this distracted, at least not in front of her father. He was much too astute and attuned to her moods.

Yanking down two large black ceramic mugs from the shelf above the coffeemaker, she filled them with the thick, potent brew. Black for her father, two sugars for her. Wiping her moist palms on her jeans, she took a deep breath and picked up the mugs. She had to get a grip on herself. It was time to go to work.

She loved the garage. Loved working side by side with her father, repairing vehicles of all kinds—trucks, cars and the more popular, and certainly more affordable, motorcycles. Cars had changed quite a bit over the years, but her father could fix them all. The man was a wizard when it came to vintage cars and had gained a reputation among collectors. Since her father wouldn't leave Chicago, wealthy clients came from all over the country to gain his expertise. Many brought their own private security team to protect their expensive vehicles.

Alex had questioned her father once about why they didn't move somewhere else. Not that there was anything wrong with Chicago. She loved the vibrancy of the city, the unique ethnic heritage that made it so exciting. But Alex had always wondered what it would be like to live in the countryside where the constant noise of humanity was silent. The city never slept. Traffic, both vehicular and human, kept the streets alive twenty-four hours a day, seven days a week.

They had enough money, as her father's specialized skills did not come cheap. "Because it's safer here," had been his soft-spoken reply. His answer hadn't made much sense to her since they lived in arguably what many would consider a dangerous area, but the look in his eyes had been so bleak and sad, she'd never brought up the subject again. But she did wonder.

He'd passed all his mechanic skills onto her and she was quickly gaining a reputation of her own. She could easily have moved out of the neighborhood and set up her own vehicle-repair business, but instead she'd settled just up the road, continuing to work with her father. She didn't want to leave him. He was the only family she had. Chicago might give the members of the city council and police force the occasional sleepless night, but to her it was home.

"What's on tap for today?" She handed her father his coffee and took a sip of hers as she reached for her muffin.

"Not much. The Mustang." He motioned to the vehicle that he'd been under when she'd arrived. "There's two Ducatis you need to check out. I bought them from a guy and he delivered them last night. Just check the work orders."

Motorcycles were Alex's specialty. She loved the speed and the freedom they offered. Her eyes lit up as she gazed at the two beauties in the far corner, just waiting for her to work her magic. "Sweet." She planned on convincing her father to give her a deal on one of these fine machines.

"Alexandra."

She stilled. He rarely ever called her by her given name, always calling her Alex. When he did, it usually meant trouble.

"Yes." She struggled not to squirm beneath his penetrating gaze.

"We need to talk. Tonight." His eyes shifted away from her and he rubbed his hand over his face. She noticed that he needed a shave. Peering closer, she realized he looked tired.

Now she was really starting to get worried. "What's wrong?" She leaned into his chest, wanting to comfort him. He wrapped his arm around her shoulders, and the huge sigh he let out ruffled the hair on top of her head.

"There are some things I've got to tell you. Things you need to know about your heritage." There was a grim note in his voice that she'd never heard before. Her father was her rock, her foundation, but she could tell this was something he was very apprehensive about.

"Is it about her?" Alex knew he would know she was referring to her birthmother. She'd never called the woman by her given name even though she knew it.

"No, it's not about Charlene. It's about me." He drew back and cupped her face in his hands. "Just remember that I love you." Leaning down, he placed a gentle kiss on her forehead. "Every decision I've made has been with your best interest in mind."

Alex was quickly moving past worried and heading directly into the realm of deeply concerned. "Whatever it is, it's okay." The need to reassure her father overrode everything else, even her fears.

"I hope you can still say that after you hear what I have to say." He dropped his hands and stepped back. "Tonight. I'll explain everything tonight. In the meantime, don't leave the garage without me. Promise me."

She could sense the tension rolling through her father. Her

own body felt tight. Stiff. "I promise." She couldn't help but sense that her world was about to change in some fundamental way and it would never be the same again. Another shiver raced up her spine and she hugged herself, wishing she'd layered another shirt under her sweatshirt.

His face softened for the briefest of seconds. "It will be all right, Alex."

"I know." She didn't know anything at all at this point, but she was desperately trying to act as if everything was normal. She needed that if she was going to make it through today. It would do no good to demand he tell her everything now. He'd said tonight, so tonight it would be.

Work. She would focus on work. She'd been handling tools and working on vehicles since she was old enough to walk. She could lose herself in the beauty of a fine-tuned engine.

The door behind them slammed open, hitting the wall with a bang. Alex spun around and came face-to-face with a stranger. Huge was an understatement. Shaggy black hair framed a rough-hewn face, all angles and planes. His lips were thin, his eyes dark and piercing as they traced her body from head to foot. Menace seeped from every pore of his skin. Alex stood frozen in her tracks.

Her father jumped in front of her, a low growl emanating from deep inside him. Tension swelled, filling every nook and corner of the room. The stranger turned his gaze from her and focused on her father, but somehow Alex knew that he was still very aware of her.

His lips parted, giving him a strangely sensual, yet cruel appearance. "They're coming for her."

Chapter Two

Joshua Striker's heart was pounding, although outwardly none of his excitement or agitation showed. He'd found her. It hadn't been easy, but he'd managed to stay one step ahead of the two roving packs of wolves searching for her. She was a treasure and they all wanted her.

He could barely see her now, blocked by the bulk of her father's body. But the one glimpse he'd had of her had been more than enough to fire his blood. He could almost feel her long, slender body bucking beneath his as he thrust hard and deep. He wanted to fuck her until she was screaming with pleasure, until they were both sweaty and spent. And then he'd do it all over again.

His cock swelled in anticipation, pressing hard against the zipper of his jeans. A fine sheen of sweat formed on his skin, making it itch. His scalp tingled, his muscles tightened. He shook his head to clear away the haze of lust enveloping him. Now was definitely not the time for this. His job was to protect her, not to claim her.

The man in front of him issued another low growl. James LeVeau, or rather James Riley as he called himself now, had disappeared from the Wolf Creek pack of werewolves in North Carolina almost fifty years ago. At the time he'd been the alpha of the pack, the toughest and smartest one of them all. After his beloved wife, Leda, had died in childbirth, he'd simply vanished.

There had been plenty of rumors over the years. The most intriguing one was that he'd had a child with a human, a daughter. Now they all knew the rumor was true and she was a prospective mate for many of the single male wolves.

The past hundred years had not been kind to the werewolves and their numbers were dwindling at an alarming rate. The past three decades had been even worse. Children were far and few between, as were females of mating age.

Personally, Joshua felt that had more to do with all the infighting between packs, but the reality remained that they needed children to expand their population. The fact that she was the daughter of one of the most powerful, most well-respected wolves in the country was a bonus. Whoever she mated with would immediately gain in status and standing.

"I come from Wolf Creek. Ian sent me."

That gave the older man pause, but he didn't back down or relax his stance. "Who are you?"

"Striker." James blinked, but gave no other indication of what he was thinking. Joshua admired the other man's self-possession.

"Last I heard Miguel was Striker of the Wolf Creek pack."

"He was my father." It still hurt for Joshua to think of his father. The large man had seemed invincible to his sons, but death had claimed him all the same.

"Was?" The very stillness of the other man assured Joshua that he was ready to spring and fight at any second.

"It took four rogue wolves and several humans to bring him down." He wanted to tip back his head and howl with the sorrow that was his constant companion. Instead, Joshua swallowed, refusing to show any of the emotion beating at him. "He was searching for you."

"You're young Joshua." James' eyes narrowed as they raked over the younger man.

"I was. Now I am Striker of the Wolf Creek pack." Striker was more than just their name, it was his family's duty within the pack. The head of the Striker family was in charge of pack security, of protecting the alpha pair and the pack as a whole. That duty had fallen to him and he would not fail, no matter the cost.

"I am sorry to hear about your father. He was the best of us." Joshua could not mistake the sincerity and the sorrow in James' voice. "I missed him."

"Why did you never contact him?" The biting question was

past his lips before he could restrain it. Joshua was angry with himself for letting his emotion show. It was a weakness he could not afford.

"It was not safe. I had too much to lose." James shook his head. "In those days they would not have accepted my child. She was not of pure blood." He gave a bitter laugh. "Times have changed in the past few decades, have they not? Back then, they might have killed her, now they want to claim her." His features hardened and the alpha warrior was revealed. "I will do whatever it takes to protect her."

"Dad?" Her low, lilting voice washed over Joshua like a physical caress, making it hard for him to breathe. "What's this all about? Who is this guy?" He could hear the uncertainty, the question in her voice as she stepped out from behind her father.

James reached out his hand and wrapped it around her shoulder, pulling her beneath the shelter of his arm. "This is part of what I needed to speak to you about." His gaze never left Joshua's face. "Lock the door and come upstairs. We have to talk."

Joshua turned away from the pair, purposely leaving his back exposed. Taking his time, he threw all six bolts on the door. When he was done, he faced them and cocked his eyebrow in question. The older man motioned to a doorway at the far end of the garage.

He strode past them, trying not to stare at the woman. He didn't know her name, but he knew that he wanted her. Something about her reached deep inside him, demanding that he claim her as his own. With his preternatural sense of smell, he caught a faint whiff of her scent and almost moaned. She was close to coming into heat, but not quite there yet. At the moment, it was just the faintest tantalizing perfume that made his head spin and sent lust surging through his bloodstream. Layered over that was the clean scent of woman, her own personal fragrance. It was fresh, like the mountain wildflowers after a summer's rain.

And he was obviously losing his mind if he was waxing poetic when there was a pissed-off alpha at his back and danger surrounding them all. If he didn't keep his mind on business, he'd never live long enough to have a chance to claim his woman.

And she was his. She just didn't know it yet.

Alex could barely breathe as she climbed the stairs with her father. What was going on? Who was this man? And what the hell did he have to do with her father? She hadn't understood half of what they'd said to each other, only that her father somehow knew this man. He was obviously part of the big secret her father had been planning to reveal to her tonight. Now that the time had come to find out, she wasn't sure she wanted to know.

Sucking in a deep breath, she kept her eyes on the stranger—Joshua Striker he'd said his name was—as he climbed the stairs in front of them. She was very aware of her father's heavy arm wrapped protectively around her. He was incredibly tense and there was a feeling of anticipation, of primal excitement, that permeated the air. It was the same electric sensation that was usually a precursor to violence.

Joshua stepped up onto the landing at the top of the stairs.

"Left," her father told him. Joshua didn't even break stride, but kept going. When he reached the door, he turned the handle and went inside.

They followed him and her father paused long enough to close and bolt the door. All this secrecy was making her extremely nervous. As if sensing her growing agitation, her father gave her a quick hug before releasing her and heading straight for the large bookcase that dominated one of the four walls in the living room. Pressing a hidden latch on the side, he waited until there was a soft click and then he pulled the bookcase forward. It slid easily, revealing a small cache of weapons in the secret cubby behind it.

"Alex." He motioned her forward and she hurried to his side, very aware of Joshua watching their every move. The fact that her father wanted her armed scared her straight down to her soul.

"Impressive." Joshua did look impressed, she thought as she grabbed two knives and shoved one in each of her boots. Satisfied, she reached for the regular handgun she used for target practice, but her father stayed her hand.

"No." He opened a small metal box on one of the shelves, reached inside and pulled out a 9mm semi-automatic. Popping the magazine, he checked the ammunition before slamming it home. He handed it to her. "Regular bullets are useless. You'll need this."

She automatically hooked the holster over her belt before checking the weapon herself. The ammunition looked different. "I don't understand."

Worry etched his face and the smile he gave her was filled with sorrow. "I know you don't, honey." He strapped a knife onto his belt while he talked. "Those bullets contain silver. What we're fighting isn't human."

Her mouth went dry and she glanced over at Joshua, who stood silently watching.

"You can't be serious." Her father was acting as weird as Divine had this morning. "There's no such thing as vampires, demons and werewolves. They're just a myth."

"Yes, there is." He tucked a knife in each of his boots. "We're dealing with werewolves and the only way to kill one is to break its neck, cut out its heart, decapitate it or poison it with silver. Regular bullets will slow it down some, but will mostly just piss it off. That's why the bullets and the knife blades are coated in silver."

Oh, God. Her father had lost his mind. There was no other explanation. Divine had been talking more and more about these creatures for the past year, even going as far as to claim she'd seen a vampire lurking in the shadows one night. Werewolves, Divine declared, mostly kept to the heavy woods outside the cities, roaming wild and free. Everyone gave them a wide berth or they paid the price, as wolves weren't exactly known for being sociable to anyone outside their species.

"Dad?" Alex didn't quite know where to begin. She wondered if she should call an ambulance. Maybe her father was having a stroke or something. Although he looked as healthy and vital as ever.

James shook his head. "I'm not crazy, Alex. Werewolves are real."

Wolf Creek pack. Her eyes flew to the man waiting patiently on the other side of the room. Did that mean he thought he was a werewolf? She swallowed hard, trying to grasp the situation. What did he want with her father and her?

Her father stepped back and pushed the bookcase toward the wall where it caught with a soft click. The whole situation was surreal. Alex had only gotten out of bed an hour ago, her life a predictable routine that she enjoyed. It was safe. Now in a matter of minutes that world no longer existed.

Joshua's eyes were flitting back and forth from her to her father. She could see the wariness in them when they glanced toward her father, but they were filled with something totally different when they fell upon her.

Lust. Pure, unadulterated lust.

She'd never seen that look in a man's eyes before. At least not directed toward her. The worst part was that it didn't disgust her or frighten her as it ought to. He was a werewolf for heaven's sake. Or at least thought he was. She wasn't quite convinced there was anything to this but deluded madness.

She felt a yearning growing deep inside her, one she didn't fully understand. Heat suffused her body, pooling between her thighs. She longed to walk up to this stranger and rub her breasts against his muscular chest and grind her pussy against the hard bulge in the front of his jeans.

What was wrong with her?

"Alex." The bite in her father's voice startled her and her eyes flew to him. He was watching her with an unreadable expression on his face. Part sadness, part determination and part resignation.

"What's going on?" Enough was enough. Time to get to the bottom of this. She had to know what was going on. Surely it couldn't be as bad as anything her imagination could conjure.

"Sit down."

She thought about arguing, but sank down in the plush, purple chair that sat next to the sofa. It was her chair, had been since she was a child. She needed the familiarity and the comfort it offered. Her father sank to his haunches in front of her. She noted that he made sure his back wasn't to the other man. "Tell me," she prompted when he hesitated.

"I was married a long time ago." His voice softened, as he got lost in the memories. Alex was shocked. This was the first she'd heard of this. "She died in childbirth. I lost both her and the child at the same time. It was more than I could bear, so I left my old life behind and started a new one."

"I'm sorry." Reaching out, she stroked her hand over his face, wanting to comfort him. His grief was like a living, breathing thing, still fresh after all these years. She wondered what it must be like to love someone so deeply it still hurt after so long.

Her father wrapped his fingers around her hand and held it to his chest. She could feel the steady thump of his heart. "When I found out Charlene was pregnant with you, I was overjoyed, but scared to death." His eyes seemed to glow pure molten gold as he stared at her. "I couldn't lose you."

"You didn't." She didn't question her need to reassure him. For the first time in her life, she finally understood why he was so protective of her.

"No. I didn't." He sighed. "But it meant I could never go back to my old life. The people there wouldn't have accepted you. They might even have tried to hurt you. I couldn't allow that to happen."

Now they were getting somewhere. "You mentioned that downstairs. I don't understand what you mean. You know these people, these werewolves, don't you?" She couldn't believe she was actually buying into the whole werewolf thing, but her father was deadly serious.

"Yes." He closed his eyes for the briefest of seconds and when he opened them again the sorrow was gone and only the determination remained. "I am one of them."

Alex jerked away, her back hitting the seat cushion behind her. She couldn't believe what she was hearing. "You..." She broke off, unable to continue. Rubbing her damp palms over her jeans, she took a deep breath and tried again. "You're a werewolf?" The implications were staggering. If what her father was saying was true, her entire life was a lie.

"Yes, I am." He paused and then took both her hands in his, ignoring her attempt to pull away. "And so are you. Not a pure-blooded werewolf, but a half-breed."

"What does that mean?" Her voice was little more than a whisper even though she was screaming inside. It was as if she no longer even knew herself. Who was she?

"It means that you will come into adulthood soon. We mature later than humans because we live much longer."

"How much longer and what do you mean 'come into adulthood'?" She was very afraid that the last thing had something to do with the unfamiliar feelings she'd been having lately. The late nights spent writhing on her bed as heat consumed her.

"We have a lifespan of about five hundred years or so. I am one-hundred-and-sixty years old."

Alex heard a buzzing in her ears. Impossible. He didn't look a day over forty. Her father tensed and swiveled, placing himself square in front of her when Joshua stepped closer.

"He's telling the truth, Alex." She could hear Joshua speaking as if from a great distance. She shook her head to try to clear it, but that only made her dizzier. "You are more werewolf than human. I can smell it. I can sense it. You will go through the change after you mate."

"Enough. Back off, Striker." Her father's voice was low and cold, cutting through the younger man's words. "It is her choice. I will not have that taken from her and I will kill anyone who tries to force her."

Joshua nodded respectfully and backed away. Alex sensed he was merely biding his time.

"Dad?" She wanted him to tell her this was all a bad joke, that her life hadn't been one big lie up until now. But from the grim look on her father's face, this was anything but a joke. This was very, very real. "Change? Mating?" She blinked rapidly as the room revolved around her.

Her father swore and she felt his hand on the back of her head pressing it toward her knees. "Breathe, Alexandra. Just take one slow breath at a time. Focus, honey."

Alex concentrated on pulling air into her lungs and finally the buzzing in her ears subsided and she felt stronger. She raised her head and met his worried gaze. "Explain it all to me. I need to understand."

"Females come into heat for the first time when they are in their early twenties. It varies from woman to woman, but it is always within a two-year span from age twenty-one to twenty-three." He sent a hard glare toward Joshua and the younger man faded back toward the kitchen. "You've been feeling restless lately, maybe having sexual feelings for the first time in your life. Your body is yearning for something, but you're not sure what for."

Alex could feel the heat creeping up her cheeks and knew she was blushing. This was definitely not a conversation she wanted to be having with her father. The fact that he knew what she'd been feeling these past few weeks was totally embarrassing. All she could manage was a single nod. She couldn't look at him.

He wouldn't allow her to hide from him. Hooking his thumb beneath her chin, he tilted it upward until she was facing him. "There is nothing to be embarrassed about. It is perfectly normal. It means you are a healthy, vibrant young woman who is ready to start a life and a family of her own."

"There's got to be more to it than just that." She wasn't stupid. If it was just a matter of her becoming an adult, it shouldn't be any big deal.

"Unfortunately there is." He offered her a smile that didn't quite reach his eyes. "For any species, survival depends upon procreation. To keep the population healthy, mother nature has built in a few extra features."

She was afraid to ask, but more afraid of not knowing. "What extras?"

"You'll soon go into heat. Your body will crave a male. You'll need him, want him with a fierceness that will shock you. It is the time that you will choose your mate. Your scent will draw any unmated werewolves for miles and they will all fight to be the one who claims you."

"You mean they can smell me?" Her voice grew louder with every word she spoke, until she was practically yelling. She tried to stay calm, but that was impossible. This was unbelievable, like something out of a nightmare, except Alex knew she was wide awake. "They know I'm aroused. In heat like some bloody animal." She didn't know whether to laugh or cry. It was crazy.

"Yes. It's called estrus and every female werewolf experiences it."

"I don't want this," she muttered, as her mind whirled, trying to understand everything she'd been told and sort out the implications.

"I know you don't, Alex. I'd hoped that maybe it wouldn't happen this way for you. There haven't been too many half-breeds in our history, so I honestly didn't know what to expect. But lately, I've sensed the change in you. Felt your wolf waiting to embrace you."

She swallowed hard. "That's what you meant when you said I'd go through the change?"

He nodded. "It's different between males and females of the species. Males come into their wolf when they mature in their early twenties. For the females, it's the mating process that unleashes the female wolf inside, allowing her to change into a wolf on command."

"That's not fair." Alex was outraged. Males didn't have to go through what the females had to go through, what *she* had to go through. Typical. It didn't seem to matter if it was humans or supernatural beings involved, men always seemed to have it easier than women.

Her father shrugged. "Fair or not, that's how it is." He paused. "It's really a wonderful thing if you allow it to happen and embrace the moment. You'll be more powerful than you've ever imagined even when you aren't in wolf form. Your hearing will be keener, your vision sharper, your reflexes faster and your muscles will be stronger. You'll also heal faster if you sustain any injuries." His eyes narrowed. "Even as a child you never got sick. You were always fast and strong. I didn't know if that was as much as my wolf blood would give you or if you'd develop as a female werewolf."

That was all fine and good, and she'd deal with it when she had to. Right now they had a much bigger worry, and he was standing in the same room with them. "But why is *he* here?" She jerked her head toward the opening between the kitchen and living room where Joshua was lurking.

"That's what I'm about to find out." Straightening from his crouch, her father motioned Joshua back into the room. "What's going on?"

Joshua prowled back into the room, his loose-legged gait

reminding her of her father. "Ian sent me."

"He is alpha?"

Joshua nodded. "He came just after you left."

"I wasn't sure he would even though I'd sent for him. How is my brother?"

Alex sat up straighter. Her father had a brother? She had an uncle? Every second seemed to be revealing something new to her. She stared at her father. It was as if he was a complete stranger even though she'd known him her entire life. It wasn't a comfortable feeling. Anger began to stir deep inside her, shoving aside the swirling confusion.

"He is well, but very concerned about you and about his niece. The pack needs both of you. Times are hard and there is much fighting among the brethren."

Her father laughed but it wasn't a particularly pleasant sound. Alex could hear the disgust in his tone. "Some things never change. Killing one another over petty grievances rather than banding together for the greater good. For survival."

"As you say." Joshua inclined his head slightly. "But the fact remains that a wolf who knew you from the past happened by your shop a little more than a week ago and saw you and your daughter. He immediately started back to the pack to tell Ian, but he must have told someone else what he'd seen.

"Word spread quickly even though he managed to get himself killed before he could give away more than the name of the city you were living in. By then it was too late. Most of the unmated males from the Wolf Creek pack, as well as the Blue Ridge and Cumberland packs, have descended on Chicago. There may be more. We've all been searching. The difference is we want to protect both you and your daughter, the other packs will probably kill you in order to take Alex and they won't give her a choice in mating. They will fight for her and she will go to the victor."

Her father's expression darkened. "You all want to claim her. Do not pretty it up."

"Of course we all want her. She is an unmated female. Not only is she beautiful, but she is your daughter as well. There are many who want her for that reason alone."

"Hey!" Anger bubbled to the surface, as she jumped to her

feet. "Don't I get a say in this?" Alex was tired of them talking about her like she wasn't even there, of discussing her life as if it were a done deal.

Joshua Striker turned to her, his dark eyes boring into her. "Unfortunately, no." He paused and ran his fingers though his hair. Alex found herself wondering if it was as soft as it looked. She shook her head to clear her thoughts. What was she thinking?

"Actually you do have two choices. Come with me to Wolf Creek and you'll have your choice of any of the unmated males. Or..." he glanced toward her father, "...you can stay here and have to defend yourself against any other males that come to claim you, putting yourself and your father in danger."

"What if I don't want to mate with anyone?" Adrenaline surged through her veins. She wanted to wake up and find out that she was still in bed and all this was just a bad dream. But it was all too real.

She could sense Joshua carefully choosing his words as if he didn't want to upset her any more than she already was. She could have told him he was wasting his time. At this point her world was so far off center it would never go back again. What was one more thing?

"You are going into heat, Alex."

It was the first time he'd said her name and it sent a bolt of desire shooting between her thighs. She had to resist the urge to squeeze her thighs together to ease the growing ache. She could feel the moisture soaking her panties and was appalled. Could he smell her arousal?

She forced herself to ignore the throbbing and pay attention to what he was saying.

"You will not be able to help yourself. You will mate. It is just a matter of who it will be with."

Alex found the very concept appalling. "That's disgusting. I'm not an animal. I'm not." She backed away from both men, holding her hands out in front of her as if to ward them off.

"Alex." Her father reached for her, but she shook her head and turned toward the door. She needed to get out of here. She needed to be by herself to think, to sort out all that she'd learned.

But it was too late. Joshua had cut off her escape, silently sliding in front of the door. His arms were crossed against his chest and his legs were spread in a wide stance. No, she wouldn't be leaving that way.

"I'm going to my old room." She stalked toward the hallway. She could always climb out through the fire escape.

"No." Joshua grabbed her arm, the heat from his fingers practically burning her through the material of her sweatshirt as he thrust her toward a corner of the living room. "There's no time."

Glass shattered and a huge wolf jumped in through the low kitchen window from the small fire escape that was below it. Several men followed. Another crash came from down the hall and Alex feared that more were coming in through her bedroom window.

Her father crouched in a fighter's stance, ready to face the threat. "Take her and get out. I'll hold them off."

"No!" she screamed. She wouldn't leave him. It didn't matter that he'd lied to her, or that her life was coming undone, he was her father. She knew he loved her and had lied to protect her. She'd rather fight and die beside him. Drawing her weapon, she took aim and fired as the first wolf attacked.

Chapter Three

Joshua watched in awe as Alex squeezed off two quick shots, hitting the largest wolf in midair as it launched itself at her father. There was no hesitation. She was definitely an alpha female, ready to fight and defend what was hers.

The wolf let out a yelp and hit the floor with a thud, its mouth opening on a snarl. Alex fired another round, this one straight into the animal's heart. The wolf went silent, its bleeding body stretched across the floor a mere foot from her.

Joshua forced his eyes away from her and toward the men racing down the hallway. There was no time for him to transform into a wolf, so he swooped down and drew a deadly, silver-coated hunting knife from the sheath tucked in his boot. He threw it at one attacker even as he launched himself at the largest of his foes.

They slammed against the floor. Joshua immediately rolled so that he was on top, his large hands wrapping around the other man's neck. His opponent bucked, his eyes and the veins in his neck bulging as he attempted to dislodge Joshua. He brought his hands up, jabbing quickly at Joshua's throat, forcing him to lean away. His attacker took advantage, rolling them both to the side. The moment Joshua's grip slipped, the other man pounced again.

Both of them were panting hard now, sweat beading on their skin. They grappled, neither of them giving ground. Joshua rolled to his feet and risked a glance over at Alex and her father. James was currently fighting two attackers and Alex was locked in hand-to-hand combat with another. Joshua growled low in his throat, the need to protect her almost overwhelming all else. Only years of discipline, and the fact that he knew these particular wolves wanted Alex alive to mate with her, kept him from doing something stupid, like trying to race to her defense before he'd dealt with the much larger threat in front of him.

The fight was primal and brutal, each of them intent on permanently disabling the other. There would be only one winner. Death or retreat were the only options for the loser. Joshua had never retreated from a fight in his life. He was the Striker. He could afford to show no weakness. To walk away would cast doubt on his abilities, would be a slur against his family heritage.

But he'd do it for her in a heartbeat if it meant the difference between Alex being safe or being in jeopardy. That thought made his heart stop beating. When it resumed, it pounded with such force it was a wonder it didn't erupt from his chest. He could not allow her to mean that much to him. He could not afford such a weakness.

Putting aside all other thought, he concentrated on his opponent. Tall and strong, with short blond hair and piercing gray eyes, he was a formidable foe. This was no young stripling, but a warrior in his prime.

But he was the Striker. Years of tradition and pride welled up inside him and a deep calm settled over him. Everything around him seemed more vibrant, all motion seemed exaggerated, as if it was in slow motion, allowing him to take in everything around him and make decisions.

When his opponent lashed out at him, Joshua ducked beneath the other man's arm and spun around coming up behind him. Wrapping his thick forearm around the man's neck, he jerked hard. The crack seemed unusually loud in its finality. The body in his arms went limp and he dropped it carelessly onto the floor, wading back into the fray.

Bloodlust was pumping through his veins, demanding a sacrifice. The fact that Alex was in danger was unacceptable to him. With a roar, he grabbed the man that was trying to corner Alex. Somewhere along the way she'd lost her revolver and was now holding him off with a knife.

As if sensing his presence, the young man turned just in

time to avoid Joshua's punch to the back of his head. Tipping back his head, Joshua's opponent howled. The remaining attackers raced across the room and dove through the shattered window, retreating to fight another day.

"Are you all right?" He gripped Alex by the shoulders, shaking her when she didn't immediately answer him.

"I'm fine." She sounded irritated. "I can't believe how fast those guys were. One of them knocked the Glock from my hand before I even knew he was there."

Joshua's lips twitched at the disgust he heard in her voice. His little alpha was pissed with herself for not being able to hold on to her weapon. He bit the inside of his mouth to keep from smiling. She definitely wouldn't appreciate his humor right now. But damn she was adorable, and sexy, when she was angry.

"Dad?" She shook herself out of Joshua's grasp and strode toward her father. James was sweaty, his shirt was torn, but he looked fine. In fact, he looked as pissed off as his daughter. Joshua was struck at that moment by how much they resembled one another.

Reaching out, James wrapped his arm around Alex and tugged her close. "I'm fine, baby. Are you sure you're all right?"

"I lost my gun." She said it as if she was admitting some dark sin.

Her father gave her a comforting hug, pride etched on his face. "You did extremely well considering you didn't know what to expect." He ran his hands over her arms and back as if to reassure himself that she was okay. "The problem is that these were, for the most part, young men. Only two of them were seasoned warriors. The next time it won't be so easy."

"Easy." Joshua could hear the growing horror in her tone. "That was easy?" Her eyes strayed to the large gray wolf lying dead on the floor and to the man with the broken neck. She swallowed hard, her hand going to her stomach.

He knew she was experiencing the aftermath of the fight. The adrenaline was still rushing through her system with no way to expend itself. He knew she must be feeling queasy. The fight was bad enough, but she'd had a huge shock on top of it. Still, she was steady on her feet. Once again, he found himself pleased with her inner strength.

James kissed her forehead before releasing her. "You must go with Striker."

"No. I won't leave you." She glared at Joshua as if he'd suggested it and not her father.

Joshua held his hands out in front of him. "He's right, Alex. They'll be back or another group will come. Next time they may be larger and more organized."

Her father gripped her shoulders, shaking her lightly. "Listen to me, Alex. I've given up everything to keep you safe and I don't regret a single moment of it. I'll be damned if I'll let these rogues have you if I can prevent it. Do you understand me?"

Joshua watched, fascinated by the play of emotions that raced across Alex's face. Anger followed by defiance and finally acceptance and sadness. She may be an alpha female but, in this small pack of two, her father was still top wolf.

She straightened her shoulders, shrugging out of her father's grip. "What do you want me to do?"

Her father nodded and Joshua could tell he'd expected no other answer from her. "I want you to go with Joshua back to the Wolf Creek pack. He will protect you with his life. There you'll have the time to get to know the rest of the single male wolves before you have to decide." He paused and dragged his hand over his face, suddenly looking tired and older. He sighed deeply as he reached out and stroked his hand over Alex's hair.

"I didn't wish this life for you. I'd hoped it wouldn't happen, that somehow there was more of your human mother in you. But the wolf is strong and won't be denied. I know this isn't what you wanted, but I have faith in you, Alexandra. I know you're strong enough to, not just face this, but to thrive."

She swallowed hard. Joshua watched the play of the muscles of her throat and had the urge to drag his tongue over that soft, sensitive skin. The adrenaline racing through his veins was searching for an outlet, and with the absence of violence, sex would suit him just as well. Maybe even better. He found it almost impossible to drag his gaze away from her, but he did, painfully aware of how tight his jeans were becoming.

"I'll get rid of the bodies," James motioned to both the wolf and the man. "Then I'll follow you. I assume the Wolf Creek pack is still in the same general area."

Joshua stepped forward, suddenly very eager to get Alex away from here. He felt twitchy, like an icy cold breeze had just skated down his spine. "It is," he assured James. "We don't have much time." He glanced out the window. The rest of the world was just beginning to wake, but he knew there were wolves prowling close. The wolf in him could sense them and they weren't friendly. "I have to get Alex back to the protection of the pack."

James stepped over the body of the wolf and opened the bookcase again. Sliding back another false panel, he exposed the front of a small safe. Quickly spinning the dial, he yanked it open and drew out a large roll of bills, handing it to Alex. He fished out another large wad of cash, stuffing it in his own pocket before closing the safe.

"If you need to stop in a motel or lay low for a few days, pay for everything with cash. Don't leave them a trail they can follow. The wolves may not live in the cities, but they're smart and resourceful. Don't ever think for a moment that they don't use whatever human technology is at their disposal." He closed Alex's limp fingers over the wad of cash. "We're just like humans really, only with a little something extra."

Alex launched herself against her father, hugging him tightly. "I don't want to leave you." Her voice was muffled against her father's shirt, but Joshua heard it all the same. He felt her pain as if it was his own. Uncomfortable with the softer emotion, he turned away to give father and daughter a moment of privacy.

"I know you don't, Alex. I don't want to let you out of my sight either, but we don't have a choice. If we split up, I can draw them away and we'll both have a better chance of survival."

She sniffed and Joshua couldn't resist peeking back at her. Alex swiped at her eyes with the back of her hand. Her father teased a laugh out of her when he lifted the tail of his shirt and used it to wipe away the telltale sign of her tears.

James took his cell phone out of his pocket, dropped it on the floor and crushed it beneath the heel of his boot. "Don't use your cell phone. We don't know if they've been compromised."

Alex nodded as she took the money her father had given her and divided it into four separate piles before placing one in each pocket of her jeans. Joshua raised his eyebrow as he stared at her. She was smart. It wouldn't do to have to haul out a huge wad of cash in front of anyone. That was something that a motel clerk or store clerk might remember.

She bent over, grabbed the handgun off the floor and jammed it into her holster. She checked her knives as well and, when she was satisfied, she turned back to her father. "Do you have any more ammunition?"

He reached into the hidden area behind the bookshelf and drew out another Glock, tucking it at the small of his back. "No. The clip was full. You fired three shots, so you have fourteen left. Make them count. Silver bullets are not easy to obtain without a lot of unwanted questions. I'd planned on acquiring more, but it's too late now."

"Will anyone call the cops?" Joshua asked.

James shook his head. "Probably not. The building behind us is vacant. And most folks mind their own business around here."

A scraping noise just outside the window alerted them all. Time had run out. James pointed to the door. Joshua retrieved his knife and whipped open the door, ready to face any threat. When he determined the coast was clear, he led the way down the stairs to the garage. The large room appeared empty, but they could all hear the loud bang from upstairs. James closed the door and bolted it shut. Joshua knew that wouldn't hold them for long.

Striding down the length of the room, James hurried into the office, returning a moment later with a heavy leather jacket and some keys. He tossed one set to Joshua as he continued on to Alex. "Put this on." He handed her the jacket and waited while she pulled it on. Then he handed her a set of keys and motioned to the corner. "Take the Ducatis. One of them has a slow oil leak; the other one just needs a tune-up. They'll get you away from here, but ditch them when you feel it's safe. They're too distinctive and easily remembered." He looked at Joshua as he said the last.

Joshua nodded as he made his way to the motorcycles in

the corner. They were first-class machines and he couldn't help but admire them. "Can you ride?" he asked Alex as she came up beside him.

She snorted before turning her back on him. He'd take that as a yes.

James laughed, shaking his head. "I'm more worried about you than I am about Alex. She can handle any machine on the road."

Alex was already mounted on her bike and had the key in the ignition. It roared to life as James hurried to the vintage Mustang and slid inside. He rolled down the window and shouted over the roar of the motors. "I'll see you in two days. Don't let anything happen to my little girl or you'll answer to me."

Before Joshua could respond the garage door began to rise. Swearing under his breath, he pulled the motorcycle off the stand and straddled it. Tires squealed and his head jerked up just in time to see the Mustang surge from the garage, barely clearing the bottom of the garage door, which was still rising.

Something pounded on the door leading down from the apartment. The bolts loosened with the blow. Another two blows and the rogue wolves would break through and be upon them. Alex tugged at his arm, shouting to be heard over the din. "Follow me." Not giving him a chance to respond, she revved the engine and shot out of the garage. He had no choice but to follow.

The Mustang roared out of the garage and down the street. The screech of tires behind James brought an immense sense of satisfaction. "That's it you bastards. Follow me."

Two nondescript vehicles sped down the street behind him in pursuit. James kept one eye on the rearview mirror and was pleased when the two motorcycles pulled out of the garage. Pushing the gas pedal to the floor, he made a hard turn to the right. He heard the unmistakable sound of gunfire and almost turned back.

It took every ounce of discipline he had to keep going forward to draw the men chasing him further away from Alex. He reminded himself that he'd taught his daughter well. She knew how to defend herself. Better still, she could drive like a demon. That's why he'd insisted they take the Ducatis. With the smaller, faster motorcycles, they should be able to evade anyone pursuing them. It was James' job to draw the bulk of the attackers after him.

He began a deadly game of cat and mouse that took them through every back street in the city. James knew them all. If he was lucky, his pursuers would know squat about the layout of the roads. His instincts proved correct and it didn't take him long to lose them. But he knew they weren't gone. They'd regroup, knowing that Alex would be heading toward Wolf Creek and the protection of the pack. James figured they'd give the city a final sweep and, if they turned up nothing, they'd head out to set up an ambush somewhere along the way. It's what he'd do if he were in their situation.

Pulling slowly out from behind a building, he turned left and headed toward the downtown district. It was time to get down to business.

Alex's heart was beating so hard she couldn't hear anything else above the pounding rhythm. The motorcycle flew out of the garage just in time for her to see the tail end of the Mustang turn right at the end of the street. Her father was safe. She was safe. That was all that mattered.

The roar of a large caliber weapon being fired made her jump. Someone was shooting at her and Joshua. Well, what did she expect? These were obviously not the sort of people you reasoned with. A whiz off to her right startled her and she automatically jerked the bike in the other direction.

Swearing at herself, she struggled to regain control and keep from wiping out. She had to just ignore the shooting and drive. She didn't even know if Joshua Striker was behind her and she didn't dare look to find out. She had to trust he'd keep up. When she reached the end of the street she didn't slow down as she turned left.

She felt something coming up on her right side and risked a quick glance. Sure enough, the other Ducati was hot on her heels. Leaning over the fast, aerodynamic vehicle, she led him through the streets of Chicago and finally into the heart of the city.

It hit her as she left the modest buildings of her neighborhood behind her that she might never be able to go back there again. The thought struck like a knife to her heart. It was the only home she'd ever known. She might never see Divine again. Mr. Bykowski at the bakery shop, where she picked up coffee and muffins every morning, would wonder what had happened to her. She didn't have any really close friends, but she and her father were part of the very fabric of life of their little section of the city.

What would happen to her father's garage? Unlocked as it was, it would probably be vandalized by the end of the day. What about her tiny apartment and all her things? She didn't own a lot, but what she did own, she'd lovingly chosen. She'd spent years scrounging through thrift shops and consignment stores to find furniture and dishes that she loved.

Her vision blurred and she blinked hard to clear it. Now was not the time. Stuff could be replaced. After all, in the end it was just stuff. What mattered was that she and her father were safe. She didn't dare think about the rest of it right now. She couldn't afford to lose her focus.

She knew that putting it off wouldn't change anything, but it would have to wait until she was safe. Then she knew she'd have to come to grips with the nightmare her life had suddenly become.

The bike jerked and the engine began to sputter. She was driving the motorcycle with the oil leak. When she glanced down, she saw flecks of dark liquid staining her jeans. Yup, there was no doubt about it. She'd just about reached the end of the line. Motioning Joshua up beside her, she pointed to the engine. He nodded and smoothly moved in front of her. She guessed that meant he wanted her to follow him.

She pushed the motorcycle as hard as she dared, knowing any moment could be its last. Finally, she had to pull over, reaching the curb just as the engine died. Joshua turned a corner, obviously not yet realizing she wasn't following.

For a brief moment, fear filled her. She was truly alone. Her home and her life had been summarily ripped from her.

Taking a deep breath, she put down the kickstand and

dismounted from the bike. Opening the side compartment, she dropped the keys inside. Slamming it shut, she stepped up onto the sidewalk and walked away without a backward glance. The city would eventually tow the bike and impound it. This was a good part of town so she wasn't concerned about leaving it here, and it wasn't as if anyone could drive off with it. It should be safe until her father hopefully got the chance to reclaim it.

She strode down the long strip of concrete, no particular destination in mind. It was a fine time to realize that she was the only one who didn't know exactly where they were going. Where was Wolf Creek anyway? Not that it mattered. Joshua would probably turn back to look for her as soon as he noticed her missing. That is, unless one or more of those nasty men chasing them caught him. She shivered at the thought. In case something happened and he wasn't able to come back for her, she needed to make a plan. She'd go to the library and look it up.

If she had to she would go into hiding on her own. She could get word to Divine, letting the other woman know where she was. Her father would look for her if she didn't show up at Wolf Creek. He would check with everyone in the old neighborhood and Divine would be able to give him her location.

Now that she had a plan, she felt better. Her stomach growled, reminding her that she hadn't eaten her muffin this morning. She was hungry and she needed coffee. With everything that had happened, she still hadn't had hers yet. Maybe it was stupid to be focused on such a mundane thing, but it was the best she could do right now. Looking around, she spotted a likely establishment. She'd get her order to go and keep moving in the same direction Joshua was headed. Hopefully, she'd be able to find him.

She glanced inside to check out the interior before pulling open the steel and glass door and stepping inside. The heat from the kitchen hit her, reminding her that she was still wearing the leather jacket. It was already heating up outside as the sun rose higher in the sky. She started to unzip the jacket only to remember she was wearing a gun strapped to her hip. She casually pulled the zipper up again, hoping no one had caught a glimpse of it. She'd definitely take her order to go. The quicker the better.

Thankfully, the service was quick. Alex paid for her order and was heading back out the door within five minutes of entering. Raising the cup to her mouth, she took a sip, sighing in pleasure as the dark, rich brew slid down her throat. It was heaven. It was normal and everyday, which was exactly what she needed.

A heavy hand descended on her shoulder. She didn't stop to think. She dropped the brown paper bag she was holding. Pivoting on one heel, she tossed her paper cup at her attacker, letting the hot liquid fly over him.

"Fuck!"

Too late she realized it was Joshua and right now he looked none too happy. Coffee stained his shirt and dripped down his jaw. Well, too bad for him. She wasn't happy either. Her fresh cup of coffee was all over the sidewalk. Thankfully, his fast reflexes had kept him from being hit too badly by the hot spray. Unfortunately, his foot had landed on her breakfast.

"What the hell is wrong with you?" Wrapping his hands over her shoulders, he tugged her to him. She thought he might shake her, but his fingers dug into the heavy leather jacket as he stared down at her, dark eyes snapping with anger. "You were supposed to stay right behind me, not stop for coffee. Of all the asinine things to do. This isn't a game you know." The last was said with a mixture of anger and exasperation, but beneath it she could hear the tinge of fear. For that reason alone, she held onto her own temper, which was hanging by a very thin thread.

She shrugged away from him and propped her hands on her hips. "First of all, the bike died. It was in the shop because it had an oil leak. I was supposed to fix it this morning. I didn't have any other choice but to stop, and you were too far ahead for me to signal you. I dumped the bike and started walking. Second, it's your fault I never got my coffee this morning. I didn't think it would hurt if I ducked into a shop long enough to get one. How the hell can I fight the bad guys if I don't have my coffee?"

"I'm beginning to think you can fight them better if you

don't have coffee," he muttered.

She took immediate offense at the insinuation that she was being bitchy. He probably hadn't had to do without his morning coffee. She opened her mouth to blast him, but stopped. Joshua was glancing around and Alex realized they were starting to attract a crowd.

"Come on." He slung his arm over her shoulders and all but forced her to walk down the street. She stopped long enough to scoop up the now flattened paper bag. As they passed a garbage can she dropped her smashed breakfast into it.

"What was that?"

"My bagel," she replied. Her voice sounded forlorn, but damn it, she'd wanted her breakfast.

"Let me guess." He grinned as he continued and she curled her fingers into her palm to keep from smacking him. "You didn't get a chance to eat your bagel this morning either."

She didn't bother to answer and tell him it was a blueberry muffin she'd missed earlier. The place she'd stopped at hadn't had any. Her stomach growled and suddenly she was overwhelmed by everything that had happened. Her coffee and bagel were the last straw. Pushing away, she glared up at him. "You might find this funny, but this is my life that's spiraled out of control. All I wanted was a damn cup of coffee and something to eat. Is that too much to ask?"

Casting him a glance that had been known to wither lesser men, she stalked down the sidewalk. He could follow her or not. She didn't care. She could take care of herself. She certainly didn't need some muscle-bound idiot male to take care of her. Okay, so he wasn't muscle-bound. He was actually sleek and sexy. But he was still an idiot.

His arms wrapped around her from behind and he lifted her right off her feet. "I didn't mean to make light of what you've gone though, Alex. I think you've handled everything amazingly well."

She absorbed his words and waited. After a minute passed, she realized that that was about as much of an apology as she was likely ever going to get from Joshua. She had a feeling he was the kind of man who didn't apologize for anything and probably didn't need to. She doubted he made many mistakes.

There was an air of self-containment and control surrounding him that was rather intimidating. That is if one could be intimidated by such things. Which, she assured herself, she couldn't. She didn't like the fact that pleasure suffused her when he'd praised the way she'd handled everything. Who cared what he thought?

He lowered her back to her feet and took her hand, threading his fingers though hers so that their palms were touching. Heat radiated from his hand into hers. "Come on. We can't stay here."

She followed him, quickening her pace until she was walking beside him. It was either that or be dragged behind him.

"Where's your bike?" she asked him.

"Ran out of gas." He shook his head, a black scowl on his face. "That's why it took me as long as it did to backtrack and find you."

Alex couldn't believe their bad luck. They were stranded without a vehicle with a group of nasty men—werewolves, she corrected herself—on their tail.

They walked for almost an hour and Alex did her best to ignore the hunger in her belly and the headache forming behind her eyes due to the lack of caffeine. She tried to focus on the city and her surroundings.

Chicago was a study of contrasts. Large, expensive homes were blocks from slums. Busy business districts existed alongside vibrant ethnic neighborhoods. Chicago was alive and ever changing. To Alex, it was home.

People scurried past them, hurrying to whatever their destinations were. Buses chugged down the roads, vying with city garbage trucks and cars for space, some of them honking their horns even though it didn't force the traffic to move one second faster. The "L"—the elevated, rapid transit system—rumbled off to their right, carrying people to work or school or wherever they were headed. Businesses were open, all trying to entice shoppers inside.

Unfortunately for Alex, the only thing that held her attention was the man beside her. She was very conscious of the fact that their palms were touching, their fingers entwined.

45

She'd never walked hand in hand with a man before. It was surprisingly intimate.

He seemed so large alongside her. She'd never thought about herself as small before, but somehow next to him she felt that way. He was probably six inches taller than her, and he was much more muscular. He exuded a sense of strength and confidence that was far too alluring.

Which didn't make sense at all. She'd worked in a garage her entire life and seen all kinds of men come and go, including handsome, well-built ones. Not once had she ever been attracted to one of them.

His black T-shirt clung to his shoulders like a second skin. The jeans he was wearing were old and soft, molding to the thick muscles in his thighs. She'd watched him walk up the stairs back at the garage and knew he filled them out from behind. He had a first-class ass. And the bulge in the front, well, that was impressive too.

His shaggy black hair fell to his shoulders, tempting a woman to brush it back, to try to tame it. She could sense the wildness lurking just beneath the controlled surface. This was a complex man with many layers. His face wasn't handsome, but strong and compelling. He exuded a sex appeal that no doubt had women falling at his feet. Alex scowled, not liking that last thought at all.

Why should she care if women threw themselves at him? She barely knew him. Yet the thought of him and any other woman naked, their bodies rubbing against one other, made her sick to her stomach. She placed a hand over her belly to settle it, blaming its upset on the fact it was far past her normal breakfast time and she still hadn't had anything to eat.

Joshua tugged her to a halt and she forced herself to look at him. The corners of his mouth turned up the tiniest bit and her stomach flip-flopped. Her nipples pebbled and moisture seeped from between her legs. His smile died, his eyes darkened, their pupils enlarging.

Oh, God. He could smell her arousal. Her father had mentioned heightened senses. She waited for some kind of crude comment, but it never came.

Reaching around her, he tugged open a door and urged her

inside. "Come on. Let me buy you some breakfast."

Alex swallowed hard and stepped over the threshold.

Chapter Four

Joshua watched the woman sitting at the table across from him, unable to pull his gaze away. Alex was on her second cup of coffee already, having practically inhaled the first one. He rubbed his hand over his mouth, hiding his smile. It faded when she took the first sip of the second cup. Her eyes were closed, her head tipped back, her expression one of pure bliss. She looked like a woman in the throes of sexual release. He swallowed hard and shifted in his seat, trying to adjust himself so that his balls weren't squashed and his cock didn't hurt.

They hadn't spoken, except to place their order, since they'd taken their seat in a quiet back corner of the small, yet surprisingly busy, restaurant. By unspoken agreement, they'd both decided to wait until they had their breakfast in front of them before they started talking. Less chance of interruption that way.

The waitress hurried up to the table and deposited his bacon, eggs, hash browns and toast in front of him. It smelled delicious. He watched Alex all but grab her plate out of the waitress's hands. Once she'd realized she was going to get a chance to actually sit down and eat, she'd opted for blueberry pancakes and bacon instead of a toasted bagel.

He quietly thanked the waitress as he watched Alex pour warm syrup over the hot cakes. Some of it dripped from the spout of the small metal jug, running down her fingers. Switching hands, she kept pouring as she brought her fingers to her mouth, licking the sweet syrup from them.

Joshua groaned and shifted again. She was the picture of sensual enticement as she popped one finger in her mouth and sucked it. Her lips were full and pink and he longed to taste them. They would be sweet from the syrup and warm. She pulled her finger out slowly, making sure she got every last drop.

She glanced over at him when he groaned again, freezing when she saw the look in his eyes. Her eyes were a misty gray, framed by long, dark brown lashes. She raised one of her slightly curved eyebrows in question. He shook his head and she shrugged, plunked the jug back down on the table and picked up her utensils. Without another glance at him, she dug into her meal.

Joshua wasn't sure he'd survive breakfast.

To save his sanity, he concentrated on eating his meal. In spite of what Alex might believe, he hadn't had time to eat this morning either. He'd spent all last night searching every privately owned garage in the city, as he'd done for the past two nights, while laying down false trails for the rogue wolves that were hot on his tail.

It had troubled him to see the area of Chicago in which James LeVeau Riley had raised his daughter, but from what he'd seen of the man and his daughter, James had obviously known what he was doing. Alex was confident and capable, more than able to hold her own with him or any other male.

The bacon was crisp, the toast golden brown and the eggs cooked to perfection. Even the hash browns weren't greasy. No wonder this place was busy. It might not look like much, but the food was exceptional. They shouldn't really have stopped for breakfast, but it was worth the risk to witness Alex's obvious enjoyment as she ate and drank.

He glanced at Alex and wasn't surprised to see her sopping up what was left of the syrup on her plate with the last bite of pancake. When she finished, she placed her utensils carefully across the plate and sat back with a sigh.

"That was excellent." She picked up her mug of coffee and took a sip before placing it back on the table. Clasping her hands over her stomach, she eyed him carefully. "So where exactly is it we're going and what will happen when I get there?"

The question and her posture were both casual, but he could see that her knuckles were white she clenched her hands so firmly. Alex was feeling anything but casual at the moment. Picking up his mug, he took a fortifying mouthful, draining the last drop.

"Wolf Creek is in North Carolina. It's about a ten-hour drive from here if we don't stop and everything goes our way. He set his mug back on the table. "It's a beautiful area in the mountains. We bought up the land about a century ago and have a compound there where the main family stays. Once we get there you'll be safe and have time to meet with all the eligible males from the pack."

"Main family?"

He noticed she avoided any mention of meeting the males of the pack, but he answered her question. "The alpha, Ian, and his mate, Patrice. My brothers and I stay there as well."

"You said something about being in charge of security or something." He could tell she was sorting through her memory, trying to recall bits and pieces of this morning's earlier conversation.

"Yes. A Striker is always the head of security. Our loyalty to the pack is unquestioned."

"So it's a big deal."

He tried to think of a way to make her understand. "Amongst our people, we are the judge, jury and executioner when there is a dispute. We are like the police, making sure the pack is protected from any outside violence as well as any upheaval from within. Our job is to protect the pack at all costs. To ensure its continued existence."

"That can't be an easy job." Her voice had softened. "Nor is it fair to put so much on one person. You know what they say about absolute power."

"That it corrupts absolutely." He tilted his head slightly, acknowledging her point. "Yet it is necessary. Besides which, my brothers help me. I am merely the head of security, not its only member. And Ian is still the alpha. His word is final."

Alex motioned the waitress over, thanking her profusely when she refilled the coffee mugs. She added sugar and stirred before picking up her mug and taking a taste. She licked her lips to catch a drop that beaded on her bottom lip. Joshua wanted to lick her lower lip, take it into his mouth and suck on it. Instead, he focused on Alex, waiting for her next question.

"Tell me about your family. You have brothers?"

He cleared his throat and kept talking, hoping to hide his growing discomfort. His erection, which had been under control, had swelled again the moment her tongue touched her lips. "My parents are both dead, but I have four brothers, one older, three younger."

"Really." She sat forward, resting her elbows on the table and propping her chin in her hands. "I always wanted a sister or a brother. It's always been just Dad and me."

"It was great to have brothers growing up, although sometimes I wished I'd been an only child." Thoughts of his siblings brought a reluctant smile to his face. "Isaiah is the firstborn, then there's me, Micah, Levi and Simon."

She stared at him, fascination in her gaze.

"I had a sister." It had been years, but he still didn't like to talk about it. "Rachel disappeared when she was a teenager. We never found her body. She would have been about fifty years old now. She was the baby of the family, about thirty years younger than me."

Alex's eyes were as big as full moons, amazement shining out of their depths. She opened her mouth to speak and closed it again. She swallowed hard. "You're saying you're eighty years old?" She glanced over her shoulder to make sure no one was eavesdropping.

"Yes."

"That's old. I still can't wrap my head around that one." Alex rubbed her hands up and down her arms.

"You will in time. I would imagine that you'll live almost as long as the rest of us as the wolf is dominant in your genetic makeup."

Alex slumped back against the seat, shaking her head. "Amazing." She swiveled her head around. "I've got to go to the ladies' room. We should probably get going."

The change in subject was abrupt. Joshua sensed her reluctance to dwell too long on her altered circumstances. He couldn't blame her, especially when they weren't safe here.

Joshua rose from the table, fished into his pocket and left more than enough on the table to pay for their meal and cover a generous tip. The delay was worth it, if only because the coffee and food made Alex happy.

Keeping his hand on the small of her back, he led her down the short hallway to the restrooms. "I'll meet you right here. Don't go anywhere without me."

She saluted smartly. "Yes, sir."

He gave her a playful swat on the behind as she pushed open the door to the ladies' room. She jumped and shot him a glare over her shoulder as she rubbed her bottom.

He smiled even as he shook his head. No one outside his immediate family treated him the way she did. Most others gave him a wide berth, fearful of drawing his attention, but Alex teased and questioned and glared at him at every turn. Pushing his way into the men's room, he decided to hurry. Who knew what kind of mischief she would get up to if he left her on her own.

Alex flushed the toilet and exited the stall, heading straight to one of the two tiny, cracked sinks. In the privacy of the stall, she'd checked on the knives, which were tucked safely in her boots, and had stashed the gun in the deep pocket of the leather jacket for now. It was late September, but it was warming up outside. It was too hot to keep wearing that coat.

Tossing it over the other sink, she stared at the image in the mirror as she soaped and washed her hands. There were no paper towels left in the dispenser, so she dried her hands on the legs of her jeans. For someone whose life had changed so drastically and who had been through so much, she looked surprisingly normal.

Her hair was disheveled, her skin pale, but the face was the same. Not even her eyes looked different, the familiar silvery gray staring steadily back at her. For some reason, she'd thought she'd look different somehow.

Her hands began to tremble. The quivering went up her arms and down through her body. She'd killed a man this morning. Rather, a wolf. But he was still a man, wasn't he? The fact that he'd meant to kill her father and kidnap her didn't make that any easier.

The first sob came from deep within her, taking her off-guard. She'd buried all her emotions up until now, needing just to function, to keep moving forward. But now that she was well fed and relatively safe, those emotions bubbled to the surface, demanding release.

Gripping the edge of the sink, she concentrated on taking one breath at a time. It was no use. She gave into the inevitable and allowed the tears to flow.

A sharp knock came on the door, but she ignored it.

The door pushed open. "Hurry up, Alex. We don't have all day."

His voice made her sob even harder. How dare he tell her to hurry? It had been her suggestion to leave. He'd been sitting there like they had all day. She'd tell him off just as soon as she got a grip on herself.

"Fuck," he muttered as he shoved the door open. She raised her head long enough to glare at him and then buried her face back in her hands. She wasn't normally a crier, but right now she couldn't make herself stop. The snick of a lock being set was loud in the otherwise quiet room and then two strong arms wrapped around her.

"Everything will be all right," he crooned in her ear as he rocked her lightly in his embrace. She felt surrounded by his heat, comforted by his unique scent. It was a fresh outdoorsy smell of pine trees and rich earth, and she pushed her nose closer to his chest, wanting to absorb it into her skin.

"I killed a man. A wolf. A man," she wailed. "Whatever he was, I killed him." She'd done it without thought, without a moment's hesitation when she'd seen him going for her father's throat. It was strange and disconcerting to realize she had a killer instinct inside her.

"You protected yourself and your father. I would expect nothing less from James LeVeau's daughter. It was self-defense, pure and simple."

"It all happened so quickly." She sniffed, surreptitiously wiping her eyes on his black T-shirt.

"I know it did, honey."

No man had called her by an endearment before, besides her father, and that didn't count. They'd called her plenty of unflattering names when she shot down their clumsy sexual advances, but this was something new and unexpected.

She tried not to read too much into it. He needed her to cooperate with him so maybe he was just humoring her. She didn't think so though. It had been more of an automatic thing. Who knows, maybe he called every woman he met "honey". All she knew was it made her feel warm inside.

They stood there for a long time. Alex was content to just be in his arms, but she knew they had to leave. Reluctantly, she pushed away. The movement brushed her nipples over his chest. She bit her lip to keep from moaning aloud. What she wanted to do was strip off her sweatshirt and bra and rub her breasts over the hard planes of his chest.

"You okay now?" He pushed a lock of her bangs back out of her face. She'd been due to get a trim and her hair was a little unruly.

"I'm fine."

"Good." He barely had the word out when he lowered his head toward her. Her lips parted automatically and she went up on her toes to meet him. His mouth was warm as it pressed against hers. It was the lightest of touches, but it ricocheted throughout her entire body, bringing it to life.

Alex trembled, but this time it felt different. Her skin was alive with sensation. She craved more of his touch. Her body needed it. Demanded it.

Joshua, however, seemed to be in no particular hurry. He nibbled at her bottom lip, tugging at it with his teeth and then stroking it with his tongue.

Her breathing was getting quicker, shallower. Her sweatshirt and jeans were confining, uncomfortably rough against her sensitive skin. The throbbing ache began low in her belly again. She felt empty, needy. For the first time in her life, she truly wanted a man.

Not just any man, but Joshua Striker. Werewolf.

The thought frightened her even as it turned her on. She didn't know herself anymore. She was drawn to his strength, his scent, the tender way he was kissing her.

"Stop thinking," he demanded as he dropped soft butterfly kisses on her cheeks, forehead and nose. "Just feel." His tongue slipped past her lips and into her mouth, tasting it, exploring it, mapping it. There wasn't a single spot that he didn't touch. When he stroked her tongue with his, she swayed. Gripping his shoulders for support, she shook off the sensual stupor swamping her and returned his kiss.

Their tongues tangled and entwined. Alex couldn't get enough of him. He tasted like forbidden fruit, hot and male and dangerous. Like thick, dark coffee, strong and potent. It was addictive. She stroked her hands up his thick neck, threading her fingers through his shaggy black hair. The strands flowed over her hands like dark silk. She wanted to feel it brushing over her breasts.

The ache building between her thighs was too great to ignore. Hooking one leg over his thigh, she tilted her pelvis forward, not surprised when she felt a substantial bulge in the front of his jeans. Moaning, she rubbed her mound over the hard ridge, searching for relief. Cream flowed from her core, soaking her panties. The seam of her jeans pressed against her clitoris, giving her some relief. But it wasn't enough. Not nearly enough. Alex wanted his hands on her, touching her.

"Joshua," she cried as she tore her mouth away from his.

"Fuck, yes," he muttered. Pushing her away from him, he reached down, grabbed the hem of her sweatshirt and tore it over her head. With a low growl, he nuzzled his way down her neck toward her breasts.

Alex grabbed the edge of the sink with both hands, holding on for dear life. Joshua cupped one of her breasts, molding it in his hand. His tongue followed the edge of her bra where it sloped over the curve of her breast to the front closure. He traced his thumb over her cotton-covered nipple before covering it with his mouth and sucking hard.

She released her desperate grip on the sink and clutched his head to her chest, feeling the moist heat of his mouth through the fabric of her bra. "More," she pleaded.

The front closure of her bra popped open. Joshua removed his mouth long enough to push the fabric aside. She looked down, wanting to watch him, wanting to see everything he did. Her nipples were puckered and tight, practically begging him to taste them.

"Pretty." His voice was a seductive purr as he lapped at first one peak and then the other. Digging her fingers into his scalp, she dragged his head to one breast and tugged him close. She could feel his lips forming a smile, but she didn't care. She didn't care what he did as long as he eased the overwhelming ache inside her.

"Yes," she hissed, tilting her head back when he took her nipple into his mouth and sucked hard. She'd never felt anything like this before. Had no idea that a man sucking on her breasts could give her such overwhelming pleasure. As he drew on her breast, she felt an echoing pulse low in her pussy. It just kept growing and growing. Alex didn't know how much more she could take.

He glided his hands down her sides, following the indent of her waist before flaring over her hips. He slid them to the front and yanked at the snap of her jeans. It made a loud pop. Gripping the zipper with his fingers, he pulled the tab downward.

She thought he would touch her then and held her breath in anticipation. Instead, he shoved her jeans down around her knees. His fingers left goose bumps on her thighs as he trailed them back up to her waist. His thumbs hooked into the sides of her cotton bikini underwear, but he didn't tug them down. Instead, he teased her skin with his thumbs.

"Joshua." She sounded petulant, but she didn't care. She wanted him to ease the ache inside her.

He gave her nipple one final suck before releasing it. "What?" His tone was so incredibly gentle and caring it brought tears to her eyes.

"Do something?" she wailed.

"Anything in particular?" he teased. His eyes, so brown they were almost black, were filled with lust, but beneath it she saw tenderness as well.

"Touch me."

"Where?"

She grabbed his hand and shoved it down the front of her panties. "Here," she gasped as his finger grazed her clitoris. "Oh, yeah," she groaned, sliding her hips forward and back so that his finger rubbed against the hard nub.

Joshua laughed as he went down on one knee in front of

her. He grasped her panties in one hand, tugging them downward until they caught on her jeans. She couldn't open her legs very wide with her clothing around her knees, but it was enough.

He leaned forward, inhaling as he nuzzled her pubic hair. "Your scent is intoxicating, Alex. Like honey and spice. And you're not even in full heat yet." She could hear the wonder in his voice.

She still didn't like the whole idea of being in heat, but at this moment, she didn't care. All she wanted was to reach for the orgasm that was growing inside her. She'd given them to herself, but she'd never had one that involved a man. She knew it would be different somehow. Richer. Fuller.

Alex leaned back against the sink for support, the porcelain cold against her bottom. Her fingers dug into the rim for support as she spread her legs as far as they could go.

His finger dipped just inside her slit and he withdrew it, bringing it to his mouth. His tongue darted out to lick the moisture from the tip. "Sweet." His eyes seemed to burn with some inner fire. "Your pussy is hot and wet and it's all for me, isn't it, Alex?"

"Yes." Of course it was for him. Did he see anyone else here?

He spread the lips of her sex wide with his thumbs and dragged his tongue over her clitoris. She cried out, unable to stop herself. She could smell her own arousal wafting in the air around her and it made her hotter. She felt sensual and ripe, ready for whatever lay ahead.

The rasp of his tongue was heavenly and she pumped her hips back and forth, absorbing every single sensation. Her breasts swayed with every movement. The tips were still moist from his earlier attention and the cool air of the room drifted over them. The sensation of the colder air on her nipples and the heat between her legs was incredibly arousing. Her scalp tingled, her skin felt stretched tight over her frame. Every inch of her was ready, screaming for completion.

He shifted one of his hands, sliding it further down her moist, plump lips. There was no hesitation as he pressed two thick fingers into her core. He was barely inside her when she felt her inner muscles clamp down hard. Her entire body convulsed. She released her hold on the sink and grabbed Joshua instead, clinging to him for support. Fluid gushed from between her legs and she cried out at the incredible sense of release. It seemed to go on forever, but she knew it was probably less than a minute. When her legs seemed to crumple from beneath her, he caught her, holding her easily upright in his arms.

It took her a few minutes to come back to herself. She felt tired, but strangely energized at the same time. She smiled at him and he surged to his feet, planting a hard, hot kiss on her lips before releasing her. She swayed slightly as he tugged her underwear and jeans back into place and pulled the cups of her bra back over her breasts, hooking the front closure.

He was finished, she suddenly realized. "What about you?" Her voice was deeper than usual and she could hear the invitation in it. She wanted to see his erection, touch it and take it into her body. As if in agreement, her core tightened and released, making her moan.

He reached down and adjusted the front of his pants. "Not now. If and when I take you it will be in a safer place. I'll need hours to fuck you the way I want to, not just a few minutes."

Alex took her sweatshirt when he handed it to her, automatically pulling it on and pushing up the sleeves. "I don't understand."

He brushed his fingers through her hair. "I know, Alex. For now all you need to know is that I wanted to do that for you. You needed the release to help ease the emotional turmoil of all you'd been through." He stepped away. "Besides, you haven't met any of the eligible males from the Wolf Creek pack. You might decide you want one of them instead."

The warm glow that had enveloped her quickly dissipated to be replaced by icy anger. "Let me get this straight. You just brought me to a screaming orgasm in, of all places, a public restroom, and you think I may want another guy to go to bed with me. What kind of woman do you think I am? No." She held up her hand. "Don't answer that. I think it's obvious what you think of me. In my neighborhood that kind of woman has a very unflattering name." She drew in a deep breath and picked up her leather jacket. "From now on don't do me any favors, okay?"

Not giving him time to answer, she strode toward the door, flicked the lock and yanked it open. "Are you coming?"

"I wish," he muttered under his breath.

The only indication she gave that she'd heard him was to tilt her nose in the air. *Hah.* He shouldn't hold his breath.

"Yeah, I'm coming." He looked as if he had plenty more to say, but she didn't care to listen.

Turning her back to him, she hurried down the hall toward the front door of the diner. She couldn't believe what she'd just done. She'd given herself body and soul to a man who'd only touched her because he thought she needed the physical release. She was absolutely mortified and embarrassed, not to mention incredibly hurt. She blinked hard to rid herself of the tears that threatened. She'd shed more than enough tears this morning. He wasn't worth them.

No wonder it hadn't been a big deal to him if he fucked her or not. He'd kept himself detached from the situation, not emotionally involved at all. She must have imagined the caring she'd seen in his eyes.

Chalk it up to experience on his part and lack thereof on hers. From now on, she'd keep her hormones contained and her sexual urges to herself. There was no way she'd allow Joshua Striker another chance to humiliate her.

Chapter Five

James downshifted, his hands smooth and steady on the gears as he brought the vintage sports car to a halt behind a bus and a truck, both of which were stopped at a traffic light. He glanced in the rearview mirror, satisfied that no one was on his tail. He tried not to think about Alex. He had to assume that Joshua would keep her safe.

He shook his head as the traffic began to move once again. Deep down in his gut he'd known that their time in Chicago was growing short. As much as he wanted to believe that his daughter was more human than wolf, he'd known that wasn't likely. He didn't like to admit that part of him was fiercely proud and glad that she was like him. That she was a werewolf.

It wouldn't be easy on her though. James was under no misconceptions about that. Even though she was being sought out as a mate, he knew that many others of his kind would look down on her, disdain her for her tainted blood. A low growl rumbled from deep in his chest. If they thought they could hurt her in any way they were in for a huge awakening. She was *his* daughter and he would protect her against any and all threats.

Even if that meant sending her away with another wolf.

He'd been shocked to hear of his old friend's death and to find young Joshua in his place. Well, he guessed that Joshua wasn't quite so young anymore. He'd always assumed that Joshua's older brother, Isaiah, would take his father's place, but it seemed that the younger brother had taken over that honor and burden.

His fingers tightened around the steering wheel. He couldn't regret the choices he'd made in his life. Because of them, he'd gotten Alexandra, and since the day she was born she'd been his life and his joy.

He did however regret that his friend had died while searching for him. James didn't know that he could have done anything differently. He'd been crushed after Leda's death. He'd lost all interest in pack life and the inevitable politics that went with it. All he'd wanted to do was to go off alone and lick his wounds in private. And he'd done just that.

He'd wandered for almost thirty years before he'd met Charlene. He'd been ready to move on when she'd told him she was pregnant. There had been no doubt in his mind that he was the father. While she'd been with him, she'd been faithful. He knew that for a fact. He'd have been able to smell the stench of any other male on her no matter how hard she might have tried to hide it. No, the child she'd carried was his and, from that moment forward, his life had had purpose for the first time in decades.

James followed the road to the downtown district. He was lucky that he'd just finished fixing the minor problem on the exhaust system of the Mustang this morning. Pulling into a parking garage next to an office complex, he drove to the top level and swung into an empty spot.

Turning off the ignition, he pocketed the keys and leaned back against the seat. It was hard to believe the life he'd built over the past two decades was now lost to him. He'd known that he wouldn't be able to stay here much longer, but he'd hoped for a bit more time, had wanted to leave on his own terms.

With Alex coming into her sexual maturity, he'd known that he would have to return to the Wolf Creek pack in order for her to meet eligible males she might mate with. There really was no other choice. A female in heat needed a male wolf to satisfy her. She could have as many lovers as she wanted, but no human male could ever sate her sexual hunger. They would bring her some relief, but she would always be left wanting, yearning for more.

It had been that way with him and Charlene. She'd filled a void in his life when he'd needed it. For that reason alone, not to mention the fact that she'd given him Alex, he would always have a soft spot for her in his heart. It didn't matter that she'd abandoned her daughter to go back to a life of drugs and prostitution. Everyone had demons of their own to deal with. He was in no position to criticize.

Then there was the pesky little detail that he hadn't aged in twenty years. He couldn't have gotten away with that for much longer. Already people were beginning to talk. It was only a casual remark here and there, but it was enough for James to know that the time had come to pull up stakes and move on.

He'd allowed himself to become a bit too attached to the garage. All his memories from Alex's childhood were associated with the place. He was sad to leave, but he better than anyone knew that life went on. He still had Alex and that was all that mattered.

Climbing out of the vehicle, he locked the door and strode away without a backward glance. When he reached street level, he ambled into the office building situated beside it.

James often wondered about people who could work in these places all day long, being told what to do by someone else. He didn't know how they did it. He couldn't imagine any other way of life except working for himself. But they were working for what they wanted, not expecting it to be handed to them for free. He could respect them for that.

He glanced at his reflection as he pulled open the large glass door. Faded jeans stained with grease and a T-shirt with a rip down the front didn't exactly help him look respectable. Ah well, he wasn't planning on staying long. His boots made no sound as he sauntered across the lobby to the security desk. The closer he got the more nervous the two men working behind the console became. He could smell their fear.

Plucking the keys out of his pocket, he laid them on the marble countertop. "These belong to Mr. Ashanti, of Ashanti Investments, tenth floor. Tell him his Mustang is running perfectly and that it's parked next door, top level, slot eight."

He didn't bother to wait for a reply, but turned and walked away. "Hey, mister," one of the guards yelled after him. James ignored him and kept going.

When he reached the street again, he took a deep breath, scenting the air. Turning left, he strolled down the sidewalk. It wasn't too busy this time of the morning. Most folks were already at work, but there were still enough people to make him uncomfortable. No matter how long he lived in the city he didn't think he'd ever get used to being surrounded by so many people. It made him edgy.

That was why he'd chosen it. Wolves didn't like crowds and cities. Too overwhelming to their highly developed senses. It was like being bombarded by sights, sounds and smells twenty-four hours a day. It was safer here for Alex so he'd learned to control his reaction to the city, reining in his ever-present desire to escape and leave it behind.

He longed to strip off his clothing and let the change wash over him. The wolf within him was restless, needing to run wild and free. He'd curtailed his wolf over the past few weeks, worried about being away from Alex for any extended period of time.

Over the years, he'd made do running in the city parks. Sometimes, he'd driven just outside the city limits where he'd allowed his wolf to take over and roam the night. The once-a-month trips beyond the city had been enough to keep the beast at bay. Barely. The thought that he wouldn't have to control that aspect of himself for much longer was one of the only good things to come out of this mess.

He sauntered down the street, ignoring the people who quickly got out of his way. He found what he was looking for a few blocks away. Pulling open the door, he stepped into the small thrift shop. An older woman with graying hair was manning the place. He nodded at her as he scanned the room.

"Can I help you find anything?" Her voice was raspy. Too many years of cigarettes if his nose was correct.

"T-shirts." He nodded again when she pointed to a rack near the back. He kept one eye on the door as he flipped through the clothing on the rack. Pulling out a chocolate brown shirt in his size, he headed back to the front of the shop. He stopped by another rack long enough to grab a faded denim shirt. Depositing them both on the counter, he waited while she rang up the total. Digging into his pocket, he pulled out enough money to cover it. The whole transaction had taken about two minutes and he was back on the street again, bag in hand.

He resumed his stroll down the sidewalk, not walking too

fast or too slow, but melding with the flow of foot traffic around him. His eyes were never still, always scanning. A smile touched his lips when he found exactly what he was looking for.

Stepping into a busy restaurant, James took a deep breath. Coffee. The half of a muffin he'd eaten this morning seemed like it was days ago. He was starving. First things first, though. He kept his head down as he headed toward the restrooms at the back.

Once inside, he took his new clothing out of the bag and laid it on the edge of the sink. He stripped off his ripped shirt and stuffed it deep into the garbage before shaking out his new T-shirt and pulling it on. Then he tugged the denim shirt on over it. He reached around to the small of his back and withdrew the gun he'd secreted there. Checking it, he returned it to its place. The metal was warm and reassuring. He was just grateful that his original shirt had been baggy enough to hide the slight bulge at his back. The denim shirt gave him better coverage.

He stuffed the bag into the garbage and left the restroom. Ambling back out to the dining area, he found a quiet table in the corner. He was barely seated when a waitress hurried up with a pot of coffee in one hand and a menu in the other. He scanned the menu and ordered while she filled his mug. When she left he allowed himself to close his eyes for a moment.

Alex. Where was she? He had no idea where his little girl was. He could only hope that her own skills combined with young Striker would be enough to get them both out of the city safe and alive. His job was to get out of the city undetected and meet them at Wolf Creek. He wanted to get there ahead of them so that he could be beside Alex when she met the rest of the pack.

But first he had to clean up the mess back at the garage and get some transportation. He opened the menu, scanned it and quickly made his choice. He'd have breakfast first. Hopefully by that time their pursuers would have abandoned the area, believing they'd all run.

If there were any of them left waiting. Well, that was too bad for them. He wasn't feeling real tolerant this morning. They'd have to take their chances. He could feel his entire body start to vibrate and took a deep breath to calm himself, conjuring up what he hoped passed for a smile when the waitress returned to take his order.

Chapter Six

Joshua felt like driving his fist through the nearest wall. He still wasn't quite certain where things had gone wrong. One minute Alex had been soft and warm in his arms, the scent of her release filling his nostrils and making his head spin, the next she'd been angry and, if he wasn't mistaken, hurt. He normally didn't care about other people's feelings. His position as Striker didn't allow for such things. But everything was different with Alex.

Her shoulders were rigid as she marched ahead of him. She pushed open the door of the restaurant and stepped out onto the sidewalk. He followed close behind. Just because she was upset with him didn't mean he'd allow her to take chances with her safety. They couldn't forget for even a second that they were being hunted. They'd gotten lucky the first time around. Next time their pursuers would probably be more skilled.

She didn't even look back to see if he was following her. His lips twitched in spite of his worry. She certainly was a sight when she was worked up over something. Her silvery gray eyes had practically singed his skin when she'd glared at him back in the restroom. Right now he was admiring the sway of her lush bottom as she strode down the sidewalk. It was a perfect handful.

He shook his head, amazed by her sheer stubbornness. He didn't have time to see how long she could go without acknowledging his presence. They had to get moving out of the city.

Quickening his pace until he was alongside her, he gave her a sidelong glance. She ignored him totally, even going so far as to look the other way, pretending great interest in the stores on the other side of the street.

"I know you're angry with me, Alex, but there's no time for that now." He scanned the area ahead of them before looking over his shoulder, searching for anyone who seemed to be out of place. His preternatural senses weren't much help in the crowded city. With so many sounds and smells bombarding him it was hard to distinguish any one in particular. Still, he tried. Alex's safety might depend on that small advantage.

"You have no idea," she muttered as she picked up her pace. People got out of her way as her long legs continued to eat up the sidewalk.

He let her go for two blocks and finally got tired of her ignoring him. Wrapping his hand around her upper arm, he tugged her into a narrow alleyway between two buildings. His senses told him that it was empty, if you didn't count the dumpster at the end with several rats poking around.

She glared at him as she tried to pull her arm from his grasp. His fingers tightened. He wasn't letting her go until she listened to him.

"Oh, right. If you can't get your own way, you'll manhandle me." She dug in her feet as he practically dragged her halfway down the alleyway. Her coat fell from her hands as she ducked beneath his arm and twisted so he was forced to either release her or risk hurting her.

Growling, he let go of her arm and ran his fingers through his hair in frustration. "What do you want from me? Whatever I did, I never intended to make you angry or hurt you." The city still marched on around them, everyone going about their business. Horns blew and the murmur of the crowd was thick in the distance. But here in the alley there was only the two of them.

"That's what makes it worse." Crossing her arms across her chest, she rubbed the spot where he'd gripped her. "It obviously didn't mean anything to you at all."

Not mean anything to him! Not mean anything to him! Did she have any idea just how hard it was for him to even suggest that she meet the other eligible males of the pack when every instinct he possessed was screaming at him to strip her naked, mount her from behind and mark her as his?

His woman. His mate.

"Maybe I will meet those other males and pick someone else," she muttered as she turned away from him.

It was the last straw.

Pouncing, he grabbed her by the shoulders and jerked her around. Whatever she was about to say died on her lips as she got a good look at his face. He moved forward, backing her up against the concrete wall. Capturing her hands in one of his, he raised them over her head. She started to struggle so he shifted his larger body closer to her, using his full weight to trap her.

"Don't you dare say that it didn't mean anything to me." His voice was low and guttural, a mixture of anger and arousal. "What you gave me was a gift. To watch you come, to smell the sweet scent of your cream, to see the ecstasy on your face was a present beyond price. Don't you dare say that it didn't mean anything."

She blinked slowly, her long brown lashes fanning across her cheeks, making her eyes disappear for the briefest of seconds. Damn, she was beautiful, her skin pale and smooth. He reached up with his free hand and traced his fingers over her cheek. The color of her eyes seemed to deepen. Her eyes fascinated him. They were so expressive, so alive.

"I don't understand." She had ceased to fight him, instead staring at him in obvious confusion.

"I know you don't, Alex. I know this is all new to you. That you don't understand our ways." Joshua lowered his head until their foreheads were touching. "First and foremost, my job is to protect you. Nothing else is more important than that. I can't relax my guard unless I know we're safe. To do anything else would be a dereliction of duty.

"I gave my oath to my alpha that I would bring you back safely. Anything less is unacceptable." He paused and lifted his head. "Besides which, I promised your father I'd look after you. I don't think it's wise to break a pledge to James LeVeau. He'd make a steadfast friend but a relentless enemy."

Alex made a small sound of agreement, but said nothing. The mounds of her breasts were pressed against his chest and he could feel their hard nubs through both their layers of clothing. She shifted slightly, her thighs rubbing against his. His shaft swelled and he leaned inward, pressing his pelvis against hers.

"See, this is what I'm talking about, Alex. All I have to do is touch you. Smell you. Hell, all I have to do is see you and I'm hard. But it's not safe here. Nor is it fair to you."

Joshua let out a long, low breath and prayed that what he was about to say didn't get her all worked up and angry with him again. He liked her this way, all soft and supple as she tried to wiggle even closer to him.

He tried not to read too much into her actions, knowing that it might just be the flood of unfamiliar hormones surging through her body, coupled with the adrenaline rush from the danger and their proximity. She had no idea just how potent those hormones and instincts were. But he did. And right now they were urging her to mate with a male of her species and, at this moment, he was the only one available.

"Alex," he began, softening his voice. "You're experiencing emotions and urges you've never felt before and unfortunately you don't have the luxury of time to deal with them. I don't want you to end up doing something you might regret." Not to mention that an alleyway where anyone could walk in on them at any second was not the place to be doing anything. The restroom was bad enough.

He swallowed back a groan as she rubbed her mound against the front of his jeans. Even through the thick fabric, he could feel her heat. He tried to remember what it was he'd been saying. He searched his mind and found the lost thread of the conversation.

"You might feel differently when you meet some of the other males." The last came out on a growl. Just the thought of another male touching her, feeling her heat, made him want to lash out. But he had to be fair to her. He was a tough, unfeeling bastard. A sanctioned killer. She deserved better.

"And you don't like that idea at all, do you?" She traced her tongue along her bottom lip, teasing him.

"Fuck no, I don't like it. But it's what I have to do. It's fair to you and it's fair to the other unmated males of the pack." He didn't even mention that if he claimed her before he brought her to the Wolf Creek pack that he'd have to fight to keep her.

Going up on her tiptoes, she kissed his chin. Her lips were soft and he knew just how damned good they tasted. He lowered his head just a fraction and she took advantage of it, melding her mouth to his.

Who knew? Alex was reeling from Joshua's confession. She didn't think he had any idea just how much he'd revealed to her. Or maybe he did. He refused her, not because he didn't want her, but because he was being honorable.

She'd never met another man who would turn away from a woman who offered sex out of a sense of honor. Most men would take what was offered and then run. But not Joshua. She suspected this wasn't necessarily a code among werewolves either. She had a feeling that this was the core of the man in front of her.

It made her want him even more.

Deep in her heart, she knew it didn't matter how many other males she met. She'd never meet another one she wanted the way she did Joshua Striker. There was something about him that drew her, made her want to be with him. Only him.

It might sound corny, but she wanted to be the one he came to for comfort at the end of a long, hard day. She was under no misconceptions of what his position in the pack forced him to do. She wanted to be able to share his burdens with him, ease them.

She also knew he wasn't ready to hear that yet, wouldn't accept it no matter what she did.

He'd explain it away as hormones or adrenaline or some other foolishness. Alex knew better. She'd always known her own mind and right now both her heart and mind were screaming that he belonged to her.

The anger in his voice when he talked about her meeting other males actually reassured her. Now that she knew he was as emotionally involved, that he did care, all her previous anger melted away.

In a way it was even kind of sweet. He'd given her great pleasure, not taking any for himself, because that was his way of protecting her against himself, against her raging hormones.

And because he'd pledged to protect her, he would at all costs, even if that meant protecting her from him.

She'd just have to convince him differently. And she'd already made a good start. When she'd touched her lips to his he'd responded immediately.

She savored the low groan that rose from deep in his chest as she slid her tongue into his mouth. His pelvis was hard against hers, his cock pressed snug against her sex. Her breasts ached, their tips swollen. God, she couldn't believe she was so hot and primed for orgasm again. Logically, she knew that part of it was hormones, but she knew that just as much had to do with the man in front of her.

He held her hands high above her head, keeping them pinned to the rough brick wall with one hand. His strength was incredible. It was also a complete turn-on, which surprised her. She'd never been the type to be impressed with muscles. She wasn't exactly weak herself and it was hard for any guy to live up to the standard set by her father. But Joshua oozed power even when he was standing still. It was an incredible aphrodisiac.

His tongue twined with hers. It was a slow, unhurried dance that made her entire body hum with pleasure. The man certainly did know how to kiss. He angled his head, deepening the pressure, taking his time as if there was nothing else he'd rather do but spend all day just kissing her.

Come to think of it, she wouldn't mind that at all. She could probably come with him doing nothing else but touching his mouth to hers, his tongue to hers. Her inner core pulsed and she could feel herself creaming her panties. Again.

Joshua eased back, the motion pushing his hips tighter against hers. They both groaned and he gave a muffled laugh. "See what I mean. It's too dangerous for me to touch you, Alex." His fingers flexed around her wrists before he reluctantly released her.

She lowered her arms, slipping them around his shoulders, feeling him tense as she stroked the back of his neck. "You live for danger," she teased.

"Ah, Alex. What am I going to do with you?" His eyes were so dark and soft they appeared almost liquid. His lashes were long and thick. On any other man they might have looked feminine. With Joshua, they only accentuated his masculinity, making the harsh angles of his face appear even sharper.

She could lose herself in those eyes. She could also think of a few things she'd like him to do, but she knew now wasn't the time. Already, she sensed his retreat from her. She was beginning to understand the man beneath the hard exterior, beginning to see what drove him, what motivated him. Even as it frustrated her, it made him even more desirable. She not only understood, but also admired his commitment to duty, his loyalty to his pack.

He took a step back, all softness fading from his expression, his face returning to its normal harsh lines. "We have to keep moving. We have less than two days to meet your father at Wolf Creek and we'll probably need every moment of it."

So much had happened this morning. It was too easy to just want to lose herself in Joshua, to forget the danger they were in, the danger her father was in. That wouldn't do any of them any good.

From now on she'd focus on the journey ahead, doing whatever she could to help them get to their destination alive and in one piece. Once they were there, all bets were off. In the meantime, she'd use the opportunity to learn everything she could about Joshua, his family and the Wolf Creek pack.

Her stomach churned. She still wasn't quite ready to face the whole werewolf thing. It was easy to accept it in Joshua, as she'd never known him as anything else. It was difficult to wrap her head around the fact that not only was her father one too, but she was as well. Or rather she was a half-breed.

He was watching her, gauging her reaction. She straightened her shoulders and offered him a tight smile. Reality had just descended again with a huge thud. It was time to go. "I'm ready."

He hesitated as if he wanted to say something further. Alex waited, but he said nothing, just continued to search her face. She wasn't quite sure what he was looking for or if he even found it, but he finally looked away, glancing toward the top of the alleyway. "I've got a vehicle stashed on the edge of town. All we've got to do is get there without anyone finding us first."

"Okay." She finger-combed her hair and straightened her sweatshirt before leaning down to snag her leather jacket from the ground. Thankfully it hadn't fallen into anything disgusting and she was able to just brush off the dirt before slinging it back over her shoulder. It was only now that she began to notice the questionable smells permeating the alley. She wrinkled her nose and tried not to breathe too deeply.

Joshua was still watching her as if he wasn't quite certain of her mood. He'd have to live with it. She couldn't exactly explain it to him. She wasn't quite sure of everything she was feeling at the moment. They'd have time to talk later. At some point they'd have to stop and rest.

"Stay close," he ordered as he led the way back to the top of the alley. With a quick glance in both directions, he turned, stepped out and headed down the sidewalk.

Alex followed close behind, doing her best to try to meld with the mass of humanity that swarmed around them. For the first time since they'd left the restaurant, she felt exposed and edgy. The reality of the situation was really beginning to sink in.

There were werewolves scouring the city searching for her. If they found her they would kill Joshua and kidnap her, maybe even kill her. From what her father had said, not everyone was enamored of half-breeds like herself. Tainted blood, he'd called it.

She wondered where her father was, praying he was safe. A huge lump swelled up in her throat, but she swallowed it back. He would expect her to do whatever it took to survive and reach Wolf Creek. She had to believe he would be there waiting for her.

She couldn't even contemplate a world in which James Riley wasn't there beside her. Or was it James LeVeau? Joshua had referred to her father by that name twice now. She'd have to ask him about that. No matter the name, he was her father and she'd never known a tougher or more capable man than him. He'd be okay and so would she. They had to be.

Strong fingers entwined with hers, making her jump. She'd been so lost in thought she'd forgotten to focus on her surroundings. That was dangerous, not to mention stupid.

"Everything will be all right." Joshua didn't look at her as he spoke, but kept them moving steadily along with the thinning crowd.

"I know." She fell into step beside him, determined to block out all thoughts, doubts and questions. Survival had to take precedence.

Everything else could wait.

Chapter Seven

Joshua tugged Alex off the "L" as soon as the doors opened, their fellow travelers giving them a wide berth. City dwellers were nothing if not smart when it came to sensing possible danger. It came naturally to them, just part of the urban survival skills they cultivated in order to live in the city. He was tall and strong, but it was more than that. His wolf was riding near the surface, radiating a sense of menace.

Humans might not need their instincts for hunting and wilderness survival, but those instincts were there, existing just beneath the thin skin of civilization. Folks may not be able to put it into words, but they recognized him for what he was—a predator.

It took them most of the afternoon to reach the edge of the city. They'd barely avoided being detected by two different groups of prowling werewolves. Joshua had no idea which packs they were from, only that they weren't from the Wolf Creek pack.

Joshua had caught the scent of one group of wolves just as they'd neared a train station. They'd jumped on the Red Line, melding with the mass of humanity to avoid detection, and ended up on the opposite side of the city. They'd walked for a while, taken the "L" again and then several buses. Joshua had purposely led them around in circles, taking a roundabout route to reach the vehicle he'd left parked in the lot of a large grocery wholesaler.

He'd figured there was less chance of someone noticing it was there for hours and, if they did, they'd just figure it belonged to one of the employees. Plus, with cars and trucks coming and going all day long, it was less likely that anything would happen to the vehicle. He'd moved it several times since arriving in Chicago two days ago, finding similar lots all around the city in which to park to avoid detection. It paid to be cautious.

Alex didn't speak much and neither did he. Both of them were alert now, watching their surroundings as they made their way down the city streets. They'd stopped at a small deli around lunchtime and picked up some sandwiches to eat as they walked, but other than that, they'd been on the move since early morning. Joshua was restless now, wanting to be out of the city and back to the forest where there was room for a man, and a wolf, to breathe.

"Almost there." He glanced over at Alex and she nodded. She'd been great considering what she'd been through. He was amazed at her resiliency and her ability to cope under harsh circumstances. His heart ached as he watched her put one foot in front of the other and keep going. It hadn't been easy to tromp around the city all day while watching for wolves from other packs. Even he felt on edge. He couldn't even begin to wonder just how she was feeling.

"Alex..." He wasn't quite sure what he was going to say to her. He was proud of her. Proud of the way she'd handled herself today with whatever situation had been thrown her way. He wasn't quite sure she would care what he thought. Why would she?

"What is it?" She'd stopped, her eyes darting up and down the street checking for danger.

"Nothing." Now that he'd thought about it, it seemed rather stupid to say something like that to her. Better to just let it go. "The car is just up the road there," he pointed. "The grocery store lot." They could just see the tip of the parking lot from where they were.

"Wonderful." She heaved a sigh and resumed walking. He looked closely at her and noticed the strain on her face and the perspiration on her forehead. She was tired and upset, but hadn't complained once.

Reaching out, he placed his hand on her arm. "I've got to scout out the area first. Just to make sure it's safe." He glanced around and noticed a sheltered doorway of an abandoned building. If she stayed back in the shadows she should be fairly well hidden from view. "Here." He guided her toward it. "Just pretend you're waiting for someone. Keep your eyes open. If for any reason you get nervous, or think someone is watching you, just go into that diner over there." He showed her the one he meant. "If you're not here when I get back, I'll come looking for you over there."

"I want to go with you." She put her hands on her hips and pursed her lips as she stared unflinchingly at him.

"It's safer if I'm alone. Remember, they'll be watching for a couple, not a lone man." He didn't want to tell her that she would also be a danger to him. There weren't as many people and odors here to mask her scent and any male wolf that passed within fifteen feet would smell her. The scent of a female werewolf going into heat was not something any of them were likely to miss. Not to mention he didn't want to have to kill anyone in front of her if it wasn't absolutely necessary. He waited while she thought it over, knowing he'd have less trouble if she agreed than if he tried to force her to do as he wanted.

"All right," she acceded. "It makes sense. But that doesn't mean I have to like it," she added.

In spite of himself, he felt the beginnings of a grin tug at the corners of his mouth. "Duly noted."

He waited until she was safely tucked in the doorway before he loped down the side of the road. The sidewalk was cracked and uneven on either side of the pitted asphalt. Turning right, he followed the wall of the building and came out behind it. All his senses were on alert now, searching for any sight, sound or smell that might alert him to possible danger. His eyes were always moving, searching out places where someone might hide. His gaze went to the rooftops, scanning as he passed behind them.

He didn't see anything, but his wolf was telling him different. The back of his neck itched as if someone were watching him. Joshua eased into the shadow of a large delivery truck and waited. Dusk was quickly falling over the city and he hoped to be well underway before dark.

Traveling at night was a dangerous proposition. There was

less traffic on the road, making them an easier target as the werewolves all knew where they were headed. But the car had some built-in safety features and a stash of weapons. He wouldn't risk it if the situation weren't critical.

Joshua crouched low and scooted behind a dumpster. Again, he waited. Watched. Listened. The air was still and filled with the stench of the city—people, garbage, grease from the few restaurants along this strip of road—making it hard for him to catch the scent of any wolves.

One slow foot at a time, he shifted from cover to cover until he was almost directly across from the grocery store. He could see the dusty, dented car in the parking lot. It was nondescript, but what was under the hood was a prime piece of machinery. Looks could be deceiving, and not only in a vehicle. It was almost too quiet. Joshua didn't trust it.

A slight movement caught his eye and he squinted to focus better. *There.* Across from the car was a man just sitting in his vehicle. Maybe he was just waiting for someone to come out of the wholesaler. Maybe not. Joshua kept searching.

A flash on the rooftop next to him caught his attention. If he hadn't been looking at just that second he would have missed it. Might be nothing. Could be a rifle of some sort.

He might be paranoid, but he didn't think so. His senses were screaming at him and he always paid attention. The wolf within him could sense more than he could in human form. It paid to listen.

Joshua glanced up at the building beside him. There was a fire escape ladder running down the side, stopping about eight feet from the ground. He hated exposing himself in that way, but he had no choice. He had to check the rooftop. Besides, going up on the roof would give him a better vantage point, allowing him to get a bird's-eye view of the entire area.

Joshua's boots made no noise as he crept across the gravel lot. Fatigue washed over him, but he shook it off. He'd been roaming around this city for the better part of forty-eight hours with only a couple hours sleep. He was hungry too. The sandwich he'd had for lunch had been hours ago and his metabolism was faster than a human's. He needed a lot more calories to function properly.

Ignoring both the fatigue and the hunger, he bent his legs and jumped, grabbing the bottom rung of the ladder. The muscles in his arms flexed and strained as he hauled himself up until he could hook his foot over the metal bar. Not making a sound, he climbed to the top. He peered over the top of the ladder and froze. There on the far side of the roof, watching the road, was a man with a high-powered rifle.

The stranger put his hand to his ear, where a small earpiece rested. "What?"

Joshua closed his eyes and focused his acute sense of hearing in order to hear the voice on the other end of the wireless communication device. Thankfully, there weren't too many extraneous sounds. If he hadn't been this close, he never would have been able to do it.

"Any sign of them yet?"

"Nothing. You sure we're in the right place?" The male swiped a hand across his forehead.

Joshua sniffed the breeze and froze. What was a human male doing keeping their vehicle under surveillance?

"Our informant said that one of those bastard werewolves had abducted a woman and would be bringing her here. It's bad enough that those mutants are allowed to live. We can't let them take our women," the disembodied voice replied as he signed off.

Shit! Bounty hunters. And these were of the type who specialized in capturing and destroying paranormal species. Although most of the population didn't even know that paranormal creatures existed, there were those who not only knew, but vehemently hated them. These people believed the only good paranormal creature was a dead one. As a result, bounty hunters had sprung up all over the world, each group specializing in the elimination of a particular paranormal creature. Obviously these were werewolf hunters.

The urge to launch himself over the top of the building, rush the man and break his neck burned in his gut. These hunters had been responsible for the deaths of one of his siblings and many of his friends over the years. They typically preyed on the younger of the species, many times slaughtering and skinning the newly transformed adults, wearing the fur hides as a sort of grim prize of war.

He'd killed his share of hunters over the years, especially after his younger sister had disappeared all those years ago. They'd never found her body, but he'd smelled the stench of a hunter in the area where she'd disappeared. He'd searched, like someone half-mad, for years, but never found the man who'd killed her.

That had been almost thirty-five years ago. By now the passage of time had probably taken care of the hunter, but the need for vengeance had never died within Joshua. It was part of the reason he'd taken over his father's position in the pack when he'd been killed. The need to protect his people from harm drove him relentlessly. And it was the need to protect that made him back away from the hunter.

Alex was out there on her own.

Joshua slowly retreated back down the ladder. Sweat rolled down his temple. Was Alex all right or had they found her? As quickly as he could, he made his way back down behind the buildings. Their vehicle was being watched. At this point he couldn't be sure if it was by just hunters or if there were also members from the various werewolf packs as well.

Obviously some of those bastards had been smart enough to trick the hunters into helping them try to eliminate him. Not that it mattered. There was no way he could risk Alex's safety by making a run for the car. It was also likely that they'd disabled it somehow anyway.

Silently sliding along the edge of a building, he peered around the corner. The doorway where he'd left her was empty. His heart stopped, time slowed down. The predator in him slowly came to the fore, rippling beneath his skin, demanding to be let out. His scalp tingled, his muscles tightened. He exerted his iron control, not allowing himself to shift into wolf form, but he utilized every other aspect of the beast. If they'd taken her, he'd kill them all—hunters and wolves alike.

Meandering down the side of the road so as not to attract attention, he headed toward the restaurant, but didn't enter. Instead, he stood to one side of the window, peering inside. It wasn't that big and he could see every table and booth.

Alex wasn't there, but another wolf was. He recognized the

bastard as one of the men who'd jumped them in the apartment this morning. He sniffed the air, but was unable to catch a whiff of Alex's scent. There were too many smells coming from the open door of the restaurant, confusing his senses and masking individual scents.

His eyes narrowed as he turned away, scanning the street. Where was she? He went back to the doorway where he'd stashed Alex and sniffed. *There!* The sweet aroma of female filled his nostrils. He took a step in one direction and stopped and sniffed. Nothing. Stepping back to the doorway, he stepped in another direction. Nothing. He did that several more times before he caught the faintest smell of Alex. Keeping all his senses on alert, he started out in that direction.

The trail led him toward an abandoned building that was boarded up. He circled it slowly, pausing now and again to listen and to sniff. He caught a whiff of Alex heading off behind the buildings and started after her. He hadn't gone more than a dozen steps when he paused. His instincts were screaming at him to stop.

Turning on one heel, he crept back to the building, circling it again until he found what he was searching for. One of the windows had several boards torn away from it. It would be a tight squeeze, but he could make it.

He crouched beside the window and waited for several minutes. There was no sound from inside. Putting one long leg through the opening, he gripped the rough edges of the window frame and angled his head and upper body through the gap.

Alex. Her scent washed over him, overlaid with fear, just as he heard the whoosh of something coming toward his head. He rolled forward, hauling his other leg in behind him as he went. Coming up on his feet, he spun around and growled, ready to protect Alex from whoever had her.

She stood not five feet from him, as pale as a ghost with a long piece of two-by-four clutched in her hands. "Oh, God. I'm sorry. I didn't know it was you." Her fingers were visibly trembling, but she held on tightly to her makeshift weapon. "I didn't want to use the gun. I was afraid it would attract attention. And what if it was just a vagrant or something. I'm not a murderer." She was talking nonstop now, obviously shaken. "Couldn't you have called out or something?" Her voice was getting sharper now, anger bringing the color back to her face. Joshua watched her, fascinated with how quickly her mood changed.

"Would have served you right if I'd bashed your thick skull in."

He let her rant until she ran out of steam and then he simply opened his arms to her. She glared at him and then her chin wobbled ever so slightly. "I could have killed you." Before he could respond, she launched herself into his arms. He closed them around her, needing to feel her next to his heart to reassure himself that she was safe.

"I'm all right. Everything is all right," he crooned as he held her. He kissed the top of her head as he rocked her in his arms, content for the moment to just stand here with her.

She leaned back, and he saw the raw determination etched on her face. Once again he was struck by how strong she was, how capable of dealing with whatever situation was thrown at her. He didn't know many people, werewolf or human, who would attack him with nothing but a two-by-four. She was something.

"What happened?" As much as he wanted to keep holding her, they needed to be gone from here. But first, he needed to know exactly what she'd seen.

"I saw one of them. One of the guys from the garage this morning." Her gray eyes narrowed. "He was with another man. I don't know if he was werewolf or human."

Joshua nodded. "I saw him in the diner I told you to go to. He was alone."

"The second I saw him I hurried around to the back of this place and found the same opening you did. I couldn't see out front. All I could do was wait. I figured if you didn't come back I could make my way back to the garage and find transport from someone in the neighborhood."

It made his blood run cold to think of Alex running around the city at night by herself. Werewolves weren't the only predators out on the streets after sundown.

She scowled at him. "I know what you're thinking, but it sure as heck isn't safe to stay here."

On that score she was correct. "You're right." He didn't have to like it, but she was absolutely right. It would have been her best course of action. In her neighborhood, she knew who she could trust and who she couldn't. He raked his fingers through his hair and sighed. "We can't stay here."

Something in his tone must have alerted her. She straightened slowly, the stick falling from her fingers to land heavily on the floor. Dust flew, but she ignored it. "What happened? What did you see?"

"They've brought in hunters to help them." He was still disgusted that fellow wolves would stoop to such a level as to associate with the hated hunters.

"Hunters?" He'd forgotten for a moment that she really had no idea of what life was really like for werewolves, for her people. She, like most humans, had no idea of the silent war that raged around them between paranormal beings and bounty hunters.

The fighting mostly took place in desolate, abandoned parts of the cities or in more secluded towns and the surrounding woods. The paranormal creatures didn't want the entire world to know about them. Survival was hard enough without government and the military hunting them. As for the hunters, they were a breed apart, men and women who didn't fit into society. Their mistrust of authorities and government kept them quiet. That and the fear they'd end up in a psych ward in some institution if they started spouting on about werewolves, vampires and demons.

He wanted to shelter Alex from the truth, but knew that wasn't possible, nor was it smart. She'd had a nice, comfortable life before today and for a brief second he regretted having had a part in destroying it, even though he knew that there had been nothing else he could have done. There was no way he could have allowed other wolf packs to take her. They might not treat her with the care and respect they would a full-blooded female wolf, but regard her as little more than a brood mare to give them the children their kind so desperately needed.

He reached out and brushed a smudge of dirt off her cheek with his thumb. She was obviously exhausted, hot and sweaty. Her sweatshirt was stained and dirty, her boots scuffed and dusty. She wore no make-up and there were dark circles beneath her eyes. She was the most beautiful creature he'd ever seen and he hated that he was going to add to the fear he saw in her beautiful gray eyes.

"Bounty hunters," he began softly. "There are many who want to eliminate our kind from the face of the planet. They kill as many of us as they can, but it is the young and the elderly who are the most vulnerable."

"Oh my God," she cried. Her eyes were huge against her pale skin.

He inwardly cursed all hunters for bringing that look of fear and disgust to her face, but he continued. She had to know the truth, if only for her own protection. "They hunt with silver bullets, with heavy steel traps coated in silver, and skin whatever unfortunate wolves they catch whether they are in human or wolf form." He closed his eyes and swallowed as memories of friends and loved ones he'd found too late washed over him. The children were always the worst.

Sounds of Alex retching pulled him out of his memories. She'd turned away to a dark corner and was bent over at the waist with her arms wrapped around her stomach. He quickly went to her side and held her until she was finished. Not that there was much in her stomach to lose, but she continued to heave long after it was empty. Finally, she stopped and her legs buckled. Swinging her up into his arms, he carried her over to the window.

"We have to leave, Alex." Comfort would have to wait. They'd already wasted more time than was safe. He needed to get her far away from this area.

"I know." Her voice was weak, but determined. "Is that what I have to look forward to? Hunters wanting to trap me and skin the flesh from my body simply because of an accident of birth?"

His arms tightened around her. "That won't happen." He would not allow it to happen.

"You might not be able to stop it." She rubbed her hands over her face and took a deep breath. "Put me down."

He stared at the window, trying to figure out how he was going to get through it with her in his arms. He'd have to tear off a few more of the boards, but that meant he'd have to put her down, which he didn't want to do.

"Joshua." She cupped his face with her hands, turning it toward her. "You have to put me down. I'm fine." She cut him off with a sharp shake of her head before he had a chance to speak. "No. You know I'm right. You need to have both hands free in case you have to fight. I need to be on my feet in case I need to defend myself."

Giving into the inevitable, he released the arm tucked beneath her knees, letting her body slide over his as her feet touched the ground. "Stay close and do exactly as I tell you."

He knew she didn't quite like his order, but she nodded. Then her face softened once again. "Thank you for coming to look for me."

"I'll always come for you, Alex." He forced himself to release her and ease himself through the window. He looked back and she was still standing there watching him, an unreadable expression on her face. He held out his hand to her. "Come. We have to go."

Taking his hand, she allowed him to help her climb out of the building and into the night that had fallen over the city.

"Where are we going?" She kept her voice pitched low so that it was barely a whisper.

"We have to hide somewhere safe while I try to round us up another means of transport."

She hesitated, worrying her bottom lip with her teeth. He almost groaned as the unconscious action sent a bolt of lust through him.

"I can get us something to drive. A car that won't be tied to either dad or me."

He shook his head. "Don't worry. I can get us another vehicle. I've got contacts in the city."

"You do?" Surprise tinged her voice.

He ignored her unspoken question, keeping his eyes, ears and nose open as he led her behind a large group of buildings before heading back out to the sidewalk. They walked in silence for several blocks and then jumped on a bus, riding it until the crowds grew thicker as they moved into a more heavily populated area.

Getting off the bus, they assimilated with the crowd of people, many of whom were on their way to dinner and then on to the clubs to dance and drink and maybe find a partner to fuck for the night as a way to forget their problems.

"Joshua?" she prompted again.

"We'll talk when it's safe. I'll answer your questions then." He could sense her irritation with him, but ignored it. Nothing was more important then her safety.

"You bet your ass you will," she muttered under her breath. But he heard her and it made him smile.

Chapter Eight

Alex kept pace with Joshua as he led her down one street and then another. It was dark now and she was glad that he seemed to know where he was going because she had no idea where they were headed.

She was still shaken from nearly coming face-to-face with one of the attackers from this morning. For a while, she'd almost allowed herself to believe that the morning attack was a one-time thing. That somehow her life might be able to go back to normal. Seeing him was a brutal reminder that this was now her reality. These men would kill to have her.

And others might just kill her. She shivered, pulling her jacket tighter around her as she thought about the bounty hunters. What kind of men hunted and killed children just because they were from a different species? She shook her head at the naiveté of her question. There were always individuals that preyed on those who were weaker or different. She saw it in her own neighborhood. It happened every day around the world. People feared anything, or anyone, who was different.

Alex swallowed, tasting the sourness in her mouth from where she'd lost what remained of her lunch. That had been weak. She needed to toughen up if she was going to survive. She straightened her shoulders and kept her eyes on Joshua. He'd killed a man today. Snapped his neck with his bare hands. While she couldn't get the wolf she'd shot out of her mind, she didn't think that Joshua had given the man he'd killed a second thought.

Not that Joshua was cold blooded or cruel. He was the exact opposite. Joshua lived by a code of right and wrong. His goal was to protect his people and he'd do whatever it took to do so. He didn't go looking for trouble, but he wouldn't walk away from it. She knew without a doubt that he'd give his life to protect her.

How did a man get to be like Joshua? What life experiences had shaped his character, making him what he was?

He exuded a bone-deep confidence in his ability to take care of himself and her. There was almost a feral quality in the way he watched the world around him. He was definitely the predator. It was in the way he held himself. In the way he walked. Men would fear him even as they wanted to be him and women would just want to be with him.

Joshua was an enigma. One minute amorous, the next totally controlled, seemingly almost indifferent. The man had more layers than an onion and she was determined to get under his skin. What did he mean that he had contacts? Did that mean he wasn't here alone? Why hadn't they gotten help before now if it was available? She had so many questions she was beginning to get a headache. Her stomach was still queasy and she desperately needed some water to rinse her mouth out.

Glancing around, she saw a convenience store that was still open. "I need some water."

Joshua turned to her and searched her face before nodding. "I should have thought of that."

That one sentence made her smile. "You're not God, Joshua. You can't think of everything."

One corner of his mouth twitched, but he didn't smile. "It's my job to think of everything." He held the door open to allow her to enter in front of him.

The lighting was harsh and she blinked, allowing her vision to focus. She headed straight to the cooler in the back and slid the glass door open, extracting a couple bottles of water. Joshua had one eye on her and the other on the customers in the store. She had no doubt that he knew exactly where everyone was, what they were wearing, and could give a detailed description of them if needed.

What must it be like to have to live like that? She guessed that she'd better start learning from him, start paying more attention herself. He might think he was responsible for her safety, but ultimately she was responsible for herself.

"Is there anything you want?" She kept her voice low as she made her way back to his side.

He shook his head. "When we get where we're going I'll get whatever we need."

She took her place in the small line, plunking her two bottles on the counter when her turn came. Reaching into the pocket of her jeans, she found a crumpled bill. The middle-aged clerk paid her no attention as he rang up her purchase, took her money and handed her back her change. She stuffed the money in her pocket, grabbed the two bottles of water and headed for the door with Joshua right behind her.

As soon as they were outside, she tucked one bottle into her coat pocket and twisted the cap off the other. Lifting it, she brought the opening to her mouth. The water felt cool and refreshing against her lips. She didn't swallow though. Instead, she swished the liquid around in her mouth and spit into a garbage can that was right outside the store. She did that several more times, trying to rid herself of the nasty taste in her mouth, before finally allowing herself to drink some of the water.

"Better?"

She nodded as she tilted the bottle up, draining what was left in it before tossing it into the garbage can. She plucked the other one from her pocket, opened it and offered it to Joshua. He took it, his fingers grazing hers as he removed it from her hand. The slight brush of his skin against hers had her entire body clenching with need. This was ridiculous.

He took a long pull from the bottle. The column of his neck was strong and his throat moved convulsively as he swallowed. His face was in profile to her, emphasizing the harsh planes and the silhouette of his nose. She'd never noticed the small bump in the center of it before. It was a fairly large nose, but it suited his face well.

He lowered the bottle and licked his lips. Alex found herself licking her lips as well. What she'd really like to do was lick his lips. Shaking herself, she managed to tear her eyes from him just before he turned back to her and handed her the bottle.

"Thanks. That hit the spot."

She was careful not to allow their fingers to touch when she took the container back from him. "You're welcome." She drank what was left and tossed the bottle into the garbage bin. "I'm ready."

"You certainly are." His low, intimate voice stroked over her skin like a physical caress. What the heck did he mean by that? Before she could get the nerve to ask him to explain himself, he was already on the move again. She had to hurry for a bit to catch up before falling in to step beside him.

Physically, Joshua was a sight to behold. She watched him as he prowled down the dimly lit sidewalk. His legs were long and thick with muscles. His jeans cupped his ass to perfection and he had a loose-legged gait that had made more than one woman stop and stare. Alex responded by glaring at them.

It was pure pleasure to watch Joshua move. The man was incredibly good looking in a rough sort of way. He had a fluid grace that she'd only ever seen in one other man—her father. She realized now that it was the wolf in them both that allowed them to move in that manner.

Alex couldn't deny that there was an animal magnetism about him that drew her. Was he right? Would she be just as drawn to another werewolf? Alex didn't think so. There was something special about Joshua. Werewolf or man, she would have felt the pull.

What would it be like to make love to him?

A shiver skated down her spine and she rubbed her sweaty palms over the legs of her jeans. It was almost enough to make her come just by thinking about all that male intensity focused entirely on her. He would be a thorough lover. Of that she had no doubt. Everything he did, he did with purpose, putting all his attention into it. It was all too easy to imagine him braced over her, driving himself deep into her core, making her scream with pleasure. She had quite an imagination even though she'd never had a lover before.

She licked her lips as she glanced away, needing to gain some control over her runaway hormones. Alex looked around and caught a few familiar landmarks, eventually getting her bearings. They were near the entertainment district. Art galleries, restaurants and trendy clubs all vied for people's money. These were, for the most part, upscale businesses, but there were clubs and bars throughout the city, ranging from chic to seedy, and everything in between.

Mind-numbing liquor, loud music and a chance to forget just how brutal and unforgiving the world could be was their appeal. There were private clubs, if you knew where to find them, offering all sorts of illicit experiences. Everyone knew about them, but most never talked about them or knew exactly where to find them.

"Where are we going?"

"We're going to see someone about getting some new transportation." Joshua caught her hand in his and tugged her along the sidewalk. She supposed she'd slowed down, although it hadn't been intentional. The colored lights and the sounds of music drifting out from the clubs had caught her attention. There was a party atmosphere in the air, but beneath it she sensed the darkness, the desperation.

She also sensed Joshua's growing tension and it made her nervous. It was too loud, too boisterous, too everything here. It almost hurt her eyes and ears to take it all in. Vendors hawked food from steaming carts, while bouncers stood outside clubs, muscular arms crossed, allowing people inside a few at a time. She noted a sharp-eyed youth lift the wallet of one unsuspecting man, and several men and women who passed them were carrying weapons. She might have been somewhat sheltered in her life, but her father had taught her how to watch others so she could protect herself. Not that she could criticize them. She had a knife shoved in each of her boots and a 9mm stuffed in her pocket.

Alex watched all the people streaming by them. Hard-looking men in jeans and leather shared the street with businessmen in three-piece suits. Women in high heels, short skirts, skimpy tops and too much makeup laughingly called out suggestive ideas to some of the men. Other women in expensive dresses and glittery jewelry were let into clubs while others waited in long lines.

Several men glanced at her, but quickly looked away when Joshua pinned them with a lethal glare. They couldn't know what he was, but it was as if they sensed he was not a man to mess around with.

"Stay close." He tugged her away from the general stream of humanity. They kept walking and Alex caught a whiff of chocolate on the air. That could only mean one thing—the Fulton River District. Here thriving businesses, that included a chocolate company, sat alongside empty warehouses and million-dollar condos. Development was fast and furious in this section of town.

Alex's curiosity was aroused. Were they headed for one of the empty warehouses or one of the fabulous condos? Apparently neither. Joshua led her down a dimly lit alleyway that ran alongside a large warehouse. Even from outside, she could hear the heavy pulse of the music pounding from the nightclub within. They passed a long line of patrons waiting outside and went to a closed iron door.

"Hey man," one guy complained. "There's a line here."

Joshua ignored him and banged on the door. Several other men began to curse and the crowd grew restless. Alex edged sideways so that she could watch the crowd. She didn't want anyone sneaking up behind them. Joshua hammered on the door again.

It was shoved open by the biggest man Alex had ever seen and she forgot all about the crowd behind them. She just stood there and stared at him. The guy had to be at least six-foot-eight, if not larger. Wearing leather pants, boots and a vest, and with his head shaved bald, he was an intimidating sight. Thankfully, he ignored her and glared at Joshua. "What?"

"I need to see Damek." Joshua didn't seem to be the least bit concerned that this guy was bigger than him.

The bouncer stared at Joshua, then at her. She felt pinned to the spot by his stare but she didn't look away, meeting his gaze without blinking. She let out the breath she'd been holding when he turned back to Joshua. "And you are?"

"Striker."

The bouncer's eyes widened, as if he recognized the name. He nodded and stepped aside to let them pass. Some of the people waiting started to complain. The big man silenced them with a single threatening look.

Alex followed Joshua into a shadowy vestibule. The

bouncer opened another door. "Wait on the dance floor. Damek will let you know if he'll see you."

Joshua nodded and led her inside. The heat hit her like a blast, the music assaulting her ears. "Who is Damek?" She hoped whoever he was, he could help them find the transportation they needed to get out of the city.

"Not now," Joshua all but yelled in her ear. She could barely hear him above the din of the music and the crowd.

It was hard to move as the mass of writhing bodies on the dance floor undulated to the rhythmic beat of the music. Drums pounded, a saxophone wailed and two guitars spilled their electric notes around the room. There were tables around the edges of the floor and they were all occupied.

Alex's eyes widened as she saw one couple openly fondling one another. The woman's blouse was wide open, her breasts spilling out into the man's hand. The woman had her hand buried down the front of her partner's pants.

She gasped when she saw another couple fucking against the back wall. The man's back was to her, but it was obvious that his pants were open and he was pounding into his partner whose skirt was shoved up around her waist. Her bare thighs were wrapped around his waist as he thrust against the woman, oblivious to the people around them.

"Ignore it." She jumped as Joshua slung his arm around her shoulder and guided her onto the dance floor.

Ignore it. There was no way she was going to be able to forget the fact that there were people all around them having sex. The more her eyes became accustomed to the flashing lights the more she saw.

One woman was kneeling beneath a table, a man's cock sliding in and out of her mouth as she sucked. Another woman was topless, her mouth open on a silent scream as two men lapped at her nipples. There was a booth in the corner that was a mass of limbs and body parts. She wasn't sure she really wanted to know what was going on over there.

Alex had never been a voyeur, but there was something almost mesmerizing about watching all these bodies intertwined, not caring if anyone else watched as they took part in the most basic of human acts.

Even on the dance floor, hands slid over bare flesh. People were in various stages of undress, touching themselves and others around them as they danced. One man was jerking himself off to the beat of the music while two women watched, their hands sliding over his bare chest. Another woman was totally naked, sandwiched between two men who had their fingers up her ass and her slit and their tongues wrapped around her nipples. Colored lights flickered wildly over the crowd, making the scene even more surreal.

Joshua pulled her to a halt and twirled her around so that she was facing him. "Ignore it," he repeated, as he placed his hands on her ass and pulled her closer.

Oh God. Her pelvis met his and she almost moaned as the hard bulge in the front of his jeans rubbed against her mound. There was no denying that the scene around her had aroused her senses and fired the gnawing need within her.

"That's it," he crooned in her ear. "They don't exist. It's only you and me." Joshua began to move to the music, his hips swaying. Alex caught the rhythm and began to move with him. Their hips swiveled and ground together, mimicking the sex act as they came together again and again.

One of his hands slid up her back and around to the front, cupping her breast through her sweatshirt. Joshua surrounded her, his heat and strength wrapped around her like a blanket.

Alex licked her lips and rotated her hips, grinding her sex against him. Even through the layers of clothing it was a delicious sensation. Her clit was swollen and each stroke against him made it throb even harder. Her panties were soaked and all she wanted was to get closer to Joshua.

A bead of sweat slipped down her back. All around them people danced and moved, intruding on their space, stealing all the air. Alex felt breathless. Lightheaded. "Joshua." His name sounded more like a moan. His dark eyes narrowed as he lowered his head toward her. His lips got closer. Almost touching.

Joshua emitted a low growl and his head jerked to the left. Alex followed his gaze and saw a large hand touching his shoulder. He released her immediately, whirling around to meet the threat, a low growl rising from deep in his chest.

The bouncer raised his hands in a gesture of peace and yelled over the crowd. "Relax, man. Damek will see you now." He pointed toward the bar area.

Joshua nodded, grabbed her hand and tugged her through the crowd. Now that the moment had passed, Alex's cheeks got hot with embarrassment. What had come over her? There was something about this place that seemed to shove aside all her natural inhibitions. She'd have made love to Joshua on the dance floor if he'd wanted. And she wouldn't have cared that all those people around them would have been able to watch.

As if he knew where he was going, Joshua led her past the bar and down a short corridor. The closer they got, the tenser she became. There was something here. Something dangerous.

"Let me do the talking."

She could have told Joshua he didn't need to worry about her saying anything. She still wasn't sure who or what they were meeting.

The door at the end of the hallway opened as they neared it. A chill went down Alex's spine in spite of the heat. Something powerful. Something—she wasn't quite sure if it was evil or not, but it was close—waited for them.

"Come in." The deep voice was pleasant, but she wasn't fooled for one moment. Her instincts screamed at her to turn and run in the other direction. Whoever this Damek character was, he was not someone to trifle with. It took every ounce of strength she possessed to walk into the office with Joshua.

"Damek," Joshua greeted the man seated behind the desk.

"Striker." The man was seated almost totally in shadow, but he stood as they entered. The door shut solidly behind them. Alex glanced over her shoulder. There was no one there.

She turned back to the man behind the desk. A dim light now shone on him and Alex realized this was no man. But what was he? If she were guessing, she'd say this was a vampire. His eyes were black, magnetic. It was incredibly hard, almost impossible, to look away. His skin was pale, but he wasn't unhandsome. On the contrary, there was something compelling about him.

"And who is your lovely companion?"

She didn't wait for Joshua to answer. "Alex," she replied.

"Alexandra Riley."

The corner of one side of his mouth twitched and he gave her a short nod. "Welcome to Inhibitions."

She jerked back as he said the name of the club. It was aptly named because a person seemed to shed all inhibitions here. Her eyes narrowed as she studied Damek. Was he powerful enough to put some sort of spell on the club? Maybe he was a wizard or something. Did wizards even exist? At this point, she couldn't discount any possibilities.

"I need a vehicle." Joshua got straight to business. Alex was glad. The quicker they got out of this place, the better. She was beginning to get a headache.

"So I understand." He indicated the chairs in front of him. "Please sit."

Alex felt compelled to sit, as if someone was whispering in her ear telling her she wanted to sit. It was disconcerting to say the least. She shook her head. "Thank you, but I'll stand."

Damek stared at her. She stared back. A slow smile spread across his face. "She is worthy of you, my friend," he said to Joshua.

Joshua just glared at the other man, but she sensed her actions had pleased him somehow. "Thank you."

"Ah, you're in a hurry. A pity you won't stay longer. It might be entertaining." Damek slanted a glance her way. "I was enjoying the performance on the dance floor."

Heat suffused her face as she realized he'd been watching her rub herself all over Joshua. Seen her grind her breasts against Joshua's chest, her mound against Joshua's erection.

A low growl of warning rumbled up from deep inside Joshua's chest. "Tread carefully, my friend. This is James LeVeau's daughter you're talking to."

Damek leaned forward and peered at her more closely. Alex felt pinned to the spot, as if she couldn't move. The moment passed as quickly as it had begun. Damek inclined his head in her direction and sat back at his desk, suddenly all business.

Alex felt relief wash over her and the very air in the room seemed to lighten. She still wasn't comfortable here and couldn't wait to leave.

"There will be a truck waiting for you tomorrow morning."

He rattled off the location and Joshua nodded.

"How much?"

Damek shook his head and returned his stare to Alex. She felt as if he were trying to see all the way to her very soul. She didn't flinch, didn't give away anything, although she reached her hand out to Joshua. He closed his fingers around hers, linking their hands together.

"Nothing." Damek stood. "I find I like the idea of James LeVeau being in my debt. We are finished here." He glided from around back of his desk, coming to a halt in front of her. "If there is anything you need, do not hesitate to ask." He tucked a heavy vellum business card into her jacket pocket. "Just show this at the door."

"Um, thanks." She forced herself not to flinch as he reached out and touched her face. His fingers were cool as they brushed her cheek. Beside her, Joshua tensed. She could practically feel him vibrating with barely suppressed fury.

Joshua dug into his pocket and dumped a roll of cash on the desk. "This should cover it. I wouldn't want myself, or anyone else, to be in your debt." He turned to her. "Come on."

Joshua tugged her away and Damek's hand fell back by his side. Within the blink of an eye, he seemed to vanish, although she sensed him there in the shadows of the room.

Alex followed Joshua back down the short hallway and through the crowd as they made their way toward the entrance. She couldn't get out of the club fast enough. The bouncer opened the door for them and they stepped out into the alleyway. Alex took a breath of fresh air, sucking it into her lungs.

"What was that all about?" She had no idea what just happened, but it felt as if something momentous had. "What is he?"

"Not now," Joshua snapped. "When we're away from here."

Alex frowned. She knew he was upset, but she wasn't quite sure why. He was the one who'd taken her to that club in the first place. Damek was his contact, not hers.

Even as she said it, she remembered the card tucked away in her pocket—the business card that came with an offer of help. That wasn't something she was likely to use any time in the future. She instinctively knew that the offer of help came with strings attached.

She'd only just met him, but Alex didn't think Damek was the kind of creature to do anything out of the goodness of his heart. With him, there would always be a price.

Chapter Nine

Joshua knew he was acting like an ass, but he couldn't seem to stop. Jealousy was an ugly emotion and one he had no experience with. He'd wanted to rip Damek's throat out when he'd touched Alex. The immortal being was more than a little fascinated by Alex, even going so far as to offer her future help. That wasn't good. The last thing he needed was a war with a vampire. Those bastards were tough and, in spite of their deathly reaction to the sunlight, extremely hard to kill.

He could all but hear Damek laughing at him, the sonofabitch. They'd known each other for about ten years now, but he couldn't say they were friends. They occasionally did favors for one another. The survival of their respective species was always paramount. The paranormal bounty hunters had given them a common foe, one that had made them reach out to one another in a way they wouldn't naturally do.

Joshua didn't know how Damek managed to live and work alongside humanity on a regular basis. But then, he was a much more social creature. There was the added fact that Damek needed blood to survive. Being close to the source was essential. He'd heard once that Damek was almost a thousand years old, although he'd never asked him if that was true.

"Where are we going?" Alex walked alongside him, stretching out her step to match his. He slowed immediately, suddenly realizing how fast he'd been going. He also loosened his grip on her hand. He'd been squeezing it so hard it was a wonder she hadn't demanded he release her.

"We need to lie low until the morning." His gaze went up and down the street, watching for trouble. He wished they were already on their way out of Chicago. He knew that the bounty hunters and groups of werewolves from other packs would be watching the roads, but he would almost be willing to take that risk if they had transportation.

It was getting more dangerous by the second for them to remain in the city. The place seemed to be swarming with werewolves. But leaving tonight was no longer an option. They'd have a vehicle in the morning and it would be safer then. There would be traffic on the roads and they'd be in a nondescript truck that couldn't be traced to either of them. Right now, he needed to find them a safe place to stay for the night.

"That club," she began. "It was different."

That was an understatement. Damek ran a den of iniquity. If you had a vice, he could cater to it. But surprisingly enough, he had scruples, lived by his own code of ethics. Damek had no trouble taking the money of the rich and powerful and foolish who ventured inside Inhibitions, but Joshua had never seen him prey on the innocent. Not that many people who crossed the threshold of Inhibitions were innocent. Usually far from it.

"Damek is dangerous."

"No kidding," she snorted. "Is he a vampire?"

"Yes."

"That place...it makes you feel out of control. Is he powerful enough to alter how people act?"

Joshua had often wondered the same thing. "I think it's a combination of the club itself and the vampire's mind-control abilities. It's more of a matter of controlling one or two people. Once a handful of people let go of their inhibitions, others tend to follow." He glanced at her and felt a cold sweat break out on his body as he noticed the flush of her skin. She was still aroused from their dance at the club. Now that they were away from the crowds, he could just catch a whiff of her sweet scent.

"It is..." She licked her lips and shrugged. "Arousing. It's very arousing to watch other people engaging in sexual acts."

Joshua wanted to howl. He wanted to back Alex into a deserted alleyway, strip off her pants and drive into her until they both yelled their release. His cock was as hard as steel and his balls hung heavy and low. He gritted his teeth and concentrated on taking one slow breath at a time.

He couldn't take her. Not here. Not now.

First of all, it wasn't safe, and her safety came above all else. Secondly, he'd promised himself he would wait until they arrived at Wolf Creek. He wanted to mate with her, but he wanted it done in a way so none could contest his claim.

The only way to gain control was to ignore her. Keeping his hand linked to hers, he led her further away from the heart of the city.

They'd left the downtown section of Chicago behind, taking the train and then a bus before finally hitting the pavement once again. But unlike her neighborhood, this area was a little more prosperous. Not by much, but enough to mark it as more upscale. Urban renewal was obviously in full swing here. Many of the buildings that housed people and businesses showed signs of being rehabbed. The folks who lived here had made an attempt to spruce them up with paint and tubs of flowers. Graffiti was nowhere to be seen and there was an air of hope surrounding the neighborhood. It was actually quite pretty.

Alex wanted to talk about what had happened back in the club, but sensed that Joshua did not. The warm lover who'd danced with her, grinding his cock against her sex, was gone, replaced by the steely eyed warrior. She sensed he was disconcerted by his lack of control. She was oddly pleased. At least she wasn't alone in how she was feeling.

The cool air of the night helped somewhat, but her body still burned with an inner fire that only he could sate. Her breasts felt heavy and tight and her nipples pushed against the cups of her bra with each step until she wanted to scream. She tried desperately to ignore the throbbing ache between her thighs. She knew this wasn't normal, but part of the change in her body chemistry as she went into *heat*. She despised that word, hated feeling so out of control of her body and emotions.

Alex still wasn't comfortable thinking about herself in that way, but there was no disputing the facts. She wanted sex, and not just any kind of sex. She wanted hard, heavy, sweaty sex. And she wanted it with Joshua.

They'd been walking about an hour, up one street and down another, when Joshua finally spoke again. "Almost there."

Alex still had no idea where there was and didn't care. It was late and she was tired, as well as horny, but at least her headache had subsided slightly. She knew they'd been walking in circles again as Joshua kept checking to make sure they weren't being followed.

Right now all she wanted was a hot shower, something to eat and a clean bed to fall into, and not necessarily in that order. The food could wait. As long as she got the shower and the bed she'd be a happy woman. Some of her sexual desire had dimmed, overcome by sheer exhaustion, which was just as well with Joshua acting so distant and withdrawn.

The motel was nothing special, but Alex guessed that's what made it a good place to stop. It had nothing to distinguish it from the dozens like it that filled the city. It was a midrange establishment, not the type that charged by the hour, but certainly nothing like the posh hotels that dotted the prosperous downtown core.

She knew that most of the rooms were accessed from inside the main building while down one side there were several ground-floor rooms where the only point of entry was from the outside. There were also a few parking spaces to allow a patron to park their vehicle in front of their motel room door. Alex was willing to bet the room Joshua got for them would be one of the ones on the outside, probably close to the end, keeping them isolated from most of the other rooms and allowing them a quick getaway down the back alley if necessary.

Joshua's pace quickened as they darted across the street. Traffic was slower here, but there were still vehicles on the road even at this time of night. The city never truly slept.

"Wait here." *Here* was a shadowy corner just beside the entrance. She stood as still as possible, barely resisting the urge to shift her weight from one foot to the other. Her eyes were half-closed before she even realized it and she jerked herself awake. She forced herself to concentrate on her surroundings, watching for anyone who looked suspicious. Besides herself that is.

Joshua was back fairly quickly, keycard in hand. "This way." She fell into step beside him again and mentally patted herself on the back as he led the way to the last door on the bottom floor.

"What's so funny?"

She hadn't realized that she had a smile on her face. She was more tired than she thought. "Nothing. It's just that I knew this was the room you'd get for us."

"You did, did you?" He inserted the card in the lock and pushed the door open.

The air was stale, but not musty, for which Alex gave thanks. "It's the farthest away from the others and no one can access it from inside the motel. This is the only entry and we can also make a quick getaway from here if we need to and disappear in the alleyway behind all the buildings that line this street."

Joshua entered the room, pulling the drapes closed over the window before flicking on the light switch. He ushered her inside, shutting and locking the door behind them. The room was not inspiring, but at least it appeared clean.

One large bed dominated the space. It had a faded brown chenille bedspread tossed across it and two lumpy-looking pillows in dull white pillowcases. A small round table sat in front of the window with two hard wooden chairs flanking it. The drapes were the same unfortunate color as the bedspread. The carpet was dark brown with flecks of other colors in it. Alex couldn't really tell if some of the colors were meant to be there or if they were permanent stains.

There was no dresser, but an open closet exposed a bare rod for hanging clothing and two built-in drawers. It didn't really matter, she supposed, as neither of them had any clothing with them. At least she had some money, thanks to her father.

Speaking of which. "How much do I owe you for my share of the room?"

Joshua, who'd just finished checking out the bathroom, glared at her. "I am not taking money from you."

"Why not?"

"Why not?" His voice was incredulous.

Alex shrugged. "It only seems fair since we're both sharing it."

Ignoring her, he stalked back to the window, pulled the

corner of the drape back and peered out into the night. "I'm going to get us something to eat. You like pizza?"

Obviously this conversation was over as far as he was concerned. She'd bring it up again later. "Yes, I like pizza. As long as it doesn't have onions or anchovies or anything yucky." She shuddered.

He twitched the drape back in place, a grin tugging at the corner of his mouth. "Got it. Nothing yucky." The grin faded, his mouth once again becoming grim. "You should be safe while I'm gone. The pizza place is only a couple buildings down. I'll be back quick as I can. In the meantime, keep your gun handy and shoot if anyone besides me comes to the door."

He came toward her, wrapping his large hands over her shoulders. "I mean it, Alex. You shoot anyone who tries to get in here."

"Okay."

His dark brown eyes stared at her until he was satisfied with whatever he saw in her face. "Okay." He gave her shoulders a squeeze before heading to the door. "Lock it behind me."

Dutifully, she went to the door, locking it behind him. She moved to the window and peeked out from between the curtains, but couldn't see him. He was already gone. The room seemed much larger and emptier without Joshua in it.

Restless energy filled her as she roamed around the room, checking it out. Turning back one corner of the sheets, she sighed with relief when she saw they were threadbare but clean. Leaving that, she headed toward the bathroom. It was small, with a shower stall, a sink and a toilet. All the comforts of home. Okay, not quite, but still it was better than nothing.

Alex suddenly felt sticky and uncomfortable. She really wanted a shower and what better time than when Joshua was gone. She wasn't sure she'd be comfortable taking a shower with him in the other room. For some reason it seemed like a very intimate thing to do. She knew she should keep watch, but really, no one knew where they were. She'd take her weapons with her and lock the bathroom door. It was perfectly safe.

There were several large towels hanging over a rod tempting her. She yanked back the shower curtain and found a bar of soap still covered in its paper wrapper. She bit her lower lip, weighing being clean against Joshua's anger with her when he got back and realized she'd made herself vulnerable while he was gone. There was no contest. No one knew where they were and the beckoning call of the shower was too great to ignore.

Going back into the main room, she removed her leather jacket and hung it on one of the three wire hangers that were soldered to the rod in the closet. She extracted her knives from her boots and the gun from the pocket of her jacket. Sitting on the side of the bed, she lay them beside her as she unlaced her short boots, sliding them off her feet. She wished she had clean clothes, but there was no help for it she supposed. Still, it would be better to be clean beneath them.

Grabbing her weapons, she went into the bathroom, shutting and locking the door behind her. Setting them on the edge of the sink, she began to strip off her clothing. Her sweatshirt came first. She held it up by two fingers, disgusted with the smell. She'd sweat a lot walking in the heat all day and at the club tonight, not to mention she'd been through a few filthy alleyways and hidden in a dirty abandoned building. Her bra followed and she hung it carefully over the doorknob. Unfastening her jeans, she shimmied out of them and her underwear. Yanking off her socks, she tossed them aside before turning on the taps.

She made quick work of unwrapping the soap as she waited for the water to heat. Once it was at a comfortable level, she stepped into the shower stall. Who knew how long the hot water would last?

The spray hit her body and she sighed with pleasure as she ducked her head beneath the water. What she really wanted was a long soak in her clawfoot bathtub at home. It was an antique she'd found in a consignment store. She'd refinished the chipped enamel and installed it with her father's help. The tub was deep and she loved to slide into its depths when it was filled with bubbles and relax after a hard day's work. It was one of the few luxuries she allowed herself.

Picking up the plain bar of white soap, she ran it over her arms and legs, but was unable to work up more than a few small bubbles. Her breasts ached and her core throbbed, but she ignored the discomfort. As tempting as it was to touch her body, she refrained. That would give her temporary relief, but would make her hornier in the long run.

For some reason, when Joshua had touched her it had felt different, had quieted some of the hormones raging through her system. At least temporarily.

Sighing, she scrubbed the soap over her torso, gritting her teeth when she washed her breasts. Her nipples were tight and red, begging to be stroked. Washing between her legs was a special kind of torture. The folds of her sex were hot and slick before the water even touched them. She groaned as her inner muscles tightened. Swaying, she groped for the wall, steadying herself as the wave of longing passed over her.

Alex pushed away from the wall and finished washing. Her feet were red, with several raw patches at her ankles and on the sides. Her boots weren't made for walking long distances like she had today, but there was nothing to be done about it.

She stepped out from under the spray long enough to rub the soap over her scalp. It took a while to get any kind of lather, but she persevered, rubbing her scalp vigorously. When she felt clean, she stepped beneath the quickly cooling spray, letting it wash all the soap from her hair and her body.

Knowing she shouldn't linger, she turned off both taps and grabbed one of the towels. She dried her body before wrapping it around herself and tucking the end over her breasts. Seeing no help for it, she reluctantly tugged her socks back on, being careful not to hit the sore spots. They might be dirty, but they were better than walking barefoot on the carpet.

She debated washing her underwear, but decided against it. If they had to make a run for it in the dead of night she wanted her underwear. Stupid as it sounded, she felt more vulnerable without them. Grabbing her panties, she tugged them on. She scooped up the rest of her clothing in one hand, her weapons in the other, and opened the bathroom door.

The steam followed her into the bedroom. She was still tired, but at least she felt better.

A metallic sound reached her ears just as she noticed the handle of the outside door begin to turn. Someone was at the door.

Dropping her clothing and the knives, she gripped the gun in both hands, aiming straight for the door. Her heart pounded, but her hands were steady as she faced the latest threat.

The lock clicked and the door began to move inward. Alex's finger tightened on the trigger. The door opened wider. Alex bit her bottom lip and waited. She'd only get one good shot.

A flat, square box came into her line of vision before the man did. Joshua looked as stunned as she was sure she must, freezing just inside the door. "Alex?"

She shuddered, lowering the gun. He shoved the door closed with his foot as he set a bag and the pizza box on the table. Calmly, he locked the door. How dare he be nonchalant about this. "I could have shot you!"

Joshua shrugged, his massive shoulders moving slowly up and down. "I knocked and called out. I just assumed you'd heard me."

"I was in the bathroom."

"So I see." He narrowed his eyes as he scanned her bare shoulders, his gaze dipping down between her breasts where the towel was anchored. His gaze continued downward over her torso and across her bare legs, all the way to her sock-clad feet. She was perfectly covered, but somehow his stare left her feeling as if she were naked before him. She felt slightly breathless and achy. Her panties were getting damper by the second and it had nothing to do with the moisture left over by her shower.

"I was perfectly all right." Even to her own ears, her voice sounded breathy, almost flirty. She cleared her throat. "I had the gun next to me the whole time."

"Nothing to be done about it now." He turned away and opened the bag. Perversely, the fact that he wasn't outwardly annoyed with her made her angry. She felt as if she'd let him down in some way. She'd much rather deal with his anger than have him disappointed with her.

"Look, I wasn't stupid about it. I took precautions." Great, now she sounded like a belligerent child when what she wanted to sound like was the mature, sensible woman she was.

"I would have preferred you'd waited, Alex. Or if I'd known you wanted a shower that badly, I could have gotten our food afterwards. I just don't like the idea of you being that vulnerable is all."

She heard it then. That note in his voice that told her he was berating himself for not anticipating what she would do. He figured he should have known even before she did what she was going to do. It annoyed her. "I told you earlier this evening that you weren't God."

"So you did." Pulling something out of the bag, he tossed it to her. She caught it reflexively in her free hand, curious as to what it was. It was definitely some form of clothing. She laid the Glock on the bed and shook out the fabric. It was a white T-shirt with "Gino's Authentic Italian Pizza" written in blazing red across the front. "I thought you might want something clean to wear."

"Thank you." She clutched it to her chest. Once again, he'd done something incredibly sensitive. It hadn't even occurred to her he would think to get something like this for her.

He shrugged. "It's nothing. You should put it on and come eat before the pizza gets cold." He was watching her with an unreadable expression in his eyes. "I promise I didn't get anything yucky."

She smiled at him, feeling as if he'd given her the world instead of just a T-shirt and pizza. It was the fact he'd thought of the shirt in the first place and tailored the pizza to suit her tastes that moved her. "Okay. I'll be right back."

Hurrying to the bathroom, she slammed the door behind her.

The second the door closed, Joshua let out a pent-up breath. His temples were pounding. Slamming his fist through the wall while he howled sounded like a good way to release some of his fury, but he did neither. He couldn't believe he hadn't realized she'd take a shower as soon as he was gone. If he hadn't been so concerned with getting some food for her, if he'd only thought the situation through, he'd have guessed she'd want to get clean after everything she'd been through today.

Instead, Alex had left herself open and vulnerable while he'd been gone.

Pushing open the door and facing a determined Alex aiming a 9mm at his chest was an experience he wasn't likely to forget. She'd been willing to face down whoever was at the door with only a skimpy towel wrapped around her.

He didn't think she had any idea just how much the towel enticed more than it hid. She might have been covered, but the thin towel had clung to her curves, outlining her waist and the flare of her hips. It had taken all his discipline not to rip the towel from her body, toss her on the bed, mount her from behind and fuck her until they both yelled with pleasure.

Digging the palms of his hands into his eyes, he pressed hard. His cock was throbbing like a damn toothache with no relief in sight. He sank down on the bed and yanked his cell phone out of his back pocket. It was a disposable one he'd dump once he was home. All of them used disposable phones, changing numbers frequently. Bounty hunters might not trust authorities, but they did love their electronic toys and he knew they'd have hackers who could get into phone records with no problem at all.

He punched in a number and waited. It was picked up on the first ring. "What?"

Joshua grinned even as he growled into the receiver. "Your day couldn't have been as bad as mine so shut up and listen."

The man on the other end snorted. "I saw just how *hard* your day was, little brother. I saw you *talking* with the woman in an alleyway this morning. If you're smart, you'll claim that woman you've been running all over town with. Fuck her so long and hard, she'll never want any other wolf but you." He paused. "It's what I'd do if I were in your position."

"You're not in my position." The thought of his brother fucking Alex brought a red haze to his eyes. "It wouldn't be fair to Alex."

"And you're all about honor, are you not, my brother?"

Joshua swiped a hand down his face, suddenly feeling very tired. "Isaiah." He didn't quite know how to answer his brother. It was a touchy spot between them that Isaiah had felt no sense of duty toward the pack, refusing to take his father's place as Striker after his death. It had fallen to Joshua, the next in line, instead. He loved his brother fiercely, but he didn't always understand him. He turned back to the business at hand. "The car was compromised."

"Shit. I pulled Simon off it as soon as I knew you were headed that way. I figured it would be more productive for us to hunt rogue wolves instead."

"It was hunters."

Isaiah swore long and loud. "Son of a bitch!"

"I got a vehicle from Damek." He gave his brother the location, hating to do even that over the phone, but knowing it was necessary.

"I know where it is. We won't be far behind you." He sensed his brother's momentary hesitation. "Joshua. Don't allow honor to deprive you of what is yours. Do not be afraid to reach out and take something for yourself."

"Isaiah," he began, not quite certain what he was going to say. But it didn't matter. His brother grunted and broke the connection. Joshua snapped his phone shut.

"Who was that?" Alex was standing in the open door of the bathroom watching him. She looked adorable in the shirt, which skimmed the tops of her thighs. He stared hard. If he wasn't mistaken, she wasn't wearing a bra.

"No one." He shoved the phone in his back pocket as he stood.

She raised one eyebrow and glared at him.

He sighed. It would be easier if she was a submissive female, but then he probably wouldn't be attracted to her at all. Shaking his head, he resigned himself to the inevitable. He held out one of the chairs. "Come and eat and I'll tell you."

Chapter Ten

Alex tugged at the hem of the shirt as she walked to the table. Thankfully, Joshua didn't seem to be paying her any attention as he was occupied digging drinks and napkins out of the bag. Now that she had something clean to wear, she'd decided to take the chance and washed her bra and panties, hanging them over the rod in the bathroom to dry. The thought of having clean underwear in the morning was heavenly. The only problem was that the shirt wasn't quite as long as she'd have liked. It just covered her behind. Barely.

Hurrying over to the table, she pulled down hard on the hem, tucking some of the cotton fabric beneath her as she sat. Relaxing now that the table was covering her from the waist down, she eyed the small mound of items Joshua was unpacking. He'd been busy and had obviously gone to more than just the pizza parlor. There were two toothbrushes, a small tube of toothpaste, a comb and a bottle of lotion. She knew he hadn't bought the lotion for himself. Again, she was touched by his thoughtfulness.

"You were busy."

He shrugged as he unscrewed the top off a bottle of water and laid it on the table in front of her. "There was a convenience store next to the pizza joint. They didn't have much, but I got what I thought you might need."

"Thank you, Joshua." Reaching out, she touched his hand.

His fingers twined with hers until their palms were pressed together. "You're welcome, Alex."

The tension in the room rose dramatically each second their hands remained clasped. A feeling of anticipation filled

Alex. A yearning grew deep inside her. Her breathing became shallower, her chest rising and falling quickly. The motion caused the fabric of her shirt to brush her nipples, making them pucker. A trickle of liquid flowed from her core and she made a tiny sound of distress in the back of her throat.

Joshua dropped her hand as if her skin suddenly burned his. "Have some pizza," he ordered gruffly as he opened the box. "You've got to be hungry."

Alex nodded, unable to speak. She'd forgotten all about being hungry for food. Her hunger was for something else all together, but something told her that particular appetite wasn't going to be appeased right now.

Taking a slice, she placed it on one of the napkins and licked her fingers. The scent of tomato sauce, basil, oregano and cheese wafted upward making her stomach growl in anticipation. She glanced over at Joshua, but he was busy consuming his first slice of pizza. He had to be starving. He wasn't a small man and he hadn't had much to eat today.

"So, who were you talking with on the phone?" She picked up her slice and took a huge bite, almost moaning with pleasure as the tangy tomato and spices hit her tongue. He'd gotten pepperoni and peppers, but true to his word, no "yucky" stuff. She watched him as she chewed, wondering if he'd tell her the truth. He polished off his slice of pizza, washing it down with a swallow of water before replying.

"That was my brother."

"Really. Which one?"

"Isaiah."

"He's the eldest, right?" Alex wasn't sure she had them all straight in her head.

"That's right." Snagging another slice, he bit into it, tearing off a huge chunk. His teeth were white and his canines looked to be incredibly sharp, reminding her once again that he was something more than just human.

She shivered as she wondered what it would be like to have him nibbling on her neck, her shoulders, her stomach and lower. She'd only gotten a taste of what it would be like in the bathroom of the diner earlier this morning.

It had certainly gotten hotter in the room in the past few

minutes. She tugged at the neckline of the T-shirt, but it didn't help. Finishing off her slice of pizza, she grabbed another. What had they been talking about? Oh, yes. "What did he say?" Honestly, trying to get Joshua to tell her anything was an exercise in frustration.

He shrugged, finished chewing and swallowed. "He'll be waiting for us tomorrow and will watch our backs. All we have to do is make our way to the truck first thing in the morning and we're out of here." He helped himself to another slice of pizza. "We'll blend in with the regular surge of traffic on the road."

That made sense. "Do you think my father is okay?" She'd been trying hard not to think about him today. She had Joshua, but her father was out there on his own.

Joshua snorted. "He's fine. The last person you need to worry about is James LeVeau."

"It's weird to hear you call him that."

"That's the only name I ever heard him called until recently. He's practically a legend where I come from."

"Really?" It was strange to think of her father as anything but, well, her father. "Tell me about him."

He hesitated. "I'm not sure how much he wants you to know, but I guess it's moot now. You'll hear all the stories when we get back to Wolf Creek. You almost done?"

She'd eaten three slices while they'd talked. Joshua had almost finished plowing his way through the rest of the large pizza. She was pleasantly full. "Yes, thanks. Help yourself." Taking her at her word, he pulled the box over in front of him and started on the two remaining pieces.

"Why don't you brush your teeth and crawl into bed. That way it doesn't matter if you fall asleep while we're talking."

Made sense to her. "Okay." She grabbed the toothbrushes, toothpaste, comb and lotion as she stood. Only when she was on her feet did she realize that with both hands full, she couldn't tug down the hem of her shirt. Joshua seemed occupied with eating so she made her way to the bathroom as nonchalantly as she could, while pretending it was no big deal that he could probably see the bottom curves of the cheeks of her ass as she went.

When she pushed the bathroom door closed behind her, she leaned back against it and groaned. A quick glance in the mirror told her that her face was indeed as red as it felt. Dumping the stuff in her hands on the edge of the sink, she buried her face in her hands and groaned again.

Yes, Joshua had already seen most of her body, and yes she wanted him, but this was all still very new to her. She was twenty-two years old, but he was the first man to ever see her naked. And that had happened when she was already in the grip of passion, which was much different than walking across a motel room floor with nothing underneath her shirt while he was casually eating pizza.

She'd better get used to it if she was going to try to seduce him over the next few days. She knew he wanted her, but he wouldn't take her because of his honor. While she respected that, she wasn't about to let the next few days slip by without trying to solidify some kind of relationship.

It would be easy for him to walk away from her when they reached Wolf Creek. That thought made her stomach lurch with panic. She wanted to make sure that didn't happen. It would be much harder for him to do so if they'd established some kind of physical and emotional bond.

"Okay," she muttered. "Get a grip on yourself." Scrubbing her hands over her cheeks, she raised her head. At least Joshua hadn't seemed to notice the fact that the shirt was just a tad too short to adequately cover everything.

She had to act like a mature woman who was used to having a man see her half-naked. No big deal. Her sex spasmed, reminding her that it was a huge deal. Ignoring the growing ache between her thighs that never seemed to fully subside, she brushed her teeth, combed her hair and slathered some of the lotion Joshua had purchased for her over her pink nose and cheeks. She'd gotten a bit of sun on her face today as they'd tromped all over town.

When she finished, she used the bathroom and washed her hands. She was as ready as she'd ever be. Resting her hand on her stomach, she tried to calm the butterflies beating within her. She was going to sleep with a man for the first time in her life. Granted, all they'd probably do was sleep, but still. His large body would be lying next to her and that bed wasn't all that big. They'd be bound to touch one another at some point. At least they would if she had anything to say about it.

Joshua dropped the piece of pizza in his hands back into the box the moment the bathroom door shut behind Alex. He was a dead man. Watching her walk across the room clad in nothing but the T-shirt and a pair of socks had been torture. His gaze had followed her every step of the way. The seductive sway of her hips, the enticing nape of her neck and the tantalizing glimpse of the milky white globes of her ass had all but made him swallow his tongue. His cock was harder than a steel spike.

His skin itched as the wolf within him fought to emerge. The animal part of himself wanted to claim her now, didn't want to leave anything to chance or to give her the opportunity to choose from the other single males of the pack. His brother's words echoed in his brain.

Take her.

Growling, he grabbed the pizza box and the empty bottles and stuffed them in the garbage can that sat beside the ancient television. When the remains of their meal were cleared away, he began to stalk back and forth across the room, trying to tame his raging hormones.

Alex was everything he'd ever hoped for in a mate. She was strong and independent, but her strength was tempered with gentleness, a kindness of spirit. She didn't know that he'd watched her walk to work this morning, seen her give her coffee to the aging prostitute who'd she'd stopped to chat with. Watching her with her father had told him even more about her. Alex was loyal. When she was committed to someone there was no half-measure. It was all or nothing.

He wanted that loyalty, strength and gentle spirit as his own.

If he were home, he'd change into his wolf and race through the night, allowing the animal part of himself full rein. The smell of the night air, the thrill of charging headlong into the dark would calm him. But he couldn't do that here in the city. The air was filled with the stench of man and all that went along with city life. Plus, there was no way he'd leave Alex unprotected.

The only other way to calm himself was with sex. Hot, hard, grinding, sweaty sex. The kind of sex that lasted for hours, only ending when the two participants were so exhausted they couldn't move and melted into sleep. The kind of sex that had been missing in his life for a long, long time.

The last time he'd had that kind of a night had been almost twenty years ago with a widow from the pack who had made it clear from the start that their short-lived relationship was only about sex. That had suited the young man he'd been then, but he wanted more than a few hours of mindless passion now.

Since that time he'd had the occasional one-night stand with other widowed females from the pack or with a human female, but he'd stopped even that about five years ago. It was unsatisfying and left him with an even deeper yearning for something more. Not that he'd had time for anything deeper over the past decade, not since his father had been killed and he'd assumed the role of protector of the pack.

He wanted sex, but he wasn't going to get any tonight, wouldn't allow himself to take it. Not from Alex. She was special. The only way he'd ever know for sure if she would have chosen him was if he gave her the opportunity. It would be too easy to take advantage of her at this moment when she was off balance and dependent on him. And that he would not do.

Call it honor. Call it pride. Joshua didn't care. He only knew that he already thought of Alex as his future mate and as such would do nothing that might bring her dishonor or shame.

But that didn't help his raging hard-on. Yanking his shirt out of his jeans, he let it hang down in front of the heavy bulge. It helped, but not much. As he paced, he began to take one deep breath after another. His brothers would all howl with laughter if they could see him now. They often accused him of having ice water running through his veins, but Alex made a joke out of his self-control. Around her, his blood ran hot and thick.

He stifled a groan and concentrated on his breathing. Yes, his brothers would never let him forget this if they ever found out. He had no intention of ever telling them.

The door to the bathroom opened and Alex stepped out, a tentative smile on her face. It slowly faded as she stared at him. He could well imagine what he looked like in her eyes. His hair was disheveled because he'd raked his fingers through it as he'd paced, his body was stiff and his face felt as if it had been chiseled from stone.

"Is everything all right?" She took a tentative step toward him.

"Everything is fine." He walked stiffly to the side of the bed and tugged back the covers. It was impossible to walk any other way with his dick at attention and his balls heavy and aching. "Get into bed."

He could see the question in her eyes, but thankfully she said nothing. As she slid beneath the covers, he caught a whiff of her arousal and a glimpse of her pussy. A picture of those slick, pink folds was forever burned into his brain. He licked his lips, wanting another taste of her sweet nectar.

She blushed as he tucked the sheet over her. Her gray eyes were soft and smoky. A man could easily fall into her seductive gaze and never find his way out again. Never want to.

"I'll be back in a few minutes. I need a quick shower."

"Of course." She picked at the top of the covers, her gaze darting away from his.

He caught her chin with his fingers and tipped her head up. "I won't bother if you're afraid to be alone."

"No! No," she replied more calmly the second time. "I'm fine. I should have thought of that and let you have the bathroom first. The water should be hot again by now." She closed her mouth abruptly as if aware she was starting to babble.

He was beginning to know her well and knew she only talked this fast when she was nervous. Joshua grabbed her knives and gun, which were still at the bottom of the bed. Laying the knives on the nightstand, he then handed her the gun. "Keep that with you and if you hear anything come and get me. I won't be long." Unable to resist, he dropped a quick kiss on her lips before disappearing into the bathroom, leaving Alex all warm and snug in the bed.

A cold shower sounded real good right about now.

Stripping off his clothes, he left them in a pile on the floor. It was only when he was naked and reaching out to turn on the taps that he noticed the cotton bra and panties. The fabric was practical but their pink color spoke of the woman who wore them. They were so like Alex, practical, yet with a softness she hid behind a layer of toughness. He doubted many people knew the true woman beneath the tough façade.

The bikini underwear looked ridiculously tiny as he lifted them off the rack and held them to his nose. Her scent was gone, replaced by the smell of soap. Sighing, he carefully draped the delicate fabric back over the rack to dry. He'd love to see her in lace or better yet in nothing at all, spread across his bed at home waiting for him.

Growling, he flicked on the taps, keeping the temperature low. Stepping beneath it, he allowed the spray to cool his heated flesh. He grabbed the bar of soap and began to scrub his body. When he was done, he soaped his hand and slid it over his cock, wrapping his fingers around the hard length. It throbbed against his palm, demanding he do something to release the pressure.

There was no way he could sleep beside Alex all night unless he got some control over himself. If he didn't she was just as liable to wake up in the middle of the night with him buried deep inside her.

The way he'd been feeling since the moment he'd laid eyes on her, he knew this wouldn't take long. Closing his eyes, he began to pump his fist up and down his shaft. The sac between his legs was heavy and he gripped it with his other hand, massaging his balls. The water beat down on his body as his hand moved quicker and quicker. Images of Alex filled his mind. He could see her standing against the sink in the bathroom of the restaurant this morning, her naked breasts swaying as she rolled her hips toward him.

His balls pulled up snug against his body. He pumped his hand harder with each stroke.

He could feel the soft slickness of her pussy as he stroked his fingers over it. Remembered the way her inner muscles clasped his fingers, drawing them deeper. His cock jerked in his hand. Yeah, he wanted to bury his cock so deep inside her that she'd never ever forget him, would always want him.

He'd barely touched her when she'd come. God, she was gorgeous when she came. There had been no holding back. She'd given him everything. Every cry, every gasp had been music to his ears. The scent of her cream had been rich and thick. He wanted to taste it, to lap it from the soft, pink folds of her pussy, teasing her clit with his tongue and his teeth until she came again. He wanted to make her come over and over until she was screaming at him to fuck her, begging him to fill her.

His harsh breathing filled the room. He kept pumping his hand as his balls pulled up tighter against his body. Semen sprayed from the tip, some of the whitish fluid covered his belly, while the rest of it was washed down the drain. Releasing his grip on himself, he leaned against the shower walls and lowered his head, spent. The cold water rained down on him as he gasped for breath.

When Joshua recovered, he raised his head and pushed away from the wall. Grabbing the soap, he lathered his belly and his relaxed penis, making sure he was clean before he turned off the water and stepped out of the shower.

He dried off and hauled back on his jeans, as well as his socks and boots. There was no way he'd do more than catch a quick nap or two tonight. He had to be on guard and ready for anything. He did leave off his T-shirt, tossing it over his shoulder as he left the clammy bathroom.

Alex was curled on her side with one hand tucked under her head, the other wrapped around the gun. Her silky brown lashes were resting against her cheeks and her mouth was parted ever so slightly as she emitted a soft snoring noise. He smiled, imagining that she'd deny the fact she snored. And it wasn't really snoring. More of a soft whistle. It was actually very cute.

Tossing his shirt over the back of one of the chairs, he stood and stared at her for the longest time. In less than a day, this woman meant everything to him. How the hell had that happened?

He had no answer. He only knew deep in his gut that she belonged to him. They belonged together. Reaching down, he carefully removed the gun from her grasp and placed it within easy reach on the bedside table. She made a snuffling noise, but she didn't wake.

Turning off the light, he eased down on the bed beside her and gathered her into his arms. She came easily, settling against his chest as if she'd been doing it for years. He sifted his fingers through her short hair. It was soft and silky, clinging to his fingers as he continued to stroke her.

Contentment filled him. He took a deep breath and felt his entire body relax. Even the wolf within him was content. All it took was this particular woman lying in his arms. There was no doubt in his mind that she was his, and he'd move heaven and earth itself in order to claim her.

Chapter Eleven

James leaned back against the outside wall of the roof of the apartment building where he was currently situated. He glanced down the fire escape that led from the roof to the first floor, making sure it was still clear. The brick was hard and warm against his back even though the sun had gone down a while ago. He'd been hunkered down here most of the day. Watching. Waiting.

After he'd eaten breakfast at the diner this morning, he'd made his way back home using a roundabout route. Making sure no one had seen him, he'd gone into the rundown apartment building across from the garage and climbed up to the rooftop. Avoiding broken glass and some abandoned patio chairs, he'd settled in. Then the long day of surveillance had begun.

As he'd suspected, there had been a few werewolves dispatched to keep an eye on the garage just in case he or Alex returned. They had all been in human form, but James knew them for what they were. It was in the way they watched and waited, patient and cunning. There had been some comings and goings throughout the day as various customers dropped by and left again with perplexed expressions on their faces. It was obvious something had happened, but it was a testament to the kind of neighborhood it was that nobody called the cops.

He'd been sitting here for almost twelve hours now and all but one of the watchers had gone. They'd left one behind skulking in the alleyway just beside the garage. James would have to take care of him first.

One slow inch at a time, he rose to his feet. Even though

he'd been in one position for hours, there was no hesitation. All his concentration was on the task ahead. He had to dispose of the bodies from this morning's fight, lock down the garage and head out of the city.

If all went according to plan, in less than twenty-four hours he'd be in Wolf Creek with Alex.

He swallowed hard as he eased the door to the roof open just enough to slide through, closing it gently behind him. Loping down the stairs, he tried not to think of his daughter. She was the light of his life and her safety was in the hands of another man. He didn't like it, but he knew it was necessary. It was also time. He'd had Alex to himself for twenty-two years. It was time for her to spread her wings, find a mate and start a family of her own. Things would be different from now on regardless of what he wanted.

He moved silently down the stairs and out the back door of the building. He knew this neighborhood like the back of his hand, had prowled it for years. That gave him a distinct advantage over his pursuers. The sky was clear, the moon visible. It wasn't full, not yet, but it was close. It hung in the sky like a beautiful yellow orb, beckoning to him, calling him to run wild and free. Soon, he promised himself. As soon as this was over he'd run long and hard.

The smell of the alley assaulted his nostrils as he stalked toward his prey. After all these years, he still hated the scent of garbage and human waste that seemed to permeate the city. It was also the reason he'd settled in this area. All these noxious odors buried his own distinct scent, throwing off any who came searching for him. And there had been a few over the years. This was the first time anyone had ever been successful though.

His boots made no sound on the loose gravel as he moved quickly and silently. He kept to the shadows, the action as natural to him as breathing. Narrowing his eyes, he sighted the young wolf peering out onto the street at the far end of the alley. He was one of the men who'd attacked them this morning.

Like a wraith, he covered the distance between them. His thick, muscled forearm went around the younger man's neck and he gave a quick, hard twist. The crack sounded unusually loud in the hush of the alley. The man was dead before his mind even had a chance to register he was in trouble. He went limp and James caught him easily, dragging his body into the shadows. He'd deal with this one after he'd finished with the mess inside.

Keeping his eyes and ears open, he sniffed the air. All the usual smells were there, human sweat and garbage and the underlying odors of booze, drugs and desperation. The street looked as it always did this time of night. The bar at the far end of the street was doing a brisk business. The door slammed open and a drunken fool staggered out. A lone, rusty, beat-up car filled with young men cruised up and down the street looking for action. They yelled and hooted at a couple of women who were walking down the sidewalk as they passed by. All in all, it was a regular night in the neighborhood.

His spine tingled as he prowled toward the garage door. Someone was inside. Reaching beneath the tails of his shirt, he withdrew his gun, praying he wouldn't have to use it. Not that the sound of gunshots was all that unusual, but he didn't want to do anything that might attract unwanted attention to the place.

He placed his hand on the door handle, turning slowly. It wasn't locked. Taking a deep breath, he released half of it and sprang into action.

Bending low, he went through the door fast, rolling behind the large metal toolbox that stood just inside the door. It was about four feet high, three feet wide and on wheels. He knew the metal was thick enough to give him some protection.

"I've got a gun." The hoarse voice was familiar. It was also female.

"Divine?"

"James, that you?" He heard a scuffling sound at the other end of the room.

"Yeah, it's me. You alone?" He could smell her now, sex and heavy perfume, overlaid with cheap whiskey. The scent of death also hung in the air, reminding him of the bodies still to be dealt with.

"I'm alone." A dim light came on over the workbench. Divine stood there, her face pale beneath the thick coating of makeup, a snub-nosed revolver hanging from one hand. "What the hell happened, James? Where's Alex?"

James stood, brushed off his jeans and tucked the Glock away again as he strode toward her. "Alex is safe."

"I don't understand." Divine licked her lips, smearing her bright red lipstick. "Otto from the bakery came and got me this morning. I hadn't even been to bed yet. I was still enjoying the coffee that Alex had given me and having a smoke while I read the paper to unwind after the night. I like to do that you know." The last was said defensively as if she expected him to scoff or laugh at her.

"Go on." he urged.

She raked her fingers through her bottle-blonde hair. "I'd just talked to Alex on the street, not a half hour before, when Otto comes running in saying he heard a gunshot at the garage. We came down to check it out and found the bodies. I told him to go back to work and I'd stay and wait. There were men watching the place, so Otto had his sons watching them all day. They all left several hours ago."

"Not all of them left," James muttered under his breath.

"Oh." Divine's eyes widened. She swallowed hard, not asking the obvious question. She already knew the answer. "What did they want? I know you're not into anything illegal, James. You've been here too long for us not to know if you were."

James sighed, needing to get rid of Divine so he could take care of the bodies. "I'm not who you think I am, Divine," he began gently.

"This has something to do with that werewolf stuff, doesn't it?" She nodded decisively.

James froze. "What do you mean?" What the hell did she know?

She shook her head and sighed. "James, did you honestly think you could live here for over twenty years and no one would ever find out? You and Alex were here about five years when I first saw you change. I'd been out late and you were just coming back to the garage. I have to say, you gave me quite the fright. I'd never seen a wolf before, except on television, let alone a werewolf. For a while I convinced myself I'd just had way too much to drink." She laughed. "But there were other signs as well. You kept to yourself and were extremely protective of Alex."

He was stunned. "Why didn't you ever say anything?"

She shrugged, the strap of her dress falling down the curve of her upper arm. She pushed it up impatiently. "What was there to say? You're a good man, a wonderful father and a heck of a great mechanic. You never judged me for what I am and you raised Alex to be the same. She's a fine young woman, James. She treats me like I'm a real person, not just some cheap, drunken whore."

"I don't know what to say." He truly was at a loss for words. Acceptance in the human world was rare for his kind and he'd never expected to find it here of all places.

"Nothing to say," she continued briskly. "I know most folks think I'm crazy, but I know what I see out on the streets. I know there are werewolves, vampires and other creatures out there."

James nodded. "You're not crazy."

She glanced toward the stairs at the back of the room. "The thing now is to worry about the bodies upstairs. I was hoping you'd show up, but Otto and his sons are bringing some tarps and the bakery truck in a few minutes. We didn't want to leave the bodies any longer. The smell is getting bad, even for this neighborhood."

"Why would you do that?" James still couldn't quite believe that, not only Divine, but also other people in the neighborhood were willing to help him. His eyes narrowed. "Does Otto know?"

"About the werewolf thing?" She didn't wait for him to answer, but continued on. "I imagine so." She cleared her throat. "Bill from the barbershop and Stanley from the bar also offered their help. I assume quite a few folks are aware that you're different." She paused. "What about Alex?"

James knew what she was asking and considering all she'd done for him he figured he at least owed her the truth. "Yeah." Sighing, he ran his hand across his face, trying not to think about Alex. He longed to know where she was, to hold her in his arms to assure himself she was safe. "I'd hoped she'd be fully human, but there were signs. She's reaching maturity as a female now. Somehow word got out that she existed and now single males from packs from all around all want to claim her, whether she wants it or not."

Divine's hand flew to her mouth. "That's barbaric."

James laughed, but it was a bitter sound. "That's nature, Divine. Humans are no different. Thing is, the years haven't been kind to the packs and their numbers are dwindling. They need females to reproduce and restore the population. The ironic thing is a hundred years or so ago they might have killed her because her bloodline is tainted because her mother was human. Now they all want her as a breeder."

"That's why you're here and not with a pack?" Once again, Divine was proving to be an astute woman.

James nodded. "I wanted a different life for Alex."

"Where is she, James?"

"Honesty, I don't know. We split up this morning and I sent her off with the son of an old friend. He's the only one I can trust until this mess is resolved."

"What will you do?"

James reached out and stroked his fingers over Divine's hair. "It's best you don't know but, rest assured, Alex will be taken care of."

"I believe you."

The sound of a truck pulling up in front of the garage had James whirling and moving in one motion.

"That should be Otto," Divine yelled after him. He pulled out his gun and hid in the shadows, not willing to take any chances.

The door to the garage was opened enough for a truck to pull in. It wasn't a large truck, but it had an enclosed box on the back with Bykowski's Bakery stenciled on the side. Still, James waited in the shadows until the truck was inside and the door closed and bolted. Two younger men waited by the side of the truck while an older man opened the truck door and climbed down from the cab. "Divine," he called. "You see any sign of James or Alex yet?"

"Hello, Otto." He stepped from the shadows, shocking the three men who stood not four feet from him.

The older man was startled for a moment, but recovered quickly, rubbing his hand over his mostly balding head. "James." He strode forward, hand extended. "Bad business up there," he motioned upstairs with his free hand as he shook James' hand with the other. "Bad business. We've got tarps in the back and me and my boys will make sure they get dumped in the lake far away from the neighborhood."

"I appreciate it, Otto." He hesitated. "I suppose you want to know what happened?"

Otto shook his head vehemently. "A man's business is his own. You are one of us and that is all that matters." Releasing James' hand, he turned to his sons. "Come. We have work to do." Both his sons were in their early twenties and were carbon copies of their father. They looked as if they were bursting with questions, but said nothing as they followed their father, tarps tucked beneath their arms.

James shook his head, feeling oddly out of control of the situation. If he hadn't returned his neighbors would have taken care of the situation for him and he'd never have known. It was strangely humbling. He'd had no idea people felt this way about himself and Alex.

Divine started upstairs, but James put his hand on her arm, stopping her. "You don't need to see this."

She looked mildly surprised. "I've seen worse."

"I know," he gently replied. "But that doesn't mean you need to see it again."

A slow smile covered her face. This one was natural without the artifice she usually displayed. James was surprised to notice she was actually quite pretty beneath her façade. "That's really sweet of you, James, but I want to help. I need to help."

Nodding, he started up the stairs with her close behind him. Otto and his sons had already wrapped the two bodies in tarps. Someone had boarded the window shut. "Who did that?" James motioned to the window, noticing the glass had been swept away as well.

One of the younger men straightened. "I did. I didn't want anyone sneaking in and stealing anything."

"My Dominik is a good boy." Otto beamed and his son blushed.

"Thank you." James didn't quite know what else to say. "Why?" He was at a loss as to understand their actions.

Otto walked over to him, his smile sad. "You think you are

a loner, keeping to yourself. You think we do not know what you do. When my Anna needed medical care, there was an envelope of money left on the counter of my store with the name of a good doctor tucked inside. When Bill was having trouble with that gang that was trying to infiltrate the neighborhood, don't think we didn't all notice when they suddenly disappeared. This neighborhood might have its problems with petty drug dealers, but there is not the same amount of violence here. It is a good neighborhood, where decent people can make a home. Don't think we don't know it is because of you, James Riley."

He'd had no idea. Over the years, he'd taken care of the neighborhood people as best he could without exposing himself or interfering in their lives too much. After all, they were human; he was not. But he was still an alpha male whether he wanted to be or not and the people around him had become his pack in a strange sort of way. He just hadn't been aware of how much they'd known. No one had ever said anything until now.

"Thank you."

"Bah," Otto swiped his hand in front of him. "There is no need for thanks. My Anna is alive because of you. There is nothing my family will not do to help yours." Motioning to his sons, they each picked up an end of one of the tarps and started back down the stairs. Otto and James took the other.

When both bodies were loaded in the back of the truck, James turned to Otto. "There's one more in the alley to the left."

He nodded. "We will stop outside and pick him up. They will be on the bottom of the lake within the hour and will trouble you no more." Otto climbed into the driver's seat while his sons opened the garage door. He eased the truck out of the building, stopping in front of the alley. As James closed and bolted the garage door, he could see both Dominik and Leon heading into the alley, tarp in hand.

"What will you do now?" Divine had come up to stand behind him.

"I have to go and meet Alex. Once I'm sure she's safe, I'm not sure what I'll do."

"You're not coming back, are you?"

Was he? "I honestly don't know, Divine. Probably not." He

left her and went into the office. Digging through the file cabinets, he found what he was looking for. Picking up a pen, he scribbled across the page. When he was done, he went back into the garage only to find Divine heading for the door. "Wait."

She turned back. "Is there something else you need?"

"No." He shook his head. "This is something I want to do for you." He handed her the papers.

"I don't understand." She squinted in the dim light to read them.

"That's the deed to the garage. I own it free and clear. The apartment upstairs is yours to live in. Feel free to rent out the garage. Check with Otto's son, Leon. I saw the way he was eyeing the place. He might want to do something different with his life than work in his father's bakery."

"I can't take this, James." She thrust the papers back at him, but he wouldn't take them.

"Yes, you can. All I ask is that you close out Alex's apartment and store all her stuff here for her." Reaching into his pocket, he withdrew a set of keys. "The keys to the garage, the apartment upstairs and Alex's place are all on here." He removed several keys from the ring before handing it to her.

"But—"

"No." He cut her off. "You didn't have to do what you did today. None of you did. The men watching this place are dangerous and you knew it, but you did it anyway. I can never repay that. Besides." He propped his hands on his hips and looked down at her. "Don't you think it's time to start taking care of yourself?" He softened his tone. "You're still a relatively young woman, Divine. Beneath that hard shell, there's a good woman. Give yourself a better life."

Her lower lip trembled and she threw herself against him, wrapping her arms around his waist. He gathered her close for a hug. She stepped back a moment later, swiping at her eye makeup and sniffing self-consciously. "I must look a mess."

He smiled as she dug a tissue out of her pocket and tried to wipe the smudged mascara from her eyes. "Yeah, you do." She laughed as he'd intended. "Just do me one favor and wait at least two weeks before you move in. Everything should be taken care of by then and there should be no danger to you or anyone else."

"Okay." She nodded. "We'll just keep an eye on the place. As far as anyone is concerned, you're on vacation."

"You okay to get home on your own?"

Divine laughed. "Honey, I'm as safe on the streets as I am in my own bed." She strutted to the door, papers and key ring clutched tightly in her hands. When she reached the door, she turned. "You take care of yourself, James Riley. And take care of that girl of yours. Alex is special."

"I will, Divine. You take care of yourself too."

"You know. For the first time in my life, I think I will." With those parting words, she was gone, the door closing heavily behind her.

James walked over to the door and eased it open, watching as she strode down the street. In spite of her assurance she was perfectly safe on her own, he kept a close eye on her until she was inside her building at the end of the street. Shutting the garage door, he bolted it and headed upstairs.

Grabbing a duffle bag from the bedroom closet, he tossed in some clothing and the few pictures and mementos that were precious to him before carrying it out to the living room. He pulled open the bookcase and removed the remaining weapons and money, stuffing them in the bag. He had the keys to a car he had stashed in another location for just such an emergency and the key to his safety deposit box in his pocket. The safety deposit box contained bankbooks for every major bank in the city.

James had money. A lot of it. He'd had decades to accumulate it and was good at making more. He had investments all across the country. He supposed it was time he taught Alex how to manage some of this stuff. Most of it was a nest egg for her future. He only hoped there was time to tell her about all of it.

Zipping the bag closed, he pushed the bookcase shut and headed out the door. He never looked back as he descended the stairs, leaving his home of over twenty years behind him. If there was one thing life had taught him, it was there was no use in looking back. It changed nothing and only brought sorrow and regrets.

The future was ahead of him. All that mattered now was Alex's safety. After that, he'd figure out what he was going to do with the rest of his life.

Shoving open the back entrance of the garage, he left the building and his former life behind him.

Chapter Twelve

Dawn hadn't yet broken when Joshua opened his eyes, although the room was getting lighter as it approached. Sometime during the night, Alex had kicked off the covers and crawled on top of him and was sleeping soundly with her arms and legs sprawled on either side of him.

How she'd managed to do that without waking him was a mystery. He was used to sleeping with one eye open, his senses attuned to anything out of the ordinary. Obviously, his wolf knew and accepted her as his rightful mate. She was intelligent, brave, kind and giving. Everything a man could want, everything he'd given up hoping for. Her place was with him. Now and always.

He groaned as he buried his face in her hair. She smelled of soap and that indefinable womanly scent that was uniquely hers. His cock was already swollen and hard, pressing against the zipper of his jeans. She shifted the smallest bit, her sex rubbing against the large bulge. Joshua gripped her hips with his hands to hold her steady. Sweat broke out on his forehead and he struggled for control. Only Alex had this effect on him.

She settled again, emitting a soft, satisfied sigh. He loosened his grip, becoming suddenly aware of the bare flesh beneath his fingers. Memories of her pink bikini panties hanging to dry in the bathroom made him groan again. There was nothing to stop him from touching her slick folds, from stroking her.

Even as he told himself he shouldn't, he slid his fingers downward, skimming the edges of the firm globes of her behind. The shirt had ridden up during the night and was bunched around her waist. He kept his touch soft, not wanting her to wake. Light was barely beginning to filter in through the thin drapes. They didn't have to get out of bed quite yet. Alex needed her rest.

His hands cupped her behind, kneading the pliant flesh. Damn, she had a fine ass. He wanted to mount her from behind, wanted to hear the slap of his stomach against her bottom as he fucked her. His chest was rising and falling rapidly now, his heart thudding heavily. Although he wasn't wearing a shirt, his torso was damp with perspiration.

He slid his fingers down the dark cleft of her behind to the treasure beyond. She moaned in her sleep, shifting again. Joshua gritted his teeth against the throbbing ache of his erection. He moved his hand lower until he was stroking her warm, moist folds. He closed his eyes and sucked in a breath. It would be so easy to just undo the button of his jeans and slide the zipper down. Within about five seconds after that, he could be buried deep in her heat.

It would feel so damn good.

Why not? a small voice in the back of his head demanded. He'd all but given his life to the pack, protecting it always against all threats. And the cost had been high. Sometimes, he wondered if he had any humanity left inside him at all. Kill or be killed had been his life for so long.

And then he'd seen Alex.

She'd reawakened something deep inside him, given him hope for the future. His brother's words echoed in his head and he could hear Isaiah encouraging him to take her, to mark her as his.

No! That wouldn't be fair to her.

Why not? that insidious voice whispered. No one would take better care of Alex or cherish her as he would. Why shouldn't he claim her?

Because she deserved a choice. Because, after everything she'd been through, Alex deserved at least that much.

Taking a deep breath, he opened his eyes and peered into large silvery gray eyes that almost swallowed him whole. They were deep and fathomless, dark pools of comfort just waiting to envelope him.

"Hi." She gave him a soft, sleepy smile that made his heart clench.

"Good morning." He barely recognized the low rumble of his own voice. He cleared his throat. "How did you sleep?"

She stretched, making him groan. "I didn't think I'd sleep at all, but I slept well." Alex leaned down and rubbed her nose against his. "Thanks to you."

His hand moved of its own volition, stroking the soft folds of her pussy. She arched against him, all but purring. "Mmm, that feels wonderful."

"This is not a good idea, Alex." He wanted to stop, but somehow couldn't tear his hand away.

"I think it's a wonderful idea, Joshua." The way she said his name had his balls clenching against his body. He wanted to hear her scream his name as she came.

She reached up and traced her fingers over his face, examining every feature. He knew he was a rough-looking bastard, but for the first time in his life, he wished his face was a bit more pleasing. That made him angry. "It won't get any better no matter how long you stare at it," he growled.

Totally unconcerned by his outburst of anger, she continued to stroke her fingers over his forehead and down his nose. "How did you break it?" She lightly touched the bump that protruded from the center.

"Fight with my older brother."

Alex laughed. "I always wanted siblings, but that doesn't sound like much fun."

Joshua shrugged, trying to act nonchalant, which was hard with his dick poking her in the stomach. "We play hard, we fight hard, but there's no one else I'd want at my back in any kind of situation."

"Mmm," she intoned as she slid her finger across his bottom lip.

Joshua didn't know what that meant, but he didn't care. He parted his lips and nipped at the tip of her finger before sucking it into his mouth. His teeth scraped gently down to the base and then he licked at the sensitive webbing between her fingers. She moaned, her hips sliding hungrily against his erection.

He pulled his head away, letting her finger slip from his mouth. "Let me touch you. Let me taste you. Pleasure you." He wouldn't take her, wouldn't claim her. But that didn't mean he couldn't taste her. Touch her in other ways.

"Yes." Her reply was little more than a whisper, but it was enough for Joshua.

"Sit up," he urged as he helped her. The motion drove her sex hard against his erection and he had to fight to keep from coming in his jeans. He shifted her so she was seated on his belly and sighed as this new position allowed him to gain control of himself again. "Let's get this off you." He grabbed the tails of her T-shirt and lifted it over her head. She raised her arms and let him tug it off her, leaving her warm and naked in his arms.

Her hair was tousled, her eyes still soft and sleepy. Her breasts weren't overly large, but they were well shaped and firm. Their rosy tips puckered, begging for his mouth. Her skin was warm and he could feel her cream seeping out of her core and dampening his stomach.

Joshua rested his hands on her thighs and slid them upward. He circled her belly button with his finger, admiring the smoothness of her skin. It made him very aware of the rough calluses on his hands and he tried to be extra gentle with her. His hands went higher, teasing the undersides of her breasts.

Alex covered his hands with hers and pushed them higher until they were covering the soft mounds, her turgid nipples poking the center of his palms. "That feels so good, Joshua," she whispered breathlessly.

"Put your hands behind your neck." She stilled for a moment and then slipped her hands away from his and placed them at her nape. The movement pushed her breasts forward, inviting him to play.

"Beautiful," he intoned as he traced his thumbs around the swollen tips. Her eyes started to close. "Watch me." Her lids rose, allowing him to see the desire burning within her. "Watch me touch you." He lightly pinched her nipples and she cried out, her eyes locked onto his hands where they were touching her. He could feel his stomach getting damper.

She started to move her hands, reaching out to him. "No," he dropped his hands from her breasts, resting them on her thighs. "If you want me to pleasure you, you have to do as I say." Her eyes narrowed and for a moment he thought she might tell him to go to hell. He kept his face impassive even though his heart was pounding.

He felt like tipping back his head and howling his pleasure when she slid her hands back behind her neck and waited. She might not understand the ways of their people, but the fact that she'd given in and accepted his dominance at this time, was the first step in his claiming her. She might be an alpha female, but between the two of them he was still the alpha male and would not be denied. He knew he couldn't take her yet, but he could subtly tie her to him with bonds of emotional and physical intimacy.

"Perfect." He gave both her nipples a teasing tweak with his fingers before levering himself up to a semi-sitting position. "I'm going to taste you, Alex. Watch." His tongue snaked out to twine around one erect nub. Her back bowed, pushing her chest closer. He glanced up and her eyes were glued to what he was doing to her. The gray in her eyes deepened as he swiped his tongue over the hard peak. "That's it. I'm going to lick every inch of your breasts and then..." he nuzzled his way over to her other breast and rasped his rough tongue over it. "And then, I'm going to eat your pussy until you scream with pleasure."

Alex could barely breathe. She certainly couldn't talk. All she could do was sit there and absorb the pleasure rocketing through her body. She'd never liked dominant men, had always fought against any kind of domineering male overtures, but with Joshua everything was different. A part of her wanted to submit to him, to allow him to do whatever he wished with her. Another part of her knew her time would come and then it would be she who would have the upper hand.

For now, all she wanted to do was soak up every ounce of pleasure. He'd been touching her when she'd awoken. His soft, gentle caress had already built the heat inside her. She was so close to coming. She wanted this. Knew this kind of closeness now would make it harder for him to leave her down the road.

It was funny, she didn't mind being naked in front of him this morning. Having his hands already stroking her body when she first opened her eyes had made it all seem so natural. Until he'd asked her to put her hands behind her head, that is. That left her feeling exposed and vulnerable.

But she no longer cared. His clever tongue lapped at her nipples. First one. Then the other. Alex locked her fingers together, squeezing tight. She wanted to clutch his head to her breast, demand he do something more. But she didn't, knowing instinctively he'd stop as soon as she moved her hands away from where he wanted them.

What he was doing felt wonderful, but she needed something else. Her core was throbbing with emptiness, demanding to be filled by him. She licked her lips, watching intently as his mouth opened to cover her nipple. "Yes," she cried as she pushed forward, shoving her breast toward him. He closed his mouth over the tip and sucked. The sensation shot straight to between her thighs and she spread her legs further, rubbing her swollen clit over his belly.

Her hands itched to touch his chest. Bands of muscle were prominently displayed, stretched across tanned flesh. A thick covering of black hair stretched from nipple to nipple before arrowing downward toward his groin. She wanted to thread her fingers through it and feel its crispness against her breasts.

Joshua released her nipple, blowing softly across the damp flesh. Alex shivered, goose bumps forming on her arms and belly. "Joshua," she pleaded.

"What, my sweet?" He nuzzled the plump mound of one breast, the stubble on his jaw abrading it slightly.

Her heart expanded at the endearment and she savored the sound of it. "I need more."

"What do you need?" He carefully tugged a nipple into his mouth and played with it with his teeth.

Alex's sex was clenching rhythmically. Her blood was pounding through her veins. Her skin felt tight and she had to swallow the urge to growl. *Growl?* She began to sweat as she sensed the female wolf within her for the first time. It frightened her even as it made her feel stronger, more desirable.

As if sensing her momentary distraction, Joshua pulled

back and blew on her damp flesh again. "Tell me what you need."

"You." Everything she was feeling came out in the emotion attached to that one small word. Joshua was all she wanted and she wanted him right now.

He lay back down on the bed and slid lower on the pillows. She started to fall forward, but he caught her easily, holding her steady. "Shift upward, Alex. I want to taste your pussy."

Her entire body seemed to clench and release as she scooted forward. She started to remove her hands to use them for support, but glanced down at him. Deciding that she wasn't going to take any chances, she kept them where they were. His deep brown eyes gleamed with pleasure as she shifted into place with her thighs on either side of his head.

"You're so beautiful. So pink and wet and sexy." His finger stroked over the slick folds, ignoring the hard nub at the apex of her sex. He sucked in a deep breath. "You smell hot, like woman and sex."

Alex bit her lip to keep from moaning aloud. She was going to come with him just talking to her. His words were almost a physical caress against her skin. Heat rocketed through her as though she were burning up with a fever. Need unlike anything she'd ever experienced shook her.

He slipped one of his hands around her, caressing her behind while the other one continued to explore her sex. "I'll bet your pussy is tight and hot." His finger dipped just inside her slit before withdrawing. Her vagina contracted and her thighs trembled. Alex swallowed back a cry when his finger slipped away.

Wrapping his hands around her hips, he pulled her downward until she could feel his warm breath brushing against the moist folds of her sex. Her breath was coming in hard gasps now, making her breasts quiver with every mouthful of air she sucked in. He snaked his tongue out, lapping at her sensitive flesh and this time she could not suppress the groan of pure pleasure that was drawn from deep within her.

"You like that, do you?" She could hear the sheer male satisfaction in his tone. If she liked it any more she'd explode. But she wasn't going to tell him that.

She closed her eyes and tipped back her head when his tongue began to taste her again. He captured her clitoris between his lips and sucked gently on it. Alex began to whimper. The stubble on his jaw brushed against her inner thighs and the sensitive flesh of her labia, sending tendrils of heat rushing though her. Every time Joshua touched her she was bombarded with a new depth of sensation. She seemed to want him more and more with each passing minute.

Alex was alive in a way she'd never been before. She felt weak and powerful at the same time, feminine yet strong. Every fiber of her being strained for completion. Tension built low in her pelvis, gathering strength, waiting for just the right touch to ignite it.

He gave one last suck on her clitoris and licked a path straight to her opening, stabbing his tongue inside her. Almost blind with pleasure, her hands flailed out to grab onto the headboard, digging her fingers into the cheap wood veneer for support, as Joshua continued to stoke the flames of desire within her.

"Joshua." It was more a demand then a plea. She was suspended on the edge of desire, unable to go back, but not yet able to go over into release.

His tongue stabbed deeper as his finger stroked over her clit. Alex cried out as the first spasm struck. Her entire body jerked and heaved as she came. At some point, she released her grasp on the headboard and gripped Joshua's head, holding it to her. He continued to lap and suck and pleasure her until she couldn't bear it any longer. The fingers that had been holding him to her so tightly now began to push him away.

"Stop," she moaned. "Enough." She half-rolled, half-dragged herself away from him, fell to the mattress and curled herself into a ball. His arms came around her, dragging her back against his chest. One of his hands rested low on her belly while the other wrapped around one of her breasts. His heart pounded against her back and she could hear the hoarse gasps of his breathing.

"You taste incredible." He feathered light kisses across her nape before nipping at her shoulder.

Alex groaned, shifting her legs restlessly. Her inner muscles were still pulsing, liquid still seeped from her core, dampening her inner thighs, but already she felt restless, as if this wasn't enough. Her body craved something more. Alex was very afraid that she wouldn't be satisfied until Joshua took her, claiming her in every way.

Joshua kept his touch light and undemanding and eventually her body began to relax. He was still tucked securely around her and she could feel the hard bulge of his erection pressing against her behind. She shifted the tiniest bit and he groaned, jerking back his hips as he tried to move away from the subtle caress.

Alex licked her lips. He'd had his turn. Now it was hers.

Chapter Thirteen

Alex straightened her legs and started to turn toward Joshua. His arms tightened around her momentarily before he relaxed and let her move. His eyes were hooded, his lips pursed together in a thin line. If she didn't know him as well as she did, the fire burning in his eyes would have frightened her. It seemed strange she'd only been aware of his existence for a mere twenty-four hours. He was such a big part of her life now that, with each passing minute, it got harder to remember life without him.

Now that was a frightening thought.

Pushing it out of her mind for the moment, she focused on the task at hand. That was pleasure. Specifically, pleasuring Joshua Striker. The man had brought her to orgasm several times now and she wanted the chance to do the same for him. She hadn't meant to fall asleep while she was waiting for him last night, but had been unable to fight against the physical and mental fatigue that had dragged her down into slumber as soon as her head had hit the pillow.

But she was wide awake now and Joshua was lying next to her, warm and hard and waiting. He watched her intently as she raised her hand and cupped his jaw. Stubble covered his chin, making him appear even more dangerous. Other than her father, she'd never known a man who emitted such raw power. She was drawn to Joshua in a way she'd never expected. Wanted to lay claim to this man who had in such a short while become such an integral and central part of her life.

"What are you thinking?" He brushed a stray lock of hair off her forehead.

She smiled as she stroked her thumb across his bottom lip. "I'm thinking that you've had your turn and now it's mine."

He froze, every muscle tensing. "Alex." The way he said her name was half-warning, half-plea.

"It's only fair." She slipped her hand higher, letting it sift through the silky strands of his hair. He moved his head against her hand in obvious pleasure. She wanted to know everything that pleased him, wanted to learn what made him groan and what made him lose control.

"Alex." There was a warning undertone now, but she ignored it. Coming up on one elbow, she leaned over him, kissing him softly. His lips were warm and supple. She didn't linger, but moved lower, peppering his jaw with kisses as she worked her way down his neck. Her tongue trailed along that thick column. His skin was rough and salty.

His hand covered her hip and for a moment she thought he would push her away. Instead, his fingers kneaded her skin, and she could sense him fighting himself.

"Let me pleasure you, Joshua," she whispered as she tangled her fingers in his chest hair. She loved the way the black curls wrapped around them as if he didn't want to let her go.

He heaved a deep sigh and relaxed. His hand dropped away from her hip, giving his silent permission for her to do whatever she chose. Alex hid her grin against his chest. Obviously, Joshua didn't like being out of control even for a minute. That was okay. Based on his reaction to her, she was rapidly gaining confidence in her own abilities to be able to rock his control upon occasion. She got the feeling he didn't relax and let go much, but that was about to change.

Nuzzling the hard muscles of his chest, she worked her way over to his nipple. A light sprinkling of hair surrounded the flat disc. Flicking out her tongue, she touched it. His entire body jerked. Leaning back, she blew on the damp nub before covering it again with her mouth and this time sucking gently.

Joshua groaned, his hand coming up to tangle in her short hair as he held her mouth tighter to him. Alex slid her hand over his torso, lightly scratching his skin. The muscles in his belly flexed beneath her questing fingers and he sucked in a deep breath, creating a space between the band of his jeans and his stomach. She skimmed her fingers just below the band. Joshua emitted a low growl. She raised her head and smiled down at him as she scooted lower on the bed. He was so tense, every muscle on his body sharply delineated as he held himself still.

She took her time undoing the button at his waist. Grasping the tab of the zipper in her fingers, she pulled it down ever so slowly. His shaft sprang upward, unhindered by any underwear. She raised an eyebrow and looked at him.

He gave her a sexy grin and shrugged. "Too confining."

Note to self, she thought. *He doesn't wear underwear.* It was hard enough to function sensibly around Joshua as it was, but knowing he was bare beneath his soft, faded jeans was going to make it even harder. The turgid flesh bumped against her hand, demanding her attention. She spread the fabric wide and pushed it downward. Joshua lifted his behind long enough for her to yank his jeans just below his thighs. She started to pull his pants off, but got distracted.

His penis was long and thick and the plum-shaped head was dark. Blue veins pulsed as his shaft flexed impatiently. Licking her lips, she trailed a single finger from the tip to the base and up again, fascinated by the texture of his skin. His erection was hard, but the flesh covering it was soft and velvety. She could feel it throbbing beneath her finger as she stroked him again.

"Alex," he groaned. She glanced up at him. His jaw was clenched tightly. She realized he was too close to the edge for her to tease him for much longer. Still, she didn't want to rush things. This was the first time she'd ever touched a man, but she didn't think she'd be near as fascinated if it were anyone but Joshua.

Lowering her head, she licked a path from the base all the way to the top, dainty little flicks of her tongue that made him groan again. She reached between his legs and cupped his testicles, massaging them. His sac felt heavy, the skin rougher and sprinkled with hair. She was enthralled with the sheer magnificence of him.

Liquid seeped from the slit at the top of his shaft and she

stroked her tongue over it, wanting to taste him as he'd tasted her. It was warm and salty and she decided that she liked it.

Her own body was reacting to what she was doing. Her nipples were firm nubs and her breasts felt swollen. She shifted her legs restlessly, unable to believe how aroused she was becoming simply by touching Joshua. Her sex was damp and soft and every now and again she would feel a trickle of liquid roll down her inner thigh.

"Alex." His voice was edged with desperation as he arched his hips upward. Opening her mouth, she sucked the head of his shaft inside, swirling her tongue around it. She could feel his testicles actually pulling tighter against his body. Giving them one final gentle squeeze, she released them and wrapped her hand around the base of his penis. Taking her time, she stroked upward and then back down, all the while her tongue and mouth continued to tease the top of his shaft.

His large hand covered hers, wrapping her fingers snugly around him and guiding her into the rhythm he wanted. When she took over on her own, he dropped his hand back to the mattress with a soft thud. She could feel the power in him, feel it collecting low in his groin, knew he was close.

Losing herself in the moment, she blocked out everything else but Joshua. She forgot the desire thrumming through her own body. Nothing mattered but bringing him the kind of pleasure that he'd given her.

"Harder, baby. Suck me harder," he groaned.

Her mouth and hand moved in tandem as she took his cock deeper into her mouth with each stroke. His hips were bucking against her now, his fingers tangled in her hair, holding her close, making sure she didn't leave him now. As if she would. She wanted this as badly as he did.

His breathing was harsh in the quiet of the room. Both their bodies were covered in sweat as Alex continued to stroke him with her mouth and hand.

"I'm coming," he gritted out from between clenched teeth. She felt him start to push her head away, wanting to give her a choice, but she was having none of that. She wanted all of him, wanted the whole experience.

He gave a hoarse cry as he came, jetting into her mouth.

She swallowed and continued to suck. Joshua's fingers tightened in her hair, making her scalp sting slightly as his shaft continued to spasm. Finally, he relaxed back onto the bed with a groan. "Enough." His hand was gentle but firm as he pushed her away and carefully untangled his fingers from her hair.

Laying her head on his stomach, she wrapped her arm around him and held him. Neither one of them spoke. Joshua rested his hand on the top of her head and it slid down until he was cupping her cheek. His thumb absently caressed her skin. Alex was content to revel in the closeness that enveloped them even as she knew it couldn't last.

Long before she was ready to relinquish the closeness between them, Joshua shifted beneath her and she reluctantly raised her head. His eyes were serious, but beyond that she couldn't read any other emotions.

"Thank you."

She shrugged. "You're welcome." The words were almost stilted, the comfortable silence of a few moments before slipping away. She became very aware of her nakedness and self-consciousness began to creep in.

Sighing, he sat up. "We've got to go." He glanced down at his watch. "It's getting late and I want to get on the road early."

Alex rolled out of bed and grabbed the bedspread, wrapping it around her body. "I'll just get a quick shower and get dressed." Ignoring his searching gaze, she gathered her jeans, socks and the T-shirt he'd bought her and hurried to the bathroom. Only when the door was closed behind her did she let out the breath she'd been holding.

She glanced at her reflection in the mirror. Her face was rosy and there were faint traces of beard burn on her jaw. Lowering the bedspread, she could see a few more light red patches near her breasts. Her skin tingled and low-level desire still thrummed within her. Partly due to her attraction to Joshua and partly due to the chemical changes she knew were taking place inside her body.

She dropped the bedspread, bolted into the shower and turned on the spray, not wanting to think about the fact her body would soon be out of her control. She shivered as the cold water hit her and quickly adjusted the temperature. Tipping her face up, she let the water cascade over her. Cowardly or not, she still wasn't sure she was ready to deal with the whole werewolf thing.

It was strange that she so readily accepted it in Joshua, but was having a very hard time accepting it within herself. It seemed natural with him. But for her, it was a shift in thinking after a lifetime of believing certain things about herself. For twenty-two years she'd been human only to be told now that she was something else entirely.

She started to scrub, but had to lighten her touch. Her breasts were extremely sensitive and so was the area between her legs. Finishing quickly, she turned off the water and jumped out of the shower. She grabbed a towel and dried off. Thankfully, her panties and bra were dry and within moments she was dressed. She ignored her sweatshirt from the day before, instead opting to wear the T-shirt Joshua had bought for her.

She smeared some of the lotion he'd given her on her face, pleased to note the redness from the sun she'd gotten yesterday had pretty much faded. She brushed her teeth and picked up the bedspread. Ready or not, it was time to face Joshua.

Joshua watched Alex hurry to the bathroom, admiring the curve of her back as she disappeared into the other room. The sound of the water being turned on in the shower made him drop back on the bed and groan. He could well imagine her naked beneath the hot spray, her body soapy and smooth.

Cursing, he rolled off the bed and yanked his jeans up, quickly zipping and buttoning them. He hadn't meant to let things get so out of hand between them, but he'd been unable to resist Alex. He was drawn to her, lured by her very essence.

He stilled. She was his Achilles' heel. Because of his position within the pack and indeed the werewolf world, he kept his emotions buried, caring for nobody but his brothers. If his enemies ever found out how much Alex meant to him, they would use her to hurt him.

He stalked over to the window and carefully pulled back a corner of the drapes, peering out onto the parking lot. There was no movement. Everything was quiet. Maybe it wasn't too late to back away from Alex. After all, she'd soon meet every eligible male from the pack. Perhaps she'd find one of them more to her liking. Someone who wasn't as controlled as him. Someone who wasn't as comfortable with killing as he was.

A growl started low in his chest and his fingers started to change, becoming long, sharp claws as they curled around the frame of the window, biting into the wooden frame. The thought of another man touching Alex, tasting her smooth skin, being the recipient of her smiles and her temper, made him feel vicious. She was his.

He swore again. Releasing his hold on the windowsill, he willed his wolf into submission. Ignoring the gouges in the wood, he turned away from the window. He took a deep breath and dragged a hand through his hair. If he had any kind of honor at all, he'd keep his distance from her. His only job was to deliver her safely to the pack. After that, he could leave, retreat to his home and lick his wounds in private. No one would ever have to know what had happened between them. That was probably for the best, he assured himself.

Then the bathroom door opened and Alex stepped out. He'd been so lost in his thoughts he hadn't noticed the water stopping. She shot him a tentative, slightly nervous smile and everything he'd just told himself, everything he'd just decided was for the best, went out the window.

She looked hot and sexy and adorable all at the same time. He was primal enough to enjoy the fact she was wearing the T-shirt he'd bought for her. She put her head down and went to the nightstand, checking her knives and gun before strapping the weapons to her body. The action reminded him not only of how competent Alex was, but also of the danger surrounding them

Alex belonged with him.

He'd tried to bury his attraction, tried to pretend it didn't really matter, reminded himself the honorable thing to do was to let her have a choice. He'd been lying to himself. From the moment he'd laid eyes on her, it was as if a switch deep inside him had gone off and all his hormones had stood up and said, "*Mine!*"

He'd just have to do everything within his power to protect her. And until he got her home to the Wolf Creek compound, where he could keep her safe, he had to shove aside all the physical attraction and pay strict attention to her safety.

"I need to get a quick shower. I'll only be a few minutes."

"Okay." There was no trace of emotion in her voice and that made Joshua unaccountably angry. He knew there was no time for emotional confessions. And even if there was time, he wasn't the kind of man to make them. But damn, he hated sensing her withdrawal from him even if it was what was necessary. And if he was standing here thinking about such things when they needed to be on the road, he was further gone than he'd thought. Swearing under his breath, he stalked to the bathroom and closed the door with a solid thunk.

Stripping off his boots, socks and jeans, he stepped into the shower and turned the water on full. It took him about two minutes to lather from head to toe and rinse. Three more minutes and he was dried and dressed. He stared at himself in the mirror and rubbed his jaw. He needed a shave, but there was no time. He wondered if Alex had beard-burn on any parts of her body and grinned. It made him feel better to know she would have a reminder of him and what they'd done as she moved through her day.

By the time he was fully dressed again and stepped outside the bathroom door, he had himself under control. He'd buried his emotions deep inside himself. It was something he'd had a lot of practice doing and he was good at it.

Alex had thrown the covers over the bed and had shoved her few belongings into the bag he'd brought back from the store last night. He almost told her to leave them, that she'd have everything she needed when she got to Wolf Creek, but he kept his mouth shut. It probably made her feel better to have some of her own stuff with her. It wasn't much, but it was hers.

She was sitting on one of the wooden chairs, obviously ready and waiting. He checked the knives he had tucked into his boots and walked over to her, crouching down in front of her. She didn't look at him, but he waited patiently until finally she gave a small sigh and tilted her head down slightly so that their gazes met.

"Everything will be all right." He'd never felt the need to reassure another person before in his life. He'd arrogantly believed if he ever found a mate she would fit comfortably into his life, not bothering the smooth running of his days. Alex was proving to be anything but convenient or easy. She made him experience deep emotions he'd never dealt with before and he already knew she would challenge his authority at every turn, keeping him constantly on his toes.

Strange as it was, that thought invigorated him. He was proud of her independent spirit and her skills at caring for herself, while at the same time he wanted to tuck her away in his home and keep her safe. He shook his head at his wayward thoughts. If he didn't claim her soon he was obviously going to turn into a raving lunatic.

She shook her head. "You can't guarantee that. No one can." She glanced away for a moment before turning back to him. "What's our plan?"

"Speed is of the essence. We're running out of time." He wouldn't tell her, but he could already smell the difference in her. She was getting closer to going into full heat and there was no time to lose. As her scent strengthened, it would make it easier for the rogue males from the other packs to find them. Plus, he wanted her safely mated to him when the time came for her to embrace her werewolf heritage.

She nodded, but said nothing.

"As much as I hate to risk it, we'll get a cab from here. We'll stop a few blocks from our destination and walk the rest of the way just in case."

Alex frowned thoughtfully. "In case of what?"

Her brows were furrowed and he longed to smooth away the lines of worry from her face. "Alex, we not only have other werewolves searching for us, but bounty hunters as well. There's no telling who is on their payroll, or who might have heard they were searching for us. I'm sure by now that our picture has been circulated in certain areas. They'll be offering money. A reward to anyone who helps them find us."

She swallowed hard. "I understand."

Joshua stood slowly. They'd already wasted enough time. It was still early, but he wanted to be on the road within the next half hour or so if possible. "Come on." He held out his hand to her. She reached out to him and he wrapped his fingers around hers, pulling her up off the chair. He gave her hand a final squeeze before releasing it.

He palmed his cell phone and quickly dialed the number he needed. Less than thirty seconds later, they were closing the door to their room behind them. Joshua headed toward the motel office to turn in their keycard. "Keep your eyes open," he warned.

Alex nodded, fading into the shadows at the side of the building as he hurried inside. He was back outside just as the cab pulled up in front of the motel.

Chapter Fourteen

Alex came awake slowly. Her head was tilted at an awkward angle against the headrest and she had a crick in her neck. Blinking, she let the world come back into focus and memory came rushing back.

After everything that had happened yesterday, their escape from Chicago this morning had been anti-climactic. They'd taken the taxicab to a restaurant where they'd ordered coffee and bagels to go. Then they'd left and walked several streets over until they'd come to a hardware store. And, as promised, there had been a slightly disreputable-looking black pickup truck waiting for them.

Joshua hadn't immediately hurried to the vehicle, but had pulled her into an alleyway close by where he could watch it without being seen. They'd hurriedly eaten their bagels and drank their coffee in the alley. Not great ambience, but necessary. Alex wrinkled her nose in memory.

She supposed he'd been looking for anyone suspicious, but after about fifteen minutes, he'd relaxed slightly. They'd dumped their garbage into a bin at the back of the alley before strolling across the road.

Joshua had brought her around to the driver's side of the vehicle and allowed her to get in only after he'd checked out the exterior and interior of the cab. Once they were both settled in their seats, he'd tugged down the visor and the key had dropped into his hand. A few seconds later, they'd pulled out onto the street, heading for the outskirts of the city. Alex assumed he knew where he was going. She certainly didn't. She'd never been out of the city in her life.

She'd had an uncomfortable ride for a while when he'd suddenly decreed that she needed to get down on the floor and hide. But she had seen the sense in it. If anyone was looking for them, they'd be searching for a male and female together. They probably wouldn't look too closely at a man by himself. Or at least she hoped they wouldn't. She hadn't liked the idea of hiding while Joshua was so exposed. She'd pulled out her gun and laid it on the seat beside him, admonishing him to use it if he had to. He'd given her an enigmatic look, pulled the weapon closer to him and kept driving.

As soon as they'd joined the steady stream of traffic on the highway, he'd let her get back up. She'd settled into her seat, strapped on her seat belt and tried to relax. Strangely enough, she'd fallen asleep.

Awake now, she sat up straight, rolling her head slowly from side to side to try to work out the kinks. She was hungry, thirsty and in dire need of a bathroom. She was also worried about her father, worried about herself and what faced her, worried about how much Joshua had come to mean to her in such a short period of time and, above all, she desperately needed another cup of coffee. She sighed. She wasn't likely to get that coffee anytime soon.

"Why the huge sigh?" Reaching out, he wrapped his hand around the back of her neck and massaged the taut muscles. She groaned as his strong fingers worked out some of the stiffness.

She shrugged. There was only so much she was willing to tell him. "I'm worried about my father. I need to go to the bathroom. And..." she opened her eyes and turned her head so that she could see him, "...I need another cup of coffee."

His grin came and went so fast she almost missed it. It made him appear younger, not quite so hard. His face had settled back into its normal serious lines, but she could see the twinkle in his eyes. "There's a truck stop about ten miles from here."

"Really?" She couldn't keep the delight from her voice.

That earned her another quick grin. "Really." He gave her nape one final squeeze before returning both hands to the wheel. "We'll stop and pick up some coffee and snacks. Or rather, I'll pick them up. You'll stay hidden in the truck."

"Sure. No problem." At this point she'd agree to just about anything to get that second cup of coffee. "What about the bathroom?"

"If I remember correctly, there's a gas station next to the diner. Less chance of anyone seeing you if you sneak in there."

Satisfied, Alex sat back and enjoyed the view. They drove in silence for another few minutes. It was a companionable silence and Alex was loath to break it, but she had questions. "I fell asleep last night before you could tell me about Wolf Creek and my father. I hadn't planned on sleeping most of the morning away either."

Joshua nodded. "I didn't want to wake you. I figured after everything you went through yesterday you needed the rest."

"I'm awake now," she pointed out.

"So you are." His eyes were constantly scanning in front of them and checking the rearview mirror. "What do you want to know?"

"Everything."

He chuckled, but it was a rough sound, as if he weren't quite used to doing such a thing. "Well, that narrows it down."

She twisted in her seat, as much as the seatbelt would allow, so that she was all but facing Joshua. "Tell me about my father."

"James LeVeau," he began. "Or rather, James LeVeau Riley, was the alpha of the Wolf Creek pack. He was the meanest, toughest son of a bitch around."

Since he'd said it in such admiring tones, Alex assumed that meant it was a good thing. She knew her father was tough, but it was hard to reconcile this ruthless image with the same man who'd tied her shoes when she was a child, taken her to see her first White Sox game when she was five, and had purchased her first box of tampons for her when she'd finally gotten her period.

"My father was Striker back then and none of the other packs messed with ours. Retribution was swift and brutal. They were good times. Peaceful times." As he continued, she noticed he seemed to get lost in the memory. "I remember your father coming to our home to talk with my father. They were good friends. All of us were in awe of your dad. He was the best of the best. The best hunter, tracker and fighter. But beyond that, he had a vision for the future. He knew that in order to survive, we had to fit in with the human population on some levels. Your father grew the wealth of the pack with shrewd investments and by cultivating some human friends at various levels of government. Then everything changed." His voice went flat.

"What happened?" She kept her voice soft, not wanting him to stop.

"James LeVeau was mated to Leda." He shook his head. "It's always a mistake for a man to love a woman that much."

Alex's heart constricted at his stark words, but she said nothing. Joshua was still talking so she forced herself to listen.

"It makes a man weak." He shot a quick glance her way. "Our women have had a hard time producing babies for the past hundred years or so. Whether it's some naturally occurring phenomena, something we did to ourselves, or a reaction to environmental changes, no one knows for sure. Not that it really matters. The result is the same. That, coupled with the pack wars and the attacks by bounty hunters, has seriously declined our population."

"You come from a fairly large family," she pointed out.

He nodded. "My mother was an exception, but even she lost one of her children, the only female in the bunch, to hunters. I think that, coupled with the death of my father a few years ago, was what finally killed her. She just didn't seem to have the will to go on after that."

Alex kept her thoughts to herself. While she couldn't pretend to understand the devastation that the loss of a child and a husband would bring, the woman still had other children. It was obvious that his mother's death had been hard on Joshua.

"My father," she prompted, hoping to lead him away from the grim thoughts of his family.

"Leda was pregnant and they were both so happy. She'd already had two miscarriages." Joshua glanced over at her before turning back to the road. "Both had happened early in the pregnancies. This time, she was healthy the entire time. I'd never seen two people look so damn happy as Leda neared her due date. I was only a young man, but even I noticed their joy. It was almost a living thing and affected everyone around them."

Alex twisted her fingers around her seatbelt. It was hard to imagine her father happily married, or mated, to someone. Did werewolves even have marriage ceremonies? Another question she'd need the answer to eventually. "Things went wrong," she prompted.

"Yes." Joshua's voice was dull and flat. "Leda died after about thirty-six hours of hard labor and James went berserk. It was a horrible thing to see such a great man brought so low by love."

Alex bit her lip to keep from crying out her denial. No wonder Joshua didn't think a strong man should fall in love. He'd seen so much tragedy and focused so much on the negative aspects that he'd completely blocked out all the positive things love brought to a person's life.

"It took about six men to pull him away from her body so that she could be cremated. He injured some of them quite seriously. In the end, his wife was cremated, her ashes scattered and James disappeared. At first everyone thought he'd gone to grieve. Then his brother showed up telling everyone that James had sent him."

"Why didn't his brother already live there?"

"Families are scattered all across pack land in sort of a loose community. They all fall under the dominion of the larger Wolf Creek pack, but they have a certain amount of autonomy. Ian LeVeau moved back to the main compound, the heart of the pack, and assumed leadership. No one had the heart to fight him for it at the time because everyone was so disheartened at being abandoned by James. Plus, my father threw his support behind Ian, so that was that."

"So Ian is still running the pack?" It was strange to try to understand the way werewolf society worked, but Alex knew she had to learn if she was going to become a part of it.

"Yes. But everyone knows he no longer wants it and it's only a matter of time until he either steps down or is challenged."

"So, what happens if he steps down? Who will assume

leadership?"

Joshua scanned the road and began to ease up on the gas. Up ahead, Alex could see a small building. That should be the truck stop. Her stomach growled in anticipation.

"Any man who wants to be leader steps forward. They all fight and whoever emerges the victor is the new leader."

The coffee was momentarily forgotten. "But that's barbaric."

"Get down on the floor, Alex." He waited until she'd undone her seatbelt and was settled on the floor before continuing. "It's the way things are among our kind. Only the strongest can lead. No one will follow a weak leader."

He pulled into the parking lot and brought the truck to a stop. Putting the gear in park, he undid his seatbelt and sat back. "We are your people now, Alex. There are many things you'll find not to your liking, but you will have to accept them if you are to survive." He picked up the gun and handed it to her before scanning the parking lot. She assumed everything looked fine because he opened the door and slid out of the seat. "Do you want anything else besides coffee?"

"Food. I don't care what it is."

Joshua nodded and shut the door. She noticed he'd kept the vehicle running just in case they needed to make a quick getaway. She gripped the handle of the gun securely as she pondered his words. The metal was warm against her palm. "Who says I need to accept anything?" she muttered aloud. "Maybe it's the pack that needs to do some changing. If things were so fine and dandy then they wouldn't have so many problems, now would they?"

Alex freely admitted that werewolf society wasn't much different from human when it came down to it. Fighting for the leadership of the pack was not that different from the many gangs that fought for territory in the city. Even supposedly civilized men fought for high positions in government, but their fights tended to be verbal, not physical. Still, that didn't make it right.

Sighing, she leaned her head against the seat. She expected there were a lot of things she was going to have to either accept or at least learn to live with. Joshua was who he was and he wasn't going to change any time soon. She would have enough of a fight on her hands getting him to claim her and admit that he loved her. Maybe she was making a huge mistake. What if all the feelings were one sided and all he was feeling was physical attraction? If that were the case then she was setting herself up for a world of hurt and disappointment.

The door to the truck opened and she jerked both her head and the gun toward it. Joshua nodded his approval as he climbed back onto the seat. He set a large sack on the seat and handed her a large cup of coffee. "Don't get up until I tell you it's safe."

As she tucked her weapon safely away and took her first sip of coffee, she watched Joshua maneuver the truck out of the parking lot and back onto the road. The cup was warm in her hands. Joshua had to feel something for her. He showed it in all the little things he did for her almost without thought. Last night it had been the T-shirt and the lotion; this morning the coffee. There really had been no need for them to stop other than the fact that she'd wanted a cup of coffee.

She took a sip of the hot, steaming liquid, warmed by more than just the heat from the coffee. He had to care. She didn't think she was imagining the depth of feeling that flowed between them. There was no way she could turn away from their relationship now. She was determined to do whatever it took to make him see he cared for her and it was okay for him to do so. She knew she might have a battle on her hands, but that was okay. She was tough. She was James Riley's daughter.

Alex sighed with relief when Joshua eased the truck into another parking lot and pulled around to the back of the building. She peeked over the dashboard and gave a prayer of thanks when she saw the restroom doors.

"Give me a second to get the key."

She nodded, but Joshua was already gone.

James pulled off the asphalt and onto the dirt parking lot that surrounded a small, run-down diner. He'd been on the road for hours and was starving. He parked his car off to the side, backing into the space. It always paid to be prepared to leave in a hurry. Taking his time, he surveyed all the vehicles parked around him and was satisfied by what he saw. His was the only car in the lot. There were a few pickups and several eighteen-wheelers.

Right now, all he wanted was a cup of coffee and some food. He didn't care what it was as long as it was filling and he could get it to go. He had no plans to linger any longer than necessary. Alex was out there somewhere and so were the werewolves who were hunting for her. He knew Joshua would protect her with his life, but it wasn't the same as being able to see her with his own two eyes. He wouldn't relax until she was safe within the confines of the Wolf Creek pack and properly mated.

He tried not to think about how Alex was feeling right now. He knew she was coping and doing what she had to do. After all, she was his daughter. He had faith in her ability to do what needed to be done.

But that didn't ease his worries. It had been a huge shock for Alex to find out about her heritage, especially in the way she had. He'd waited too long to tell her the truth about himself and about her. That was *his* mistake, and one he wished he could rectify. If he could turn back the clock he would. But that was impossible. The only thing any of them could do at the moment was to move forward and deal with whatever came next.

Climbing out of his car, he kept his sunglasses on as he scanned the area, letting his heightened senses flare outward. Nothing seemed out of the ordinary as he strode across the gravel parking lot. The sun was high in the sky and the heat felt good against his face. He could see and smell the surrounding forest and for the first time in years felt as if he could truly breathe. He was going home.

He yanked open the door and his nostrils were assaulted by the smell of burnt toast, bacon, eggs, coffee and unwashed bodies. Barely resisting the urge to curl his lip in disgust, he went to the counter, ignoring the stares directed his way. An older woman with a stained uniform and a worn look on her face scowled at him from behind the counter. "What will it be?"

James scanned the printed menu posted behind her. "I'll have the number two special and a large coffee to go." He figured the breakfast special couldn't be too bad.

She yelled his order through the open window that led to the kitchen. Turning back to him, she rang up his order. "That's six seventy-five."

"That's fine." He pulled a couple bills out of his pocket and paid for his order.

"Where you headed?" The woman squinted at him, her eyes missing nothing as she sized him up from head to toe. She poured his large coffee, plunking it down on the counter in front of him.

James knew her type. She liked to gossip and would remember him. He cursed himself for stopping. "Chicago," he lied easily. She'd had no way of knowing which direction he'd come from.

"Business or pleasure?"

He ground his teeth together. Why did he have to stop at the diner with the nosey waitress and why didn't anyone in this joint need another cup of coffee? As if hearing his unspoken plea, a man shouted from near the back of the room. "Hey, how about some more coffee back here, Gladys?"

"Hold on to your britches, Hank, I'm coming." She scowled at James as if this was somehow his fault before she grabbed the coffeepot and left her spot behind the counter.

James breathed a sigh of relief when the cook, a big, burly man with tattoos running up and down his arms, brought his order out from the kitchen. "Anything else?"

"No." Grabbing his coffee and his meal, he left the diner behind him. James could feel the woman's eyes burning into his back as he strode back to his car. Opening the door, he stashed his meal on the floor on the passenger side. He'd eat somewhere less visible.

Starting the engine, he grinned as lady luck smiled at him. A large transport truck slowed and began to pull into the parking lot. James used the bulk of the vehicle to shield him as he put his car in drive and turned out of the lot. Even if someone had been watching, they'd have no way of knowing which direction he'd taken.

Whistling under his breath, James drove down the road searching for a place to pull off so he could eat his breakfast before continuing on to Wolf Creek. It wouldn't be long until he was with Alex again. His fingers flexed hard around the steering wheel as he wondered where she was.

Chapter Fifteen

Alex was enthralled by the countryside as it passed by her window. The truck cruised along, Joshua pushing way above the speed limit whenever he could. She knew he was in a hurry to get home.

They'd been on the road all day, stopping only long enough to relieve themselves at a gas station and even once in the bushes before moving on once again. She knew they were on a deadline and they were being chased by bounty hunters and other werewolves, but right now she was doing her best just to enjoy the moment. The countryside seemed so vast and empty compared to the cramped quarters of the city. They'd driven through parts of Indiana, Kentucky and Tennessee already today, and had passed a sign that had announced they were now in North Carolina.

The paper bag beside her crinkled as she groped for it. One thing about traveling, there wasn't much else to do but watch the scenery and eat. Thankfully, Joshua had bought sandwiches, chips, drinks and chocolate bars at the diner early today.

"I think it's empty." He glanced at her as she opened the bag and peered inside, finding only wrappers.

Unfortunately, Joshua was right. She folded the bag down and shoved it away from her.

"Are you hungry?" She could hear the concern in his voice and it warmed her. Only her father had ever worried about her.

"No, I'm not hungry." She ran her finger over the material of her jeans, tracing the outer seam. "Just anxious, I guess. I mean I don't really know what to expect when we get wherever it is we're going to. Yes, I know we're going to Wolf Creek, but I really don't know where that is, what it looks like, what will happen, who I'll meet..." She trailed off when she realized she was babbling. Great, that was sure to make her appear strong and self-assured.

Joshua took one hand off the steering wheel and held it out to her. She gripped it like a lifeline, holding it harder than she wanted to. The further from the city they went, the more nervous she became. Her world was far behind her. This was *his* world now and she didn't know if she'd find a place within it.

"We're almost there. The hills of North Carolina are home to Wolf Creek and some of the most spectacular countryside around. It's wild and untamed and incredibly beautiful." He glanced over at her and the look in his dark eyes had her squirming on her seat. "Much like you," he whispered as he turned his attention back to the road. His low tones stroked over her skin, making her burn with sudden desire.

She swallowed hard. "Tell me more about it."

"The Wolf Creek pack land covers literally thousands of acres of land. Much of what we don't own in the area is parkland. We've had to adapt to the changing world just like everyone else has. Our people are artisans and farmers."

"I'm sure they're all as meek as lambs," she snorted. The men who'd broken into the garage had been more like thugs then farmers.

Joshua shot her a quick grin. "We're all werewolves underneath our skin, Alex. We cannot change our nature. But that doesn't mean that we can't be more than that."

He stroked his thumb across the top of her hand, reminding her that she was still clutching his hand a tad too tightly. She loosened her grip, but she didn't let go. She liked the feel of their hands joined together. He shifted his grip and threaded their fingers together so that their palms were touching. "Artisans and farmers," she prompted.

Even though his eyes were busy watching the road and the woods that ran alongside, he seemed more relaxed than she'd ever seen him. Maybe it was because he was heading home.

"Many of the men and women farm the land, growing as

many of the vegetables and fruits as they can. What we can't grow ourselves, we buy or barter for. Meat is no problem, as all of us are skilled hunters and the woods are teeming with game."

He tensed as a convoy of several large trucks came toward them, but he relaxed again when they passed by in a flurry of wind and dust. Maybe they were heading to Chicago, she thought wistfully. For a brief moment, Alex wished she was going with them. She turned her head and watched them until they disappeared into the distance, sighing when they vanished from sight.

Joshua gave her fingers a reassuring squeeze. "We also have skilled artisans—potters, carvers, woodworkers, sculptors, jewelry-makers and others. Our goods are sold in stores all across the country."

"Really." In spite of her melancholy, Alex found herself very interested. "I've always been curious about wood carving and pottery making."

"The others will teach you anything you wish to learn."

"They will?"

"Of course they will." She could hear the surprise in his voice. "It is our way, Alex. We are a pack and all members work together to ensure the pack's survival. Many of them would be honored to teach James LeVeau's daughter."

Alex absorbed what he'd said, mulling it over in her mind. Maybe her new life wouldn't be so bad if she had the opportunity to learn some things that she'd always wanted to. Then she remembered something else her father had mentioned. "Won't some of them dislike me because of my mixed blood?" She didn't want to use the words half-breed or tainted.

Joshua growled. It started low in his chest and grew until it practically filled the cab of the truck. When he glanced over at her, she could swear his eyes were glowing. "Anyone who treats you with anything but the utmost respect will answer to me."

She nodded her head, feeling a trickle of sweat rolling down her back. Fury rolled off him in waves and she had to fight her impulse to pull away from him. Then her sense of humor came to her rescue. "Does that include you too?"

He appeared startled and then the corners of his mouth

kicked up and the heat in his eyes switched from anger to passion in a blink. "I'm excluded from that because I'll always treat you with respect. Whatever I do is for your safety and well-being. You won't always like it."

Alex glared at him, her eyes narrowing. "Don't think for one minute I'm going to allow you or anyone else to dictate my life." There was no time like the present to get that idea right out of his head. She was her own boss. Just because she was attracted to him didn't mean she'd let him take over her entire life.

His fingers squeezed hers and then they were gone. Joshua swore as he grasped the wheel with both hands and jammed his foot down on the gas pedal. Instinctively, she knew he wasn't angry at what she'd said. He wasn't the type of man who would let a little thing like her disavowal get in his way. No, he'd just go ahead and do whatever he felt was right and let the chips fall where they may. She was going to have her hands full with him.

He swore again. The low, even tone of his voice was more frightening than if he'd been yelling.

"What is it?"

"Behind us."

She swiveled around and found a dark green truck gaining on them. "Maybe they're just in a hurry." She didn't believe that any more than Joshua did.

"Open the glove box, Alex. There should be some sort of weapon there."

Ignoring the request, she took the time to check her knives and gun before she opened the glove box. It was empty except for a large handgun. She removed it, taking the time to make certain it was loaded before handing it to him. He shook his head as he laid the weapon on the seat beside him.

"Put your head in your lap and stay down."

"I can shoot."

"Damn it, Alex. I can't do this if I have to worry about you." His yell startled her. A vein throbbed on the side of his head and she could see a small tic just beneath his eye.

"All right. All right," she groused as she lowered her head, placing it on her lap. She kept her grip firm around the butt of her gun. "I'm doing this under protest."

"Duly noted." His voice was grim, but she thought she detected a note of pride in his voice. She couldn't be sure though. The only view she had at the moment was of what was left of the stained and ripped black carpet that covered the floor.

"I could shoot while you drive," she muttered, still not happy with this arrangement. If she thought she could help, then she'd damn well sit up and take her chances. She felt like an idiot, cowering while he continued to drive. Even worse, she hated not knowing what was going on. "Where are they?"

"Almost alongside us. Their vehicle's got more power than ours. We can't outrun them. This wouldn't have happened if we'd gotten the car yesterday."

She could hear the disgust in his voice and knew that, once again, he was blaming himself for this. Really, the man took way too much on himself. "It's not your fault, Joshua. You're not responsible for everything or everyone around you. You can't know everything."

His lips pursed into a grim line. "Don't tell anyone else that."

"Joshua—"

"Hold on." He cut her off.

She could hear the roar of a powerful engine moving up alongside them. Joshua slammed on the brakes and the truck went into a skid. Tires squealed. Rubber burned. Alex's entire body jerked and she tried to brace herself. The muscles in both Joshua's arms strained as he struggled to keep them on the road. When he had the truck back under control, he pressed down on the gas pedal once again. Now they were behind the other vehicle. Holding the steering wheel with his right hand, he grasped the handgun with his left and held it out the window, firing off a series of quick shots.

Alex peeked over the dashboard, her fingers digging into the seat to help her keep her balance. She was just in time to see the dark green truck go into a skid and roll into the ditch, finally landing upright at the bottom.

They didn't slow down.

As they passed, a man was already dragging himself out of the front seat. Blood was dripping from his forehead, but his hands were steady as he fired off several shots with the rifle he held.

"Get down," Joshua roared. This time, she didn't think, just ducked. The window behind her shattered and shards of glass exploded into the air around her. She covered her head with her hands, protecting herself as best as she could.

Two more shots echoed. Alex knew that the rifle had a much farther range than either of their guns. A tire exploded and the truck lurched. "Hang on," Joshua shouted.

Alex braced one hand on the dashboard. The other still had a death grip on her gun. The truck pulled to one side as Joshua wrestled to keep it under control. It skidded off onto the soft dirt shoulder and the world tilted around Alex. Her stomach lurched as the vehicle rolled. Alex was jerked forward, then back, smashing her head against the side window. The seatbelt bit into her shoulder and chest, keeping her from flying through the windshield as the truck flipped over again. They weren't as lucky as the men in the other truck had been. When they finally came to a halt, Alex was hanging upside down.

Shocked, she hung there, trying to get her bearings. Her mouth was dry. She opened her mouth to speak, swallowed and then tried again. "Joshua?" she croaked.

She turned her head slowly, biting her lip to keep from crying out when she caught sight of him. He was hanging upside down like she was, blood dripping down the side of his face. His eyes popped open as she watched him. He blinked twice, then immediately turned to face her. "Are you all right?" His voice was little more than a rough rasp.

She nodded and then groaned and grabbed her head. She groaned again when she accidentally struck her temple with the gun that was still grasped securely in her hand. Through it all, she hadn't let go of it.

She heard a click and then Joshua half fell, half lowered himself until he was on the roof of the truck, which was really the floor now that they were upside down. Alex wondered about her own state of mind that her last thought had made perfect sense to her. As she watched, he levered himself out of the driver's side window, which had been smashed out during the crash. He'd made it look easy.

She fumbled with the buckle on her seatbelt and it came unsnapped just as Joshua appeared on her side of the truck. She barely had time to register his grim expression before she fell. With all the strength leached from her arms, she was unable to support herself as he had. Instead of lowering herself out of the seat, she ended up in a crumpled heap. She'd be sporting a few extra bruises after that, but she was free.

Joshua was swearing as he all but ripped the door off its hinges and knelt beside the opening, carefully helping her out of the tangled mass of metal and alloy that had been their truck. Where Joshua had levered himself out of the truck almost effortlessly, she had to be practically dragged from the wreckage. His strong arms gently eased her toward him.

She closed her eyes and leaned against Joshua, trying to absorb some of his strength as she sucked in a deep breath. She was glad to be sitting on the ground, even though it was hard and rocky. Anything was better than being tumbled around in the truck. Her head was pounding and her stomach was none too steady, but she knew they couldn't stay here. The men from the other vehicle wouldn't be far behind them. Although she wanted to bury her face against his chest and rest there, she knew there was no time. It wasn't easy, but she forced herself to push away from him. "We have to get going."

She opened her eyes and got her first really good look at him as he stood. She'd thought he'd appeared dark and dangerous before, but she'd been mistaken. The man before her was almost a stranger. There wasn't an ounce of softness anywhere in him. His rough-hewn features and the blank stare on his face reminded her of a picture of a barbarian warlord she'd seen in a history book once. This was a man who would have no trouble killing his enemies. In fact, he appeared as if he'd enjoy doing so. He looked ruthless, powerful and deadly.

She was damn glad that he was on her side.

Joshua felt all his emotions turn cold as he watched Alex gather herself. Tiny cuts dotted her arms and there were several other nicks on her face. A huge bruise was forming on the right side of her face and he wouldn't be surprised if she had a mild concussion.

The hot fury churning within him had quickly solidified into molten ice. They had hurt *his* woman. *His!* They would pay for that mistake. Watching her as she rolled over onto her hands and knees and struggled to stand made him want to howl with rage. But rage would work against them. He needed to be clear-headed and detached if they were going to survive.

His job was to protect her and he had failed her. Kneeling in the dirt with her face and arms bloody, her shirt ripped and her jeans torn, she glanced up at him and gifted him with a wan smile. "I could use some help here."

Shaking himself from his grim thoughts, he wrapped his arms around her and lifted her to her feet, not releasing her until she was steady. "We have to move." He hated to have to rush her, but they had no choice. Thankfully, their seatbelts had kept both of them from serious injury. Otherwise they'd be sitting ducks.

"I know," she reminded him. "I was the one who told you that. Remember?" She reached out and placed her hand on his cheek. "Are you sure you're all right?"

He thought his heart would surely burst it seemed to swell so large in his chest. This woman in front of him was everything. There was nothing he would not do to protect her and to keep her. If he'd ever had any doubts about that, they were gone. He was in awe of her courage. Any other woman would be crying or screaming at him for getting her into this mess. Instead, Alex was worried about him. "I'm fine."

He ignored her concerned gaze as he stepped away and returned to the truck long enough to grab her jacket and a lightweight windbreaker he'd found stashed behind the driver's seat this morning. The nights would be cold and right now he had no idea how long they would be out here.

Yanking his cell phone out of his back pocket, he flipped it open. No service. He wasn't surprised. Cell phone service was spotty at best in the mountains. There was also the possibility it had been damaged in the crash. Closing it, he jammed it back into his pocket.

Alex was still standing in the same spot waiting for him and he took her hand in his and started to pull her toward the trees. They would be safer there than they would be on the road. The woods were his domain.

He moved as quickly as he could. Alex did her best to keep up, but she was still shaky. Still, she kept moving and didn't complain. She knew the score as well as he did. "Do you think they were alone?" Her question didn't surprise him. She had a quick, intelligent mind.

"No. I'm sure they've probably already contacted others spread out along the route. Most likely all of them are converging on this area."

"Did you recognize the men in the truck?"

He'd gotten a good look at them when they'd come up alongside the truck. "Yeah. One of them was the bounty hunter I saw yesterday. I'm assuming his buddy is one too." She stumbled over a downed tree and he caught her, holding her for a brief moment. He could hear her heavy breathing and knew she was struggling to keep up with him. It worried him. "How bad is your head?"

She grimaced. "I'd love a hot bath, some pain relievers and a good night's sleep. Other than that, I'm a bit banged up, but I'll be all right."

He noticed then that she still had her gun clasped in her hand. "Why don't you tuck that away for now."

She stared down at her hand and almost seemed surprised to still see the gun there. "I'd forgotten I was still holding it." She finally had to reach down with her free hand to pry her fingers from around the metal. Once she had it tucked into her jeans at the small of her back, she flexed her fingers. "I didn't want to lose it this time."

No, he thought. She'd lost her weapon during the fight in the garage and his little warrior wouldn't want to do that again.

Alex slipped on her leather jacket and he tied the windbreaker around his waist as they hiked onward. It didn't matter to him what the terrain was. He knew he could take care of both Alex and himself. He was headed in the direction of Wolf Creek and that was all that mattered. Eventually, his brothers would know something had gone wrong and they would come looking.

If he'd been on his own, he would have shed his clothing and shifted. In his wolf form he could have run for hours, outpacing the hunters. But Alex couldn't change yet and he wouldn't leave her.

He sniffed the air constantly, testing it for smells that didn't belong. He ignored the sweet smell of Alex that drifted up to his nostrils. Yes, she was sweaty and dirty and he hated the scent of blood that surrounded her, reminding him of her injuries, but beneath it all was the sweet smell of woman.

A bird flew up from the trees behind them. Joshua whirled around. Instinctively, he leapt at Alex, catching her in his arms as he threw them both to the ground, sheltering her so that his much larger body took the brunt of the fall. He heard the telltale whistle before he felt the pain. A large silver-tipped bolt from a crossbow pierced his left shoulder. If he hadn't jumped when he had, it would have been buried in his heart.

Chapter Sixteen

Alex stared in horror at the large arrow protruding from Joshua's body. He seemed oblivious to it as he drew his gun with his other hand and crouched beside her. She tried to scramble to her knees, but he knocked her back down with his shoulder. "Stay down," he hissed. Beads of sweat dotted his forehead, but in no other way did he give any indication he was in any pain at all.

The man was unbelievable.

Reaching behind her back, she pulled out her gun. The weight felt solid in her hand. "How did they find us so quickly?" She'd thought that with Joshua's skills in the woods the hunters would have a harder time finding them. Which was a stupid assumption when she really thought about it. If these were professional bounty hunters they would be skilled trackers. She excused her brief mental lapse, telling herself the blow to her head from the accident had momentarily scrambled her brains.

"We've got to move." His eyes scanned the woods around them. "The two hunters are coming from the east, but they've got company. Keep low."

She scrabbled to her feet, but kept her head and body as low to the ground as possible as she followed him behind some heavy brush. She could hear a shout in the distance but couldn't make out what was said. "More hunters?" Her voice was hushed, but it still sounded incredibly loud. She knew she shouldn't be talking, but she had to know what was going on.

"Werewolves," he growled, disgust dripping from that single word. *Betrayal.* He didn't say it, but Alex could all but hear it.

The fact that a werewolf would join forces with bounty hunters to destroy another of their kind was an abomination. These hunters routinely killed women and children in their efforts to destroy the species.

Alex didn't speak after that, but concentrated on putting one foot carefully in front of the other. She tried to match Joshua's steps. He was absolutely silent as he moved fluidly and quickly through the forest. He didn't lead her in a straight line, but had her moving over rocks and fallen logs, zigzagging their path. He always seemed to know where to step to avoid making any sound. It seemed as instinctive to him as breathing. This was the wolf inside him, she realized. This was the predator, at home in the woods.

It occurred to her that if she weren't with him, he'd be stalking those hunters and rogue werewolves instead of running from them, wound or no wound. Her fingers tightened around her weapon. He stopped behind a large boulder and pulled her down beside him.

"The arrow has got to come out. It's getting in my way."

Of course it was. Not that it hurt him in any way. It was just getting in his way. She was filled with the totally unreasonable urge to yell at him. Instead, she pushed back her anger. "What do you want me to do?"

He gave a single nod of approval as if he'd expected nothing less from her. "You'll have to break the end off the bolt. It's tipped in silver and is too big to pull back out without causing more damage." Reaching down into his boot, he withdrew a wickedly sharp hunting knife. "If you can't crack it off, cut it with this."

Laying the gun down on the ground next to them, she stared at the arrow protruding from his body, trying to figure out the best angle of approach.

"Just do it. We don't have time to waste." He braced himself against the rock, the muscles of his good arm tensing as he waited.

She wasn't trying to waste time. She was trying to build up enough courage to do this. Taking a deep breath, she wrapped her hands around the top of the shaft just below the tip and put all her strength into the task at hand. Doing her best not to jolt him, she cracked off the deadly silver end and tossed it to the ground.

Joshua was breathing heavily now, and a bead of sweat rolled down his temple. "Good. That's very good. Now come around to my front, brace your hand on my chest and pull the rest of the arrow out."

Alex swallowed hard, but did as he instructed. His body was warm beneath her hand, his heart beating steadily beneath her palm. There was no give in the wide expanse of muscle that banded across his chest. She gripped the shaft with her other hand, took a deep breath and pulled in one hard motion, much like ripping off an adhesive bandage.

He sucked in a breath between his clenched teeth, but other than that he gave no sign she'd hurt him at all. His body was rock steady, but she was feeling a bit wobbly. Kneeling in the dirt, she wiped a hand over her damp forehead. Blood welled from the hole. "That needs to be cleaned so it doesn't get infected."

"Later." He glanced back toward the direction they'd come from, his eyes narrowing. "Help me get my shirt off. I need to wrap something around this to stop the bleeding."

God. She'd been sitting here just watching him bleed. Her head must be more muddled from the crash than she'd thought. Galvanized into action, she shucked her jacket and tore her own shirt over her head. Using the knife he'd handed her, she cut it into strips. She had a momentary pang over destroying the shirt because he'd given it to her. Which was actually quite a silly sentiment at a time like this.

She also wished she had her grimy sweatshirt to pull on. But that was back in the wrecked truck, rolled up in a paper bag with the rest of their belongings. She hadn't even noticed the bag when she'd crawled out of the truck. Obviously, it had gotten tossed somewhere during the accident. No matter where it was, there was no going back for it now.

Alex ignored his questioning stare as she carefully cut away the short sleeve of his shirt. She folded several of the strips she'd cut in to thick pads, placing one at the entry point of the wound and the other at the exit. She then used several more strips to wrap his shoulder, hoping this would stem, if not stop the bleeding. When she was done, she hauled her leather jacket on over her bra. "You should wear your jacket."

He shook his head as he used the windbreaker to clean most of the blood from his arm. "I'm going to use it to try to lead them away from us." His eyes softened as he cupped her jaw in his hand. "Thank you, Alex." His thumb stroked her bottom lip before he pulled away and gathered his hunting knife, placing it safely back into his boot. He picked up his handgun and nodded. He was ready to go.

Alex grabbed her gun and checked her knives, which were still safely tucked in her boots. Joshua was already moving, but she stared down at the long broken arrow that lay discarded on the ground. The arrow was tipped in silver, which was deathly poison to werewolves. They'd meant to kill him and had come close. She could not allow that to happen. Tightening her grip on the cold metal in her hand, she decided then and there she would have to be more vigilant. He was prepared to protect her with his life. She could do no less for him.

They walked for about fifteen minutes, when he stopped and crouched beside a birch tree that had fallen in some storm. Using his hand, he scooped away some of the soft ground around the base and partially buried his windbreaker. As he stood, he swiped his dirty hand over the leg of his jeans. Then he had them backtrack for several yards before he led her off in another direction, telling her to make her steps as far apart as possible.

Time moved onward. She wasn't sure how long they'd been walking, but it must have been at least an hour. Joshua was very careful. Every now and then he'd stop and listen. Neither of them spoke, both of them conserving their energy in case they had to run or fight. She ignored the worried glances that Joshua kept giving her and tried to look energetic and alert whenever she felt his eyes on her. But it wasn't easy.

Every ache and pain in her body was making itself known. She felt as if she was one big throbbing mass. Her face hurt and her head was pounding. The muscles in her legs burned with the unfamiliar exercise and her feet hurt. She imagined she had more than one blister on each foot. Her boots had not been made with this kind of activity in mind, plus they were fairly new and not quite broken in yet. After spending all day yesterday walking, her feet were beginning to complain.

The gun in her hand was beginning to feel as if it weighed a ton and she kept flexing her arm, trying to relieve the strain. She wasn't willing to tuck it away any longer. Their enemies were too close for her to risk it.

All she wanted to do was to lie down in the dirt and sleep. Right now, she could probably sleep standing up. Every now and then her eyes would start to drift shut and she'd have to jerk herself awake. She figured it was her head injury making her tired. She probably had a mild concussion, but there was no time to worry over that minor detail. They had much bigger problems chasing them through the woods.

Joshua held up his hand and she almost plowed into him before she could stop. She curled her fingers into the back of his shirt and held on for a moment, longing to just snuggle against him and rest. Grabbing her arm, he pulled her low, practically shoving her behind the trunk of an oak.

He held up two fingers and pointed off to their right and then one finger and pointed to the left. Gripping her right hand, he pointed her gun with its silver bullets toward the left. *Werewolves.* She knew then it wasn't the bounty hunters who had found them.

Joshua then pointed two fingers straight ahead and shook his head. So it wasn't just werewolves, but bounty hunters as well. She nodded so he'd know she understood. His dark eyes were fathomless as he leaned forward and dropped a quick, hard kiss on her lips before disappearing into the forest around them. One moment he was there, the next she was alone.

Cold sweat broke out on her body as fear filled her belly. She knew he was going out there to fight them, possibly even to draw them away from her. If she'd have known his intent, she could have stopped him.

No, she honestly told herself. She couldn't have. The look in his eyes had told her that nothing could stop him. Not until all their enemies had been eliminated.

She shivered beneath the leather jacket, suddenly chilled to her bones. Only two days ago, she'd had no idea this world existed. Now she'd been plunged into the middle of a war that had apparently been ongoing for quite some time. Right now, she longed for her old life with its predictable, if slightly boring, routine. She wanted to work alongside her father at the garage and drink in his familiar, comfortable presence. She wanted to curl up in her living room and read a book while she sipped a huge mug of coffee or wander out onto the street and shoot the breeze with Divine.

But that was over. She knew those days would never return. All she had now was the life ahead of her and that included Joshua. She grasped her weapon more firmly and risked a glance around the tree trunk. A rustling sound came from ahead of her. She took a deep breath and let it out slowly.

Her arm was steady as she extended it in front of her. Time seemed to slow down as the wait became unending. Her fingers flexed as she heard the faint sound again.

She blinked away the sting from a bead of sweat, not willing to move to wipe her eyes.

It got closer.

And closer.

Her finger caressed the trigger.

A small furry animal burst from beneath a pile of leaves and scurried across the ground in front of her.

Alex sucked in a breath and dropped her chin down to her chest. Her heart was pounding and she had the sudden urge to laugh. She could just imagine how she looked, the fearless hunter facing down a killer squirrel.

Swiping her free hand across her face, she shook herself.

She got no warning at all, but suddenly she knew there was someone, or something behind her. Instinct? Or maybe she felt the subtle shift in the air? Whatever it was, Alex suddenly threw herself to the right as she turned. A huge gray wolf was already airborne as she fell to the ground, raised her arm and fired off several quick shots.

The large animal yelped and jerked in midair before its heavy weight came tumbling down on top of her. All she could see was a huge muzzle with large teeth coming toward her. She fired again, but the wolf kept on coming.

The impact knocked the air out of her lungs. Frantic, she dropped the gun and shoved at the animal's head. It took her a second to realize it wasn't moving. It was dead. She'd killed it. Him. It.

She shook her head and tried to clear her vision. The impact with the wolf hadn't helped her already battered body, but she knew she couldn't stay like this. There were more of them out there and she was vulnerable just lying here.

Arm muscles straining, Alex thrust the animal's head away and then concentrated on moving the heavy body off of her, but it took some doing. This was no regular-sized wolf and it was a deadweight. She half-pushed, half-squirmed out from beneath it, flopping onto the ground beside it to catch her breath.

As she lay there, she silently thanked her father for all the shooting lessons she'd had since she was a kid. She hadn't had to think in order to act, but had done it purely on instinct.

Her limbs were shaky, but she managed to grab her gun and crawl back to the trunk of a tree. Briefly, she rested her forehead against it. Where was Joshua?

A low, menacing growl echoed around her and her fingers closed around the hilt of her weapon. How many bullets were left? She thought she'd fired seven shots—four today and three back at the garage. Had it been more?

Steadying herself against the base of the oak tree, she took several slow, deep breaths to calm her breathing. She didn't hear a sound, but suddenly a man stepped into view about fifteen feet away. Had her shots given away her position to the bounty hunters? Man or werewolf? She didn't know and couldn't take a chance. She fired off a round.

She swore when he ducked out of the way just in time to avoid being hit. Bark exploded from the tree just above her head and she ducked before popping up again to return fire with two quick shots. As she pulled back behind the tree, she admonished herself for wasting her ammunition.

"That's what he's trying to do and you're obviously playing into his hands," she muttered as she shifted to the next tree. The man shot at her again, but this time she didn't return his fire. She'd already wasted three of her precious bullets on him. She needed to make every shot count.

"Come on out," a male voice yelled. "We don't want to hurt you. We only want the wolf."

Yeah right. Like she'd believe that. She crept as quietly as possible through the trees, scooting from one to another. Another shot grazed the tree in front of her and she flinched.

Suddenly, a bloodcurdling scream echoed through the forest. Alex wanted to cover her ears against the horrid sound, but couldn't move. Then silence. Joshua had found one of the bounty hunters.

Alex swallowed, but it wasn't easy. Her mouth was as dry as sandpaper. Her stomach churned. She took a deep breath and then another. She dropped to her knees and sucked in air just as another shot rang out, shattering the bark just inches from her chest. Splinters of wood flew wildly and she was thankful for the protection of her leather jacket.

Flinging her body to the side, she fired from flat on her stomach, sending three quick shots in the direction of the shooter. She was swearing even as she was dragging her body across the forest floor. They had somehow surrounded her. And just where in the heck was Joshua?

Several more shots were fired in quick succession. One of them plowed into the ground beside her. She felt a sharp sting in her arm. Whether it was a rock from where she'd flung herself to the ground or a shard from the exploding tree trunk she didn't know and she didn't have time to check.

She saw a tiny movement in the trees just a few feet away. Saying a quick prayer, she fired. A man's body jerked into sight and he swung his rifle toward her. She fired over and over, emptying her gun into his body. He toppled backward, his rifle dropping to the ground beside him.

There was no time to breathe as two wolves, both a dark brown, sauntered into view. "Shit!" She dug her feet into the ground and scuttled backward. They lowered their heads and growled menacingly.

She raised her weapon and pulled the trigger. The metallic click reminded her she was out of ammunition. Dropping the Glock, she grabbed her two boot knives out of their sheaths, flinging them in rapid succession. Both animals were quick, their reflexes astounding as they managed to sidestep the blades at the last possible second. She was well and truly screwed.

Keeping one eye on them as they stalked closer, she groped her hand out, trying to find a stray branch. A rock. Anything she could use to protect herself.

The larger of the two wolves growled menacingly as it slunk forward, saliva dripping from its powerful jaws. It gathered itself to jump. She could see the bunching of the muscles in its hind legs and braced herself for the attack.

The animal sprang, its powerful body practically flying as it launched itself into the air.

It never touched her.

Out of nowhere, a massive black wolf plunged into its side, sending the brown wolf hurtling back to the ground.

Alex sank to the ground. Joshua had finally arrived.

Chapter Seventeen

Joshua didn't think as he launched himself into the air. He didn't have to. Instinct had taken over. He was in the fight of his life. He could allow no one or nothing to harm Alex.

He plunged into his opponent's side, taking him to the ground in a flurry of fur and snapping jaws. Sinking his teeth into the other beast's neck, he held on.

Alex cried out and he swiveled his head toward her in time to see the other wolf lunge at her. He flung his opponent away and leapt at Alex, knocking her out of the way. Taking the full impact of the wolf on himself, he barely avoided being bitten before nimbly gaining his feet.

Positioning himself in front of Alex, he faced off against his two opponents. The first one was slowly staggering back to its feet, bloodlust in its eyes. The second was pacing to the side, trying to go around him. He backed up, all the while keeping his gaze on the other two wolves. He herded Alex back toward the base of a large oak tree. He'd left his clothing behind it when he'd shifted. If he could get her back there she would be able to find his hunting knife. He didn't know how much ammunition was left in the handgun, but it wouldn't be much help against werewolves. The silver-coated knife would be much more effective in slowing them down.

He bared his teeth, emitting a low, powerful growl as his opponents shifted closer. Both bounty hunters were dead. He'd killed one and Alex had shot the other. He'd smelled the other carcass and knew she'd also managed to kill a werewolf. Most women would be cowering or screaming. His woman looked pissed off as she continued to scout around for a weapon.

He'd killed two more werewolves in the woods, ones he hadn't recognized. He'd also taken a few hits. These wolves, unlike the ones from the city, were seasoned warriors and no easy target. They'd gotten in their share of blows and he was bleeding from several different places along his sides. His shoulder was also bleeding again from the crossbow arrow. Because it had been silver-tipped, the wound would take longer to heal. Thankfully, the damage to the bone itself had fused and healed during his transformation to his wolf form.

The two wolves before him were gathering themselves to attack. He could sense the anticipation in the air, along with the stench of blood, fear and excitement. These wolves didn't want to mate with Alex. They wanted to kill her. That's why they had joined forces with the bounty hunters. These wolves were obviously part of the extreme packs who didn't want to water down the blood of the species with half-breeds.

Well, too bad for them. They weren't getting anywhere near Alex.

He'd managed to push her back to the base of the tree. Hopefully, she'd find his belongings. Not that it truly mattered. He planned on protecting her. But he knew she'd feel more secure if she had a weapon.

He could hear her deep breathing. Smell the stink of fear and blood that mingled with her sweat. He longed to coddle her, to take her away from all this death. He wanted to strip her naked and bathe away the stench that now coated them both. His body responded immediately to thoughts of her naked. His muscles flexed, rippling beneath his fur coat.

He was truly losing his focus if all he could think about was Alex being naked when he was faced with two vicious opponents. Shutting off his thoughts, he turned all his attention to the beasts in front of him.

Deciding the best defense was offense, he launched himself without warning. He landed on top of the larger of the two and sank his fangs deep, drawing blood, tearing flesh. He immediately leapt off the wolf's back, kicking it backward in the process, as he jumped at the other one, bringing it down as it moved toward Alex.

In a blur of motion, he jumped from one opponent to the

other, always inflicting some damage. He knew he couldn't kill either of them like this. That wasn't his goal. He planned to weaken them first and then move in for the final strike.

The smaller of the two brown wolves cut away suddenly, racing toward the safety of the woods. Joshua growled in fury. He knew he couldn't allow the wolf to escape and bring back reinforcements, but he didn't really have any choice. There was no way he could leave Alex unprotected.

Channeling his rage, he jumped at the remaining large wolf. They rolled to the ground, churning up the dirt as they growled and snapped and clawed at one another. Joshua knew his opponent was weak from the prolonged battle. He heaved himself on top of the wolf, clamping down hard on his neck.

This time he didn't let go. Bones crunched beneath his powerful jaws.

A few minutes later, he dropped the deadweight, flinging it away in disgust. He stood there, lungs heaving, as blood dripped down his flanks.

Alex faced him bravely, hunting knife in hand. He'd known that she'd find it. Her face was stark white, but her hand was steady. As he trotted toward her, she began to tremble. "Oh, God," she muttered as she sank to the ground, dropped the knife and buried her face in her hands.

Worried, he hurried up to her and licked the side of her face. They didn't have time to waste. He had no way of knowing how close reinforcements were. There could be dozens more hunters and werewolves searching for them.

He wanted to change back into his human form, but he knew he couldn't expend that much energy. Not until they were safe. He was more powerful in his animal form, his senses keener and sharper. And at the moment, that was more important than appearing human for her. Alex had to accept him for what he was.

Opening his muzzle, he carefully took one of her hands into his mouth and tugged gently. She raised her head, swiping at the sweat on her brow and the tears that clouded her eyes.

He tugged again.

"What?"

He backed up, pulling at her.

"All right. All right," she groused. "Hold your horses." She clambered to her feet and picked up his hunting knife.

He dropped her hand and padded to the side of the tree and pawed at his clothing.

"I suppose you want me to take that."

He nodded and she groaned. "I'm talking to a wolf. Do you have any idea how weird this is for me?" She didn't wait for an answer, but kept on muttering to herself as she grabbed the handgun, checked the safety and stuffed it in the waistband of her jeans. She jammed the hunting knife back in its sheath and shoved it in her coat pocket before gathering up his clothing and boots.

"I need to find my Glock and my knives." She started to go around him, but he moved in front of her, blocking her path. There was no time. The wolf that had escaped was moving fast. There was no way of knowing how close the other members of his group were. There would be more of them. Of that, Joshua had no doubt. They had to move. Now.

"I guess that's a no."

Bitterness filled him. He wished they were mated. If they had completed the mating ritual, if he had claimed her for his own as his wolf was demanding, she'd have been able to hear his thoughts and to communicate with him mentally. That would have been a huge advantage when he'd been fighting the others. He'd have known what was happening to her at all times. When the shots had rung out, his heart had almost stopped. It was only when he'd heard the return fire that he'd managed to start breathing again.

Sometimes honor was a bitch.

They'd talk about this later. The important thing now was that they needed a safe place to hole up for the night. Their enemies were still searching for them, the sun was sinking and total darkness wasn't too far away.

Alex was holding his clothing in her arms, her body swaying with fatigue. He hated the fact she couldn't rest, but since there was nothing he could do about it now, he put it out of his mind as he nudged her body and then padded into the woods. He paused and glanced over his shoulder. Alex was staring at him.

"We're just going to leave them, I guess." She stared down at the carcasses that were flung carelessly across the dirt. She sighed and swallowed hard. He stood motionless, watching her gather her strength once again. Pride filled him when she shook herself, tilted her chin upward and stalked toward him. She never looked back as he led her deeper into the forest.

There was a cave not too far from here that would afford them some safety. Joshua recognized the area. He'd scouted this land when he'd been little more than a boy. Now, he was glad he had. Being familiar with it would give them an edge. And right now they could use any advantage they could get.

Alex stumbled behind the gigantic black wolf. *Joshua!* It was amazing to her, yet all too real that this magnificent predator was the same man who'd brought her a T-shirt because she needed clean clothing and who'd stopped and bought her a coffee earlier today for no other reason than because he'd known she'd wanted one.

She'd seen more blood and death this afternoon than she had in her entire lifetime. And she'd kill again if she had to. Staring down at her hands, she was unable to believe that they weren't coated in blood. Sure, they were stained from where she'd bandaged Joshua's injury, and from where she'd struggled to shove the dead werewolf off her, but that was it.

Somehow, she felt as if there should be more. She knew she'd done what she'd had to do to protect herself and Joshua, but still, it wasn't easy.

The new life that had been thrust upon her was certainly more violent than the one she had left behind, and that was saying something considering where she'd grown up.

Swiping the back of her hand over her forehead, she then wiped it over the leg of her jeans. She was exhausted. Her legs and feet had long passed the burning-muscle stage and were almost completely numb. Her arm ached from carrying Joshua's clothing. It wasn't a large bundle, but it seemed as if she'd been lugging it around forever.

Realistically, she knew it had probably only been for two hours, maybe less, but it was hard going. There were no trails and she was constantly having to scramble over fallen trees and push her way through thick brush. She almost resented how easily Joshua maneuvered through the woods in his wolf form. She wondered what it must feel like to be that strong and agile. She guessed she'd eventually find out.

If she lived long enough.

She bit her lip to keep from asking to stop. There was no way she'd give in to weakness. Besides which, she knew they couldn't stop. One of the wolves had gotten away and that could only mean one thing. There would be even more enemies on their trail.

When Joshua finally stopped at the base of a rather large hill, she almost cried with relief. Then she almost cried in agony when he started up the steep incline. She sucked in a deep breath and stared at the rocky hill. She could do this. There was no other choice.

Sighing, she put one foot in front of the other, being very careful where she placed her boot. As tired as she was, it wouldn't take much for her to lose her focus and stumble. She couldn't afford a sprained ankle or something worse at this point.

She concentrated on her breathing, which was becoming more labored with each step. Her sweat-stained clothes were sticking to her and she felt curiously detached from her body. One step. Then another. There was nothing else she had to think about. Nothing else she had to do. She trusted Joshua to stay alert.

She stumbled when she reached the top. Flinging out her hand, she managed to keep from ending up facedown in the dirt, but it was close. Her hand skidded out from beneath her and Joshua's clothing went flying. She rested there on her hands and knees, her head bent as she sucked some air into her starving lungs. It hadn't been a long climb, but it had taken what little energy she'd had in reserve.

Warm fur brushed against her cheek and she managed to raise her head. She found herself peering into concerned brown eyes. "I'm okay." Lifting one of her hands out of the dirt, she stroked it over his side. She frowned when her fingers encountered something wet and sticky. Drawing back her hand, she stared down, horrified by the blood that dripped from the tips of her fingers. "You're hurt!"

She scrambled to her feet, her fatigue washed away in a rush of adrenaline and concern. His black fur and her exhaustion had hid the fact that he was badly injured. The wolf backed away from her and if an animal could shrug, then this one did. The total unconcern for the state of his health was so familiar she wanted to scream.

"Oh yeah. You just go ahead and bleed to death. See if I care." Stomping past him, she continued to beat a path through the woods. She had no idea where she was going, but what did it matter? "You get yourself killed and they'll eventually find my petrified bones at some point I suppose." She knew her anger was unreasonable, but she wasn't feeling really reasonable after everything she'd been through the past few days.

Her hand was captured in the wolf's strong jaw again, and when she tried to pull away, he clamped down tighter. Not hurting her, but letting her know who was in charge of this expedition. She glared down at the huge beast. "So which way are we going?"

He tugged her back in the opposite direction from which she'd been traveling. "It figures," she muttered. Resigned, she tromped after him, stopping to scoop up his now dirty clothes as she went. Her adrenaline rush was giving her a much-needed boost. She knew she was on borrowed time though. When she crashed this time, there would be no going on until she rested. She could only hope they were getting closer to whatever destination Joshua had in mind.

The wolf stopped at the top of the path and disappeared behind some heavy brush. She paused when she reached the spot she'd last seen him and really looked around her. Being high up, she had a good view of the area. It was strange and unsettling for a city girl like herself to see nothing but forest as far as the eye could see. She was well and truly out of her element.

Although he didn't make a sound, she knew when Joshua came up beside her. She could feel the sheer power of his presence like a ripple in the air. "I'm not sure I can get used to all this nature."

Ignoring her, he headed off again. Her ears perked up a

couple of minutes later. If she wasn't mistaken, she was hearing water. Cool, wet, running water. Her throat burned and her skin itched, especially her arm. She was going to drink her fill and then strip off her clothing and wash every inch of herself. She smelled rank and felt worse.

But Joshua stopped before they reached the water. It was so tantalizingly close she was tempted to go on alone. Then she remembered his injuries and began to worry. Just because he acted as if everything was okay, didn't mean it was.

He led her in between two large rocks and she was shocked to find there was actually a small cave nestled behind them. She assumed there were no other critters inhabiting the dwelling at the moment, but she still waited just outside until he poked his large furry head outside and peered questioningly at her.

"I'm assuming there are no surprises in there? No furry creatures, besides yourself that is?" There it was again, that wolfish grin. She'd almost swear he was laughing at her. "Well, you won't be laughing if I find a mouse or a spider or anything," she warned as she stomped past him.

The cave wasn't actually a cave. More like an indentation. It only went back about ten feet and was about fifteen feet wide. And thankfully, from what she could see in the fading light that shone in from between the two large rocks, there didn't seem to be any other inhabitants. It was dry and comfortable.

Laying Joshua's clothing on the ground, she changed her mind at the last second and grabbed his T-shirt. That would do for a towel. She was having a bath before she was doing anything else. He was blocking the entrance now and she put her hands on her hips and glared down at him. "I'm having a bath and unless you want your furry butt kicked, I suggest you get out of my way."

She'd had enough of alpha-type men in the past thirty-six hours. They either wanted to kill her or mate with her, with the exception of her father and Joshua, who wanted to protect her. Either way, she'd had enough. Apparently Joshua must have thought so too because he nodded and led the way out of the cave and headed toward the sound of the water.

The stream wasn't far from the cave at all, for which she

was grateful. Her poor feet couldn't take much more abuse today. Falling to her knees in the moist dirt that lined the bank, she stuck her face right in the water. The cool wetness soothed her skin. She yanked her head back and took a deep breath before lowering it again. This time it was to drink.

It was awkward to try to slurp up water, but she didn't stop until she'd had her fill. When she raised her head, Joshua was sitting beside her, watching her with that wolfish grin in place. Obviously he'd seen her make a fool of herself while she was drinking. He'd apparently had no such problems in his animal form. And why would he. Drinking from a running stream would be natural to a wolf.

He stared at her, his eyes going even darker. Lowering his head, he heaved a sigh before stretching his neck upward.

She sank back on her heels and waited, knowing what was coming. The first crack took her by surprise. It was strange and frightening to watch him change. Yet she couldn't make herself look away. This was Joshua, the man she loved. And for better or for worse, this was now her life, her fate.

Bones lengthened, reforming into familiar limbs as hair began to disappear. His jaw cracked, shortened and reset itself in a familiar line. The hair on his face receded until there was nothing but the black slashes of his brows and heavy stubble on his jaw. His shaggy hair hung to his shoulders. It took only seconds for him to transform from beast to man. Only those deep, fathomless eyes were the same.

She sat there in the dirt, amazed and horrified.

It was... She didn't know what it was. Incredible. Unbelievable. Enthralling. If she hadn't seen it with her own two eyes, she never would have believed it. Her heart was pounding and her palms were sweating, which was stupid. This was Joshua. She knew him and certainly wasn't afraid of him.

He slumped forward and then pushed himself upright again. That's when she saw the wounds. His shoulder was bleeding again and there were several large gashes opened up on both his sides.

"You're hurt." Although she'd seen the blood earlier, she hadn't been able to see just how badly he'd been injured. Scrambling closer, she all but crawled through the dirt to reach him.

"It's nothing." His voice was rough. His eyes steady.

"It's not nothing. Of all the lame-brained idiotic things..." Her tirade trailed off as she examined his injuries, trying to be as gentle as possible. "We should have stopped earlier so I could have taken care of this for you."

He seemed more bemused than angry as she trailed her fingers over his ribs checking for broken bones. "I didn't have enough energy to change and still get us here. In my wolf form I have more strength and my senses are keener. I needed to be alert."

She supposed he was right. She had no idea how hard it must be on a body to go through such a transformation, but having just witnessed it, she had a feeling it had to take something out of a person, especially if they were already injured. "Come over by the water so I can clean these."

He followed her, his movements fluid as he settled on a flat rock that rested along the bank of the cheerful little stream. She plucked the hunting knife from the sheath and held up his shirt. He stayed her motions, his hand wrapping around her wrist. "If you cut that, I'll only have my jeans to wear." It was then she remembered he'd sacrificed his coat earlier to throw the hunters off their trail.

"I have to have something to wrap around your arm and you can wear the leather jacket. It's my father's so it should fit you."

He shook his head. "Then you'd have nothing to wear."

He had a point there, but she shook her head bravely. "I have my bra. It's enough."

His fingers stroked the back of her wrist, soothing the skin over her pounding pulse. "It's a fairly long T-shirt. Cut a few strips off the bottom."

Nodding, she did as he'd instructed and laid the rest of the shirt and the knife to one side. She dipped one of the strips into the water, wrung it out and began to clean his wounds. She flinched several times, but Joshua never moved a muscle.

And it had to hurt. The long gouges, obviously from the other wolves' claws, were jagged, but thankfully, upon closer examination, not deep. They had almost stopped bleeding. She knew werewolves healed quickly, but this was incredible. Still, she wasn't taking any chances. Cleaning each wound carefully, she made sure all the dirt had been removed from the area.

She tried her best to ignore the fact that his thick muscles rippled beneath her fingers as she stroked the thin piece of cloth over them. His flesh was deeply tanned and very appealing. She swallowed, not daring to look any lower than his waist.

Wringing out the cloth again, she focused on his shoulder. That wound was seeping blood once again. She did her best to wash it clean before making two pads out of one of the other strips of cloth. She picked up the final strip and wrapped it around the pads to hold them in place. She supposed he'd lost the original bandage when he'd shapeshifted into his wolf form.

She sat back on her heels, swiped her hand over her forehead and was immediately reminded of her own grungy state. "That will have to do until we get somewhere that has some real medical supplies."

Joshua shrugged. "I've had much worse. I'll be fine in a few days."

"You may be fine, but I might not be." Alex staggered to her feet and tossed the wet piece of cloth down onto a rock. "I need a bath." Ignoring his blatant stare, she eased the leather jacket down her arms. The darn thing was heavy and her arm still stung from earlier. She sure as heck hoped she didn't have a splinter or something sticking out of her arm.

Joshua surged to his feet, swearing pungently as he stalked toward her. The leather jacket fell to her feet, forgotten in the face of his anger.

"What's wrong?"

He looked wild, his body practically vibrating with anger. "What's wrong? What's wrong?" he growled menacingly. "Why the hell didn't you tell me you were shot?"

Chapter Eighteen

Joshua grabbed Alex just as her knees crumpled. Her face was completely white as she stared up at him in growing horror.

"I didn't know." She twisted her head so she could see the wound better. "I thought a piece of one of the trees had splintered or I'd bruised it on a rock or something." Her voice got fainter with every word.

He eased them both to the ground and examined her arm. "It seems to have just grazed you," he told her gruffly. "You were lucky." He didn't want to think about how close he'd come to losing her just when he'd found her. If the hunter responsible weren't already dead, he'd find him and kill him.

"Yeah. I feel really lucky these days." He ignored her sarcasm as he grabbed the wet rag, dipped it into the cool water and began to clean the six-inch furrow that stretched from just above her elbow to just below her shoulder. She flinched and he could hear her breath hiss out from between her clenched teeth, but she didn't cry out.

Easing himself into a seated position behind her, he wet the cloth again and resumed cleaning. There was dried blood and bits of cloth from the lining of the jacket embedded in the wound. "Lean against me." He pressed against her stomach with his free hand, loving the way the soft skin felt as he slid his palm over it.

She seemed to hesitate, keeping her body erect, but finally she slumped against him. He concentrated on cleaning the dirt and blood from her arm, but he was very aware of the warm weight of her pressed against him.

Her head was tucked beneath his chin and he could still

smell the slight scent of the soap she'd used in the shower this morning. He moved his head back and forth, brushing the top of her head with his chin.

She was still wearing a bra, but the thin pink cotton didn't leave much to the imagination. Besides which, the firm, silky texture of her breasts was burned into his brain. He knew exactly what they looked like. Felt like. And how they tasted.

His body stirred and his cock lengthened and thickened in response to her presence. She definitely brought out the elemental side of his nature. He shifted so that he was closer, his erection pressing against the small of her back. He swallowed a groan of pure pleasure as he touched his hard flesh against her softer skin.

"Joshua?" Her voice was shaky and he could feel her trembling. He was an idiot. Here she was injured and he was busy copping a feel.

He inspected her arm and, satisfied he'd cleaned it as best he could, he tossed the cloth to one side. "I don't think we should cover your wound. It's probably better to let the air get to it."

She tilted her head back to look at him. "Okay." He could tell he was confusing her. Hell, he was confusing himself.

"Do you want to get a quick bath before we go back to the cave?" He stood, leaned down and lifted her easily.

A light rosy flush covered her cheeks as she glanced at him and then away. "Yes."

He settled her on a rock and went down on one knee in front of her and unlaced her boots.

"I can get that," she protested.

He pushed her hand away. "You need to take it easy." He slipped one boot off and swore when he saw the blood on her sock. "Why didn't you tell me your feet were hurting?"

"We couldn't stop." She shrugged as if it were no big deal. Technically, he knew it was just some blisters that would heal, but it still hit him like a punch in the gut. He removed her other boot and sock very carefully, lifting and examining her other abused foot.

He sat back on his haunches and stared at her. A bluish-purple bruise covered part of her face, a blatant reminder of the truck accident earlier in the day. She also had a long bruise across her chest and he knew it was from where her seatbelt had kept her from going through the windshield when the truck had rolled. Circles could be seen beneath her tired gray eyes, making them appear almost sunken in her face. Her lips were pursed and he could tell she was in pain.

Her arm had a six-inch gash from where a bullet had grazed her and her hands were covered in dirt and blood from her forced trek through the woods. Her feet were bloody and raw in places and he knew she wouldn't have an easy time walking tomorrow, but he had no doubt she'd march along beside him without a word of complaint. He almost didn't want to remove her jeans, afraid to find more bruises.

Joshua scrubbed his hand over his face. All he wanted to do was to take care of her and get her to safety. Instead, she had been battered and bruised and was running for her life. Some protector he was. Disgusted with himself, he got to his feet. "Can you stand?"

"Of course."

"Of course," he muttered.

"Look," she snapped, her hands on her hips. "I don't know what's sticking in your paw buddy, but don't take it out on me. All I want is a bath and some sleep. No one is forcing you to stay."

He stood there amazed and amused by her feistiness. Only a few moments before she'd looked like she would collapse any moment and now she was giving him hell.

"I'm definitely staying." Reaching out, he unbuttoned her jeans and tugged down the zipper while she batted ineffectually at his hands. "And I'm certainly helping." He whisked her jeans down around her ankles and had her step out one foot at a time.

"I can do it by myself," she muttered, taking a step back when he reached for the clasp of her bra.

"Surely you can't be shy." But he realized that she was. "Not after this morning."

Her scowl deepened as her cheeks got redder. "It might be no big deal for you to run around naked, but it's not something I'm used to, okay."

Shaking his head, he scooped her up into his arms and waded out into the stream, aiming for a rock right in the center of the slow-running water. He settled her on the rock so that only her legs from the knees down were actually in the stream, and waded back to the shore for the makeshift washcloth. The water barely touched his thighs, but it was cool and wet and that was good enough for him.

He tossed her the cloth as he lay down in the stream, submerging himself totally. He heard her protest and knew he was going to catch hell for getting his bandaged shoulder wet. She didn't understand it wasn't that big a deal to him. He'd been hurt worse so many times before that today's injuries barely qualified as scratches.

Raising his head out of the water, he barely had time to snag the wet rag out of the air before it struck him.

"Now I'll have to bandage your shoulder again."

Shaking out the cloth, he rubbed it over his neck and chest, working his way lower. Her eyes seemed to glaze over as she watched his every move. Her scantily clad breasts shifted up and down with every breath. Her nipples were visible beneath the thin fabric. She shifted, parting her legs slightly.

He swallowed a groan.

He continued to wash his body, paying particular attention to his groin and thighs. She licked her lips as he stroked the cloth over his erection. The sac between his legs was heavy even as it pulled closer to his body. Damn, but he wanted her.

Knowing he was playing with fire, he took the two steps necessary to bring him to her side. "Your turn." He handed her the cloth, took a step away and waited.

Alex could barely breathe. Her lungs didn't seem to want to function properly at all. Joshua was like something out of the perfect female fantasy as he washed himself, totally unabashed by his nudity and his obvious arousal. Sculpted muscles rippled and flexed with every movement he made, showcasing his sleek, hard body. He was the quintessential male predator preening for the female of his choice.

She had no doubt Joshua could have any woman he chose. There was an animal magnetism, a latent sensuality, about him that would draw any woman's attention. Just watching him wash himself had liquid arousal flowing between her thighs. She knew that should probably embarrass her, but she was too turned on to care. Her nipples were hard buds, completely outlined against the tight cotton fabric of her bra.

She knew they still weren't safe, couldn't linger here any longer than necessary, but she couldn't summon the energy to move. After all the death of today, a part of her simply wanted to experience the sensation of being alive.

Laying the cloth down beside her, she reached for the clasp of her bra, but Joshua stopped her. "I think it might be better for you to leave that on."

She stared almost unbelieving at him, but he was deadly serious. "All right." She dropped her hands away from her bra and picked up the cloth. As best as she could, she washed her hands, arms, torso and legs, at all times aware of Joshua's eyes on her, watching every single stroke of the cloth as she moved it over her skin. She might still be wearing her bra and panties, but his hot gaze made her feel as if she were totally naked.

It felt like heaven to have the cool water rushing around her feet as she kept them submerged in the water. As the dust and dirt and sweat began to vanish beneath her scrubbing, she felt almost human again.

She grimaced at the thought. She wasn't really human was she? Being part werewolf definitely made her something more than human. Alex shoved that thought to the back of her mind. She'd deal with it later. When they were finally safe in Wolf Creek.

Dipping the cloth into the water, she then twisted it until almost all the water was gone and then held it out to Joshua. "Can you do my back?"

His expression was totally unreadable as he took the thin strip of fabric and stepped behind her. There was no hiding the fact he was still turned on. His cock was at full attention as he'd watched her rubbing the cloth over her body. Intense heat rolled off him as he shifted closer to her.

She leaned forward to give him better access and groaned when his large hands covered her shoulders, kneading the tense, stiff muscles. "That feels good," she moaned when his thumbs found a particularly sore muscle. He used just enough pressure to work the kinks out the stiffness, but not enough to hurt her. The man had magic hands.

He continued down her back, sweeping his hands down her spine, easing aches she didn't even know she had. She slumped further forward until her head was almost touching her knees. With her eyes closed, she relaxed, allowing his caressing fingers to lull her.

She muttered a protest when he finally stopped, and shivered when she felt the damp coolness of the cloth being dragged over her back. The sun was sinking behind the mountains and the temperature was dropping rapidly. Goose bumps broke out on her arms and legs and she wrapped her arms around herself, flinching when she accidentally hit her bad arm.

Joshua quickly finished washing her back and handed her the cloth. Without a word, he scooped her up into his arms and waded back to the shoreline, setting her on her feet long enough to gather their clothing. He handed her the bundle and then picked her up again, carrying her through the woods and back to the cave. Alex was much too tired to protest, and Joshua didn't seem to even notice his injuries. At this point she didn't mind the ride at all.

Closing her eyes, she rested her head against his chest, conscious of the deep, steady beat of his heart. She must have dozed because one second she was being carried through the woods and the next her feet were being lowered to the floor. She swayed, but he kept his arm around her until she was steady.

"You need to put your jeans on," he murmured. "And your socks." She made a small sound of protest and he smoothed his hand over her hair and down her back. "I know they're grungy, but it's going to get cold tonight."

Knowing he was right didn't make it any easier. She stepped away and set the bundle of clothing on the ground, fishing through it until she found her jeans and blood-stained socks. The light was almost negligible inside their hideaway now and she hurried before she lost what little there was.

Once she had her jeans on she sat on the hard dirt floor and carefully eased her socks over her sore feet. The cold water of the stream had helped soothe them somewhat, but Alex knew tomorrow would be no picnic. She shrugged. She'd deal with that when she had to. There was no point worrying about it now.

She opened her mouth to speak, but yawned instead. It wasn't a lady-like yawn either, but a large, jaw-cracking one. Joshua lowered himself to the hard ground beside her, clad in his jeans and socks as well.

"What about your shoulder?"

"Don't worry about it. The bleeding has stopped and a damp bandage won't hurt it." Gathering her into his arms, he lay back on the hard-packed ground using what was left of his T-shirt to cushion his head. Plucking the leather jacket off the ground, he draped it over her torso, making sure her shoulders were covered.

Alex relaxed immediately as the heat from his body began to seep into her chilled skin. She could feel his erection pressing into her stomach and lifted her head slightly so she could look at him. It was hard to see him in the dark, but she could just make out the outline of his face and the gleam of his dark eyes. "Why?"

There was no need for her to clarify further. He knew what she meant. His large hand pressed against her bottom, holding her close to him. "Don't ever think I don't want you." She could hear the strain in his voice as his low, rasping tones made all the hair on her body stand on end. "But I won't take you. Not yet."

"Why not?"

His hand slid over the curves of her behind making her gasp with pleasure. "Because once I come inside you, mate with you, I'll mark you with my scent. When we get to Wolf Creek, everyone would know that you were mine."

She blinked hard, wishing she could see him better. "You're serious. They'd be able to smell your scent on me?" That didn't seem fair to her at all.

He nodded. She felt the slight movement of his head rather than saw it. "Very serious. It's a way of letting all the single males know that a female has been claimed. Once we are mated, they know if they approach you they will have to deal with me."

She drummed her fingers against his chest. "That seems to favor the males and not the females. I mean, you can have sex with whoever you want, but a female has sex with a male werewolf once and she's marked for life."

He trapped her hand with his, flattening her palm over his heart. "It is nature's way of ensuring the survival of the race. Besides, if a female's mate dies, she is free to sleep with whomever she wants and even mate again if she chooses."

"Great." Exasperation tinged her voice. "I should have experimented when I had the chance."

The low, menacing growl startled her. She found herself flat on her back before she knew what was happening. Joshua loomed over her large and fierce as he clasped her face in his hands. "You are mine."

Why she was teasing the already enraged beast, she didn't quite know. But something inside her made her taunt him back. "I thought I had a choice."

"You have made your choice." He became very still above her. She could feel the tension rolling off him, filling the cave until it sucked almost all the air out of the confined space. "Or have you changed your mind?" His fingers tightened almost imperceptibly on her face. "Do you think that I cannot protect you?"

She was horrified at his misinterpretation of her words. "No, you big idiot. Of course I trust you to protect me." Honestly, who could understand the workings of the male mind? "And, God only knows why not, but I haven't changed my mind."

He gave a bark of laughter and she could feel the tension slowly seeping from him. "You are the only person who dares to speak to me with such disrespect."

"It's not disrespect," she protested. "But Joshua, sometimes you take way too much on yourself. You're only human. Well, werewolf, anyway." Her attempt at humor didn't even make him crack a grin. She sighed. "You're not all-knowing, all-seeing." Reaching her hand upward until she found his jaw, she lovingly traced the hard line. "You were willing to die for me. What woman could ask for more?" Just thinking about his actions today made her insides melt. He hadn't put into words what he felt about her, except in sexual terms, but she felt his actions spoke for him.

He lowered his head until their foreheads were touching. She could sense his hesitation and held her breath, hoping he'd tell her how much he'd come to care for her. Instead, he sighed and kissed the tip of her nose. "What am I going to do with you?"

She could think of quite a few things personally. "If you've got to ask," she teased. Alex had a feeling nobody teased Joshua or made him laugh. He needed more of that in his life.

He shook his head, leaned down and pressed his lips against hers. He hadn't laughed, but she could tell he was smiling. That small sign made her extremely pleased with herself. Joshua definitely wouldn't be an easy man to live with, but he was the one she wanted. She knew no other man would make her feel the way he did.

She opened her mouth to try to coax his tongue inside, but he pulled away. Rolling quickly, he returned to their original position so that she was draped across his body again. "Enough of that." He coaxed her head down to his chest and she was tired enough to let him. "When I mate with you and claim you as mine, it will not be in some dark cave in the dirt."

The possessiveness in his voice made her shiver. She knew he would be a demanding lover. Her core dampened and softened, the inner muscles rippling as she arched her hips against the bulge in his jeans. He opened his legs and trapped hers between them, holding them still, but keeping her locked close to him.

"Sleep," he muttered gruffly. She smiled as she felt the leather jacket being tucked gently around her shoulders again. He sifted his hand through her hair, relaxing her further. She yawned again and nestled her cheek against his soft chest hair.

Lying in the dirt, bruised and battered and sore, she'd never felt more content. With the beat of Joshua's heart against her ear, she drifted off to sleep.

Chapter Nineteen

James drove down the long, winding road, watching the sun slowly sink behind the mountains. He could feel the tension seeping into his muscles and rolled his shoulders, trying to relax.

He hadn't been back this way in years, but it was all so familiar. He recognized landmarks and noted changes to the landscape as the car moved steadily forward. The hum of the tires on the pavement and his steady breathing were the only sounds he could hear. He hadn't bothered with the radio, knowing any reception he got would be spotty at best.

He tried not to think about Alexandra, but it was no use. He wanted to know where his daughter was. His fingers tightened around the steering wheel until his knuckles turned white.

After protecting her for so many years it was sheer torture to leave her in the hands of another man. Yet it was what he'd had to do, and he knew he'd do it again in a heartbeat. He'd seen the way Joshua had looked at Alex. The man wanted her.

And for the first time in her life, Alex had shown interest in a man. He'd seen the spark in her eye when she'd looked at young Striker. It would be a good match. One he could live with.

For right or wrong, he'd sent them off together to give their attraction time to grow. He'd wanted a different life for his daughter, but fate and genetics had overruled him. Alex was a werewolf, whether she wanted it or not. The best thing he could do for her was to encourage her to accept all aspects of herself, to show her she was the same person, only with a little something more.

He emitted a low growl as he thought about what might happen between Joshua and his daughter as they spent another night on the road. It wasn't something a father wanted to think about, yet it was why he'd sent them off together in the first place.

James knew Joshua would protect Alex with his life. Furthermore, if he was Striker for the Wolf Creek pack he had the skill, intellect and muscle to do so. But any man or werewolf, no matter how skilled, could be brought down. There were rival werewolves searching for them. Not to mention bounty hunters were always a problem.

He pushed his foot down harder on the fuel pedal. James knew he'd soon have to stop for the night. The daylight was fading and he didn't want to approach Wolf Creek after dark. At this point, there was no way of knowing who was friend and who was foe. He started scanning the sides of the road, searching for a place to pull over and wait out the long, cold night.

Joshua opened his eyes and stared at the dim light creeping in through the slim opening in the rocks. Dawn was breaking and he damn well deserved a medal for sainthood after the night he'd put in. Alex was draped across him, her body almost boneless. It had been an exquisite torture to hold her in his arms all night long.

A quick flick of a few buttons and two zippers, a quick roll to put her beneath him, and he could have been buried inside her moist, welcoming heat. The thought was enough to make even the strongest man sweat, knowing all that was his for the taking.

He knew she wanted him as much as he wanted her. Her sexual drive was heating up and was getting closer to its peak. He wanted her home safe within the confines of the compound and tucked into his bed when the time finally came to claim her.

Not that it would be easy. In spite of her claim that it was him she wanted, they'd still have to go through the ritual of allowing other males to state their case unless he wanted an all-out battle on his hands. Although the way he was feeling at the moment, a bloody brawl sounded like a good way to work off some of his tension.

Alex chose that moment to stretch before shifting around to find a comfortable spot. Joshua gritted his teeth and clamped his arm around her waist to keep her from squirming around on top of him. The throbbing of his cock matched the painful throbbing in his shoulder this morning. Although his shoulder wasn't causing him near as much discomfort.

He looked down at her, but all he could see was the top of her head. She had her face buried against his chest and her arms tucked snugly around him. She was usually so vibrant and full of life when she was awake, it was strange to see her so still and restful. She was a tall woman, so it was easy to forget she was slender of build.

Joshua slid his fingers over the small of her back and then upward. She arched toward his fingers. "Mmm," she moaned. "That feels nice."

The hard points of her nipples were pressing against his chest. He could feel them through the thin fabric of her bra. It would be so easy to just ease her over onto her back, open her bra and spread the fabric apart, exposing her breasts for him to touch and taste. It was so tempting.

"We have to get going." His voice sounded deep and raspy after a night of sleep. Of course, the fact he had a raging hard-on didn't help either. He hated to disturb her, but he expected that today was going to be as bad, if not worse, than yesterday. They were closing in on the Wolf Creek pack territory and the males from the other packs, as well as the bounty hunters, would be getting desperate.

Alex raised her head and blinked at him like a sleepy owl, her eyes a pale silvery gray in the early morning light seeping into the cave. He loved her eyes. With their unusual color and thick, brown lashes, they were a sight to behold. And extremely expressive.

He loved to watch all her emotions flash through them. If eyes were the mirrors of the soul, then she had a beautiful one.

Not that he had any doubts on that score. Not after the few days he'd spent with her. And what the hell was he doing waxing poetic over her eyes? They had to get going.

Still, he didn't sit up and dislodge her. She'd had a hard day yesterday and deserved a few minutes to wake up on her own. It had nothing to do with how damn good she felt cradled against his body.

The bruise on her forehead was a lovely shade of purple and yellow this morning. He touched it gently with his fingers, probing carefully around the edges. "How do you feel?"

She closed her eyes and sighed. "Good. But then again, I haven't moved yet." She started to lever herself away from him, but that drove her hips into closer contact with his groin. He hissed out a breath and rolled, shifting her to the ground beside him.

"Sorry about that." She ducked her head, but not before he caught a glimpse of the light blush covering her cheekbones.

"No problem." He grunted as he sat up, his own muscles protesting. He swiveled his neck from side to side, feeling his bones crack as he climbed to his feet. The hard, cool ground had made his muscles stiff, so he raised his arms in the air, stretching them. He bent his elbows and let his hands fall behind his head when he clasped them behind his neck. It felt good to work the kinks out of his body. If he'd been alone, he would have changed into his wolf form last night and curled up in a corner of the cave, but that would have meant leaving Alex to lie by herself.

She seemed accepting enough of his wolf form when he was fighting, but he didn't think she was ready to accept a wolf sleeping beside her at night. Or maybe it was him who wasn't ready to test her. Either way, he wouldn't have traded last night for anything. Having Alex lie so trustingly in his arms was something he wouldn't soon forget.

He watched her as she rolled up onto her knees and then carefully placed one foot flat on the ground and pushed herself upward. She groaned and he could hear the slight crack of her bones as she rolled her neck and shoulders.

"Now how do you feel?" He lowered himself back to the ground, hauled on his boots and began to lace them.

"Like I was in an accident and then trekked through the woods all day yesterday." She groaned again as she lowered herself back to the ground and reluctantly pulled her boots over to her.

"Wait." Joshua grabbed what was left of his T-shirt and tore two long strips off the end. He scooted over in front of her and pulled her right foot into his lap, carefully removing her sock. Her foot was sore in several places. He knew she needed some healing salve and a few days of rest for her feet, but that couldn't happen yet. Taking one of the strips, he carefully wrapped her foot and then tugged her sock back on. Then he did the same with her left foot, carefully inspecting it as well. One wasn't any worse than the other. She could walk, but it wasn't going to be fun.

When he was done, he helped her put her boots on, brushing her hands aside as he laced them up himself. He stood and then pulled her up beside him. "How does that feel?"

She took a few steps and smiled at him. "Better, thanks." She glanced down at the remains of the shirt in his hand. "I don't think there's enough left for you to wear." She bent down and hefted the jacket off the ground. "You should wear this."

He shook his head. "You need it more." He could already see the goose bumps on her arms. The morning was cool, but it would heat up as the day wore on. "Here." He handed her the T-shirt. "There should be enough for you to wear. It will help keep you warm." He took the jacket from her and held it while she slipped the remains of the shirt over her head.

It fell to just below her bra and was more of a crop-top than a shirt, but it was something. Shaking out the jacket, he held it while she slipped her arms inside. He didn't miss the slight wince on her face as she moved. He knew the wound on her arm was sore, not to mention the fact that the muscles across her chest and shoulders were stiff from yesterday's accident.

Not for the first time, Joshua wished she had already gone through her change. Once her werewolf had integrated fully within her, she would heal much faster. She'd be less vulnerable too, able to shift to her wolf form and run swiftly and silently through the forest.

Very carefully, he pulled her into his arms. She melted

against his bare chest immediately, rubbing her nose against his chest hair. He buried his face in her hair and inhaled her scent, letting it soothe him.

"It's going to be another rough day." He wouldn't hide anything from her. She had to be prepared.

"I know." She continued to rub her cheek against his skin as if she couldn't get enough of him. He knew her actions were unconscious, part hormones, part instinct. His erection, which had gone down slightly, sprang to life again.

"If there were any other way..." he trailed off, uncertain what else to say. They both knew there was no other way, no going back.

"I know," she whispered again, her arms tightening around him one final time before she stepped away. Straightening her shoulders, she reached into the pocket of the jacket and pulled out the sheath with his hunting knife. She handed it to him hilt first. "My gun and two knives are gone. This and your handgun are all we have."

He closed his hand over the knife sheath and pushed it back toward her. "You keep it." She started to protest, but he held up his hand. "If I sense anyone else near us, I'm going to shift. I can protect you better that way."

She nodded, but still seemed concerned. "All right." The sheath hooked easily over the waistband of her jeans and she adjusted it several times until she was satisfied it was within easy reach.

He checked his gun. "There are only two bullets left in here and they're not silver." He handed it to her and watched as she tucked it into the pocket of her jacket.

Her stomach growled loud enough for him to hear, reminding him that neither of them had eaten since around noon yesterday. But she never said a thing about being hungry. Then again, he'd known she wouldn't. She was an amazingly practical and resilient woman.

Her hunger probably hurt him more than it did her. For him, it was another reminder of how he had failed to take proper care of her. He also knew she'd be pissed with him if she knew what he was thinking.

Taking her hand in his, he twined their fingers together.

"Remember, if I tell you to do something, just do it. There may not be time for me to explain."

She nodded and gave his hand a squeeze as he led her out of the cave and into the early morning sunshine.

Alex squinted against the glare, which really wasn't all that bright. But after being in the dark cave all night, her eyes needed time to adjust. She would have loved to have the time to just look around and explore the area. The birds were singing an early morning song and the air was clean and crisp. She pulled the jacket more firmly around herself and then stared at Joshua's naked back wondering if he was cold. Not that he'd tell her. Heaven forbid he admit to any kind of weakness.

She glanced over her shoulder and watched as the cave disappeared from sight. She hated to leave. At least there had been the illusion of safety while they'd been tucked inside. Now that they'd left it behind, she felt vulnerable again.

It was only a matter of time until one group of enemies or another found their trail. These were all experienced woodsmen, both hunters and werewolves, and there were God only knows how many of them after her and Joshua. Still, she'd rather be with Joshua than with anyone else. No matter what happened, she'd fight by his side until the end.

It had felt strange, yet amazingly familiar to awake in his arms this morning. It was the second morning in a row she'd done so, but it seemed as if she'd been doing it for years. She hadn't wanted to leave the comfort and warmth of his large body. He'd held her securely throughout the long night, cradling her against him, keeping her safe while she slept.

Joshua had already been aroused by the time she'd opened her eyes and became aware of her surroundings. There had been no mistaking the rather large erection pressing into her belly. She'd responded immediately, her inner muscles contracting and softening. There was something about Joshua that her body recognized. They belonged together and she planned to make that a reality once this ordeal was over.

They walked in silence, and as the minutes became hours he had to release her hand and go ahead of her to forge a path though the dense woods. He moved silently and easily through the forest, obviously at home in his surroundings. Every now and then he'd glance over his shoulder to check on her. She always smiled at him, but still his frown deepened.

Truthfully, her feet were killing her again. They'd been pretty good for the first hour, thanks to the extra padding he'd wrapped around them. But now they were beginning to throb again. She passed her time imagining how wonderful it was going to feel to soak them in a tub of warm water. When this was over, she was going barefoot for a week.

He held up his hand as he stopped in his tracks. She immediately came to a halt, knowing he'd sensed or heard something. Silently, he prowled the area before coming to stand beside her. "We have company." His low, almost toneless words were mouthed next to her ear. She nodded to let him know she understood.

He bent over and quickly unlaced his boots, yanking both them and his socks off quickly. Shucking his jeans, he folded them and handed them to her. Alex swallowed as he turned from her and began to shift.

She'd seen it once, but not like this. This time the man was becoming the beast. Bones cracked and changed, some lengthened and others shortened as he bent forward and placed his palms on the forest floor. Muscles rippled and flowed beneath his skin. Thick black fur seemed to spring from his flesh as his face contorted and his jaw elongated, forming the familiar muzzle of the wolf.

Her heart pounded so loudly she couldn't even hear her own breathing. She clutched his jeans to her chest, needing something to hold onto. She swayed and stiffened her knees. This was no time to act like a ninny. She knew what he was. Accepted what he was. At least intellectually. This whole change thing was going to take her some time to get used to.

She couldn't even begin to imagine what it would be like to go through this metamorphosis herself. That was something she'd deal with when she had to and not one moment before. Right now, it was taking everything she had in her just to keep putting one foot in front of the other.

Even though it seemed to take forever, she knew it had only been a matter of seconds. The man was gone. In his place was a powerful, magnificent predator—a huge black wolf—king of the forest.

He turned his head and peered at her through familiar eyes, so dark that they appeared black. There was no doubting the intelligence or determination in that gaze. She'd seen it many times before.

Bending over, she picked up his boots and added them to her load. He was still staring at her when she faced him again, obviously waiting for her. She gave him a quick nod. He turned and loped off ahead of her, his muscular body sliding gracefully across the ground. She couldn't take her eyes off him. Even in this form he was enthralling.

He turned and shot her a disgruntled look. She didn't need to be able to hear him to read his thoughts. "I'm coming," she muttered under her breath as she crept as silently as she could behind him.

Chapter Twenty

They'd only been walking stealthily along for about five minutes when Joshua stopped again and ducked behind a cluster of fir trees. Alex quickly followed him, lowering the bundle of clothing to the ground and drawing the hunting knife from its sheath.

She thought about Joshua's handgun and the two bullets left in it, but felt the knife was the better choice. A gunshot would be heard for miles. She'd use it if necessary, but for now the knife would have to do.

Hunkering down behind the trees, she listened. The woods had gone silent. The birds had stopped singing, the insects were silent, even the wind seemed to pause.

Her fingers squeezed the hilt of the knife. Who was after them this time? Bounty hunter? More werewolves? It didn't really matter she supposed. An enemy was an enemy.

Joshua tipped his head to one side, as if he were listening intently to something only he could hear. Suddenly, she wished she could change too. If she could transform herself into a wolf then they would be able to speed through the countryside to their destination. She would be a help to him, not a hindrance. If he were by himself, he'd already be back within the safety of the pack.

Her ears perked up as she thought she heard a sound off to the left. It was faint. The sound of something brushing against the leaves that littered the ground. Her hands were moist and she shifted the knife, wiping her hand on her jeans before gripping the hilt again and moving it into position.

The longer she stayed in a crouched position, the more her

legs began to cramp and her feet throbbed. But she stayed in the uncomfortable stance. There was no way she was moving until Joshua gave her the okay. His senses were much keener than hers and she knew he was hearing or smelling things she wasn't able to.

A man stepped out into a small clearing a few feet away from them. He was tall and well built with a wide chest and long, muscular legs. "Striker." His voice was low, but it carried well. "We've taken care of a couple of bounty hunters and a rogue wolf that were on your trail. It's safe to come out." He reached behind him and dragged the carcass of a brown wolf into the clearing. Alex recognized it as the one that had escaped from yesterday's fight.

Joshua didn't move, but turned his head to study the man. Alex wondered who he was. He obviously knew Joshua. Still, they waited.

"Come on man. We're your escort back to the compound." The man turned his head, his long blond hair ruffling in the slight breeze. "I know you're close. I can smell her." He turned his face from side to side, his nose in the air as if trying to find her.

Alex buried her face against her knees, huddled closer to the tree and tried to make herself as inconspicuous as possible. *He could smell her?* How humiliating was that? She felt something brush against her face and jerked her head up. Joshua rubbed his face against hers as if offering silent comfort.

She reached out, clutching her fingers in his soft fur, needing the reassuring contact. She didn't think she was ready to meet anyone from his pack yet. But time had obviously run out.

Joshua changed back into human form. The transformation was quick. The strange thing was it was beginning to seem almost natural. And how weird was that? He bent close to her, his hair brushing against her cheek as he whispered in her ear. "You stay here. I'm going to go and talk to Luther."

She nodded, but didn't speak. Joshua faded into the bushes, circled around and stepped out behind the other man.

"I wasn't expecting you, Luther."

The blond man spun around. He was slightly shorter than Joshua, but not by much. In terms of build, they were evenly matched. Still, there was something more dangerous about Joshua. Menace seemed to just emanate from him.

Luther took a step back and then seemed to check himself. "Thought you might need some help." He jerked his head toward the dead wolf.

"How did you know where to find me?" Joshua was totally naked and should have seemed vulnerable next to the other man, but nothing could be further from the truth. He appeared even larger, more imposing and totally unconcerned about his nudity.

Luther shrugged. "Me and my brothers have been out scouting the perimeter of the pack land for the past two days. We figured you'd be along soon. And you found her, didn't you."

It wasn't a question because he'd already said he could smell her. His eyes gleamed with lust. Alex shivered when the blond stranger licked his lips. Suddenly, she felt like the girl in the fairytale her father used to read her when she was a little girl. What was it? Oh, yeah, Little Red Riding Hood. This particular wolf looked like he wanted to eat her for lunch.

"She is safe." Joshua kept his arms by his sides, his stance loose. She could tell he was ready to move or fight at any second.

Luther scanned the trees, searching. "Where is she? I want to see her."

Revulsion filled Alex. She didn't want to be anywhere near this guy.

"You will see her when the time is right. I'll bring her back to the compound. You and your brothers can go on ahead."

"I don't think so, Striker." Luther motioned off to his left and two wolves slunk out from beneath the brush. "We'll take her from here."

"You think you can take her from me?" Joshua asked, his tone almost mild.

"You Strikers think that you are so special," the other man all but spat. His handsome features were contorted with rage. "Why should you have her? The Carlos family is just as deserving and furthermore, we don't mind sharing. Do we boys?" The two wolves seemed to smile.

Oh shit. She was in trouble. The hilt of the knife dug into her palm she was gripping it so hard, but she took comfort from the pain. There was no way she'd allow herself to become some pass-around treat for Luther and his brothers. She tried to swallow, but her throat was impossibly dry. Sweat beaded on her forehead, but she didn't dare move to swipe at it. The last thing she wanted to do was draw any attention her way.

Joshua bared his teeth as a menacing growl came from deep in his chest. "You are refusing a direct order?"

The other man smiled with smug satisfaction. "Things have changed since you've been away."

Joshua stilled. Energy seemed to coalesce around him, making him appear even larger. "I always thought your family was short on brains, Luther. But now I'm certain of it."

The blond man laughed as the two wolves slunk closer. "With all the Striker brothers gone looking for the little she-bitch, there was a change in the leadership of the pack." He shrugged and crossed his arms over his chest.

She was almost afraid to blink, afraid she'd miss something as the tense scene played out in front of her. Her position from behind the trees allowed her to watch even as she was hidden from view. Joshua's eyes narrowed, becoming even darker.

"I wouldn't want to be the one to have to tell James LeVeau that you killed his brother." Joshua's tone was mild, but the other man jerked backward as if he'd been struck.

"He's still alive?"

"Did you expect it to be otherwise?" Joshua shifted the tiniest amount, but the others didn't seem to notice.

"Those damn hunters guaranteed they'd get rid of him."

"It was you who fed information to the bounty hunters. You betrayed our people to those monsters who have preyed on our women and children." His entire body seemed to vibrate with barely suppressed anger.

Luther shrugged. "Whatever it takes to get the woman. With James LeVeau's daughter by my side, no one will gainsay my right to lead the Wolf Creek pack."

"You think not?" Joshua shook his head as if addressing a

wayward child. "The Striker family would definitely object."

"Not if there are none left to do so." Luther puffed out his chest, full of bravado now. Alex couldn't believe he didn't seem to realize the danger he was in. Joshua was only one man, but at this moment she'd put all her money on him.

The fine hair on the back of her neck stirred and a shiver skated down her spine. She turned her head slowly, careful not to make a noise. He was standing right behind her, a large brown wolf with dark brown eyes and very sharp teeth. He growled as he started to lope toward her.

Jumping to her feet, she ignored the shout she heard behind her, focusing on nothing but the animal in front of her. She kept the knife in her hand hidden by her side as the wolf raced closer. All her senses were heightened. She could hear the pads of his feet pounding against the ground as he ran. She could feel the breeze on her skin, the sweat on her back and the deep pounding of her heart. The forest seemed to recede into the background. There was only her and her attacker.

The animal took one final step and launched itself at her. She swung her arm upward with all her might and buried the silver-coated hunting knife in the wolf's chest, aiming straight for the heart. She threw up her free arm, covering her face and blocking it from the animal's large jaw.

She heard the yelp of pain, felt the gush of liquid as blood coated her hand. Leather tore as sharp teeth shredded the thick fabric of her jacket. Alex fell over backward, striking the ground hard. The wind was knocked out of her, but she managed to twist the knife deeper in the wolf's chest. Claws tore at her jacket and she screamed out as he struck her bad arm.

The beast thrashed about and Alex's already abused body took another beating as she fought to keep the wolf's teeth from her throat. Finally, after what seemed to be an eternity, the wolf gave one final shudder and went limp. She lay there panting for breath, unable to move with the weight pinned on her chest.

She gathered her remaining strength and managed to roll to her side. The muscles in her arms and legs burned as they bunched and strained to shift the bulk of the large wolf off her. She flopped back to the ground, gasping for breath. She started to wipe the sweat from her brow and stopped when she realized her right hand and arm were covered in blood.

Alex rolled to her hands and knees. She sucked in a deep breath as her stomach heaved. She yanked off her jacket and cursed when she hit her bad arm. Using the lining of the jacket, she wiped off as much of the blood as she could.

It was only then that she heard the sounds of a fight in the clearing behind her. *Joshua.* She jumped to her feet and almost fell back to the ground again. She swayed and grabbed a tree for support, blinking as the world came back into focus. Joshua had shifted again and the massive black wolf was locked in a life-and-death struggle with two other wolves. Luther lay flat on his back on the ground, his sightless eyes staring at the sky, his head at an unnatural angle.

Although it made her stomach roil, she grabbed the hilt of her knife and yanked it out of the chest of the wolf beside her. What was it her father had said about how to kill a werewolf? Silver was poison. Breaking their necks or decapitating them would also kill them.

She stared at the knife and gave thanks that this was no ordinary blade, but one coated with a layer of silver. The shiny edge was now speckled with the blood of the creature on the ground. She'd never have been able to break its neck, but she'd certainly sunk the silver blade straight into its heart.

Alex swallowed hard and turned away from the carnage beside her. Reaching down, she grabbed Joshua's gun from the pocket of her mangled jacket and jammed it into the waistband of her jeans. It wouldn't kill a werewolf, but it might slow one down. Clutching the knife tight, she stepped into the small clearing.

The three wolves ripped, clawed and bit each other. Blood sprayed the ground as they growled and fought. Alex had never witnessed anything so brutal in her life. She swayed, but locked her knees. She had to be able to fight, to help Joshua.

Sucking much needed air into her lungs, she steadied herself as a deep calm settled over her. She and Joshua would defeat their enemies or die together here in the woods. Determination fired her blood as she took a step closer to the mound of growling fur that thrashed on the ground.

Joshua had one of his opponents by the neck, his teeth

locked into the creature's flesh in a death grip. The other wolf jumped on Joshua, sinking his teeth into Joshua's black fur. Alex lunged forward and drove her knife into the rogue werewolf's back. It raked Joshua's sides with its claws as it jumped away.

Alex stumbled back as the wounded animal turned on her. The hilt of the knife was sticking out of its back. The wolf had moved so quickly, she'd lost her grip on her weapon.

Drawing the gun, she fired off the two remaining shots in quick succession. The wolf jumped to the side, but one of the bullets nicked him. Rather than slow him down, the regular bullet just seemed to piss him off.

She tossed the empty gun aside. She was on her own, weaponless. With one eye on the predator moving closer to her, she searched the ground for a rock or branch. Her back hit a tree and she stopped, but the wolf kept creeping closer.

The werewolf growled, saliva and blood dripping from its massive jaws. Alex braced her legs and got ready. If she was lucky, she could hold him off long enough to grab the knife from his back. Who was she kidding? She'd have her hands full trying to keep those large, sharp teeth from ripping out her throat. Not to mention the damage those long claws could do.

These guys were playing for keeps. Now that their leader was dead, she didn't think mating with her was still on the schedule. Even if it was, she didn't care. She was a fighter. If she was going to die then she was going to take this creature with her. "Come on," she taunted. "Or are you too afraid to fight a woman. I've already killed a couple of you mangy critters."

He leapt so suddenly she stumbled. She stuck out her arms and prayed for strength, as she was knocked backward. A low rumble seemed to fill the air and then the weight was gone from her chest. She turned her head and watched as Joshua dragged the smaller wolf away from her, his powerful jaws crunching the bones of the other beast's neck.

She tried to sit up but fell back to the ground, swallowing a moan of pain. The wolf had raked her arms with his claws and they were bleeding. She watched, unblinking, as Joshua finished off the other wolf and dropped its body to the ground. The small clearing was littered with bodies, the stench of blood and death permeating the air.

Alex gagged and dragged herself as far away as she could get, which in reality was only a couple of feet. Soft fur brushed against her as she felt Joshua settle beside her. His tongue stroked over the torn flesh of her arms as if trying to soothe her. She gave a small hiccup—half-laugh, half-cry—and then began to cry in earnest.

Wrapping her arms around her wolf, she buried her face in his fur and sobbed. She didn't cry for long, because in the back of her mind she knew they had to move. If these werewolves had found them, then others could as well.

Pulling her face away, she dried her eyes with the tail of her cropped shirt. Most of the bleeding on her arms had stopped. Hopefully, that meant the gouges weren't deep, but just long and mostly superficial. Or maybe it was because her wolf was pushing more to the surface with each passing minute.

The massive black wolf lay quietly by her side, his chest moving up and down in a slow, steady manner. She came up on her hands and knees in a hurry, all pain and injuries forgotten. Joshua wasn't moving.

She ran her hands over his sides and back and found several serious wounds. Jerking off her shirt, she began to tear what was left of it into strips and began to bind the worst of them. Joshua stared at her though his dark, liquid eyes, his expression unreadable. He'd taken on three opponents at once and won.

His tongue came out to lick her hand as if in reassurance. "I know that you're fine, big guy. Just indulge me and let me tend to those injuries, okay?"

He nodded and closed his eyes again. She gave a watery laugh. Even exhausted and wounded, he wouldn't admit to being hurt and tired. God, she loved him.

A twig snapped in the distance. Oh, shit, there were more of them. Jumping to her feet, she stumbled over to the body of the wolf with the knife still sticking out of its back. Getting a firm grip on the handle, she tugged with all her might. The blade came free and she hurried back to Joshua's side.

How many of them were there? Joshua was in no shape to fight and neither was she. Grabbing him by the shoulders, she began to pull him back into the woods. She'd have to try to hide them. Joshua stumbled along beside her still in his wolf form, doing his best to help her. The rustling sound was getting closer. Alex stopped and hunkered down beside Joshua who was already getting to his feet. The man was amazing.

Four gigantic wolves entered the clearing. The largest of the bunch was dark brown with patches of black. He padded over to the body of the man and then the other two wolf carcasses and sniffed. His eyes bespoke of death as he studied the clearing.

Oh shit!

Alex swallowed, suddenly more afraid than she'd been since this entire mess began several days ago. This wolf was different from all the rest. Like Joshua, this wolf was lethal.

The other three wolves, all of whom were various shades of brown and black, fell into position behind the larger one. The leader swiveled his head in Alex's direction and began to stalk toward her. He didn't growl, didn't make a sound, and the silence was all the more frightening.

But she had moved beyond fear and was ready to face death. There was no way she could defeat this latest threat. There were too many of them and she was too tired and injured. But she would defend Joshua and herself with every breath that was left in her body.

Slowly, she stood and stepped in front of Joshua. The knife was once again clutched in her hand. She held the blade low and at the ready. "Come on then," she growled. "What are you waiting for?"

The large wolf cocked his head to one side and stared at her. She stared right back, refusing to flinch from its menacing gaze. Joshua suddenly appeared beside her, his huge black body inserting itself in front of her. He bared his teeth and emitted a low growl. The other wolf growled back.

Alex wasn't sure what the heck was going on, but she stepped out from behind Joshua to stand next to him. He was her mate, official or not, and she would stand beside him.

A majestic gray wolf suddenly appeared from out of nowhere. Muscles rippled as it positioned itself between her and Joshua and the other group. It stared first at one group and then the other.

Alex's breath caught in her throat. She recognized those golden brown eyes as they swept over her. They showed the same love and concern they had her entire life. The gray wolf emitted a huge rumbling growl when it caught sight of the blood on her arms and the bruise on her forehead and body. He pinned his golden-eyed glare on Joshua and then faced the group of four.

The tension in the air was so great, Alex thought her nerves would snap. Oh, God, her father was going to challenge the other werewolves. She swallowed the lump in her throat, almost afraid to breathe. The largest of the challengers growled and surged forward, stopping just short of her father and crouching low on all fours.

Joshua calmly padded over to stand beside her father, earning a black glare from the challenger. The large gray wolf and the massive black one stood shoulder to shoulder as they faced down the other four.

Finally, Joshua tipped back his huge furry head and howled. The mournful sound echoed around them and was carried away on the wind. The other four tilted back their necks, raised their heads to the sky and howled in return.

Alex blinked, wishing she understood what the heck was happening. She'd be much happier when she finally understood all this wolf stuff. Silence reigned as the group of four wolves all gave her one final look before turning and fading back into the forest. Her father stared at her for a long moment before he too, turned and padded away.

Now she was totally confused.

She dropped to her knees and sat in the dirt as Joshua came toward her. He nudged her face with his muzzle. Then he disappeared behind a tree on the other side of the clearing. She was too tired to move and too exhausted to think. All that mattered was that she didn't have to fight.

Less than a minute later, Joshua reappeared clad in his jeans and boots once again. He strode over beside her, lifted her to her feet, wrapped his strong arms around her and held her. She buried her face against his chest, appalled by the gouges and claw marks that covered his arms and torso. She didn't want to see his back, knowing that had to be as bad.

Before she could speak, four men strode from the woods, this time making no attempt to conceal their footsteps. Joshua turned her in his arms until she was facing them. Like they had been in wolf form, the largest of the four stood slightly in front of the rest. They were big men, their hair dark and shaggy and their features eerily familiar.

"Alex." Joshua wrapped his arms around her as the men moved closer. "I want you to meet my brothers."

Chapter Twenty-One

Alex didn't know whether to laugh or cry. This was certainly not the first impression she wanted to make on Joshua's family. She was dirty, bloody, exhausted and she knew she had to stink. And, oh my God, she was half-naked as well. Her muddled mind cleared long enough to remind her that only the thin pink fabric of her bra shielded her breasts. Her coat and shirt were both in shreds.

She didn't know what to say to these men. She was slightly embarrassed and intimidated by the united picture they made standing with their arms crossed across their massive chests, watching her, judging her and obviously finding her lacking.

She'd raised her arms to cover herself, but dropped them back by her sides, tilted her chin up and glared at them. Who were they to judge her? They hadn't arrived until the fighting was over. Where were they when their brother was fighting for his life?

The largest one in the front cocked his eyebrow at her, but she didn't so much as blink. He was even bigger than Joshua and that was saying something. His hair was a deep mahogany brown that hung down around his impossibly wide shoulders. She had a feeling this was the eldest brother.

Joshua gave her a slight squeeze of encouragement. She took a deep breath, hoping no one noticed her hands were shaking, and prepared to meet his family. She opened her mouth to speak, but the men were no longer looking at her. All heads were turned toward the forest and even Alex could feel the surge of power coming toward them.

Her heart leapt with joy as her father stalked back into the clearing. She was so glad he hadn't left. She automatically took a step toward him, but was unceremoniously hauled back into Joshua's arms. "It is my duty to comfort you now. Not his."

Her eyes flew to Joshua's and she could see that he was deadly serious. All this male posturing was making her head pound. He was her father for heaven's sake and she hadn't seen him in several days.

"She's not yours yet, Striker." Her father kept coming toward them, ignoring Joshua's brothers who looked none to happy with this announcement. "There has been no formal ceremony and my daughter is yet unmarked."

That bit of information made her cheeks heat and she shuffled her feet uncomfortably. She dipped her head down to her chest, wishing her hair was longer so that it would cover her face. Honestly, listening to her father talking about her being marked by some wolf was just too much.

Joshua began to growl as her father stopped in front of them. Her father emitted a sound unlike anything she'd ever heard before. Part growl and all challenge, the two men faced off against each other and she was the prize caught in the middle.

She wrapped her arms around herself. "No more." She stumbled back and a large hand caught her from behind. Her stomach lurched as she pulled away before Isaiah could get a grip on her. "No more fighting. No more death." She was finding it harder to breathe now, her chest rising and falling rapidly.

"No more," her father promised as he took a step toward her. "Come here, Alexandra." He opened his arms, offering comfort. She glanced at Joshua and then at her father, totally confused, knowing whichever one she went to the other one would be hurt.

Turning her back on all of them, she started toward the trees. All she wanted to do was to curl up somewhere, close her eyes and sleep. Maybe when she woke, she'd be able to think more clearly.

Thick forearms wrapped around her, stopping her in her tracks. She didn't need to turn around to know whose arms they were. Sighing, she leaned back against Joshua's chest. He leaned down, his breath brushing across her neck as he whispered in her ear. "I'm sorry. I didn't mean to make you choose between us. That was uncalled for. Unworthy of you after all you've sacrificed." His lips grazed her ear, making her toes curl in her boots. "Your father needs you. Go to him."

With his hands on her shoulders, he turned her around so that she was facing the group again. She ignored the four brothers who were watching the scene unfold with avid interest. Her only concern was her father. He stood apart from them, his feet braced apart, his hands open by his sides. It was his face that told the tale. His golden brown eyes were filled with such sorrow and pain that her heart began to throb.

Everything she'd been through the past few days rose up to haunt her. She had no idea where her father had been or what he'd had to deal with, but he was here right now. He'd come for her. To protect her as he always had.

Giving a small cry, she ran to him. Her feet tripped on an exposed tree root and she stumbled, but before she could fall, strong arms caught her. The familiar smell of sandalwood washed over her as her father hauled her into his embrace and held her as though he'd never let her go. "My Alexandra. My precious little girl," he crooned as he rocked her slightly in his strong embrace.

She didn't mean to cry. Didn't want to cry. She wanted to be tough and confident. But tears leaked from the corners of her eyes, staining the front of her father's shirt. She felt a hand on the small of her back and realized that Joshua had come up behind them. Reaching out blindly with her hand, she tugged him closer, needing both of them.

Taking a few deep breaths, she got control of her wayward emotions and raised her head. A shiver shot through her body and goose bumps rose on her arms and chest, reminding her that she was only partially dressed. Her father swore as he stepped back and ripped off his shirt and wrapped it around her. He helped her tuck her arms in the sleeves, being careful of her injuries, and then buttoned it like he had many times when she'd been a child.

"Dad."

He finished slipping the last button through the hole before he looked at her.

"I'm really okay."

"No you're not," he growled. She could hear that anger in his voice and knew he was angry with himself. Her father and Joshua had much in common.

"Yes, I am." She caught his face in her hands and made him really look at her. "By rights I should be dead, or at the very least captured, and I would have been without Joshua." Going up on her toes, she kissed her father's cheek and released him. Taking a step back, she stood at Joshua's side. "I need to see to your injuries." She was worried about the long gashes on his chest, back and arms even though they were no longer bleeding.

Joshua twined his fingers with hers, but his gaze was still on her father. The two men stared at one another as the tension rose again. Finally, her father gave a curt nod. Joshua inclined his head and at last gave her his attention. She wanted to be indignant over the fact that the two men had just seemed to have decided her future between them, but she was just so relieved they weren't going to fight that she couldn't work up a good mad.

Honestly, the testosterone level was enough to suffocate a woman. They could decide whatever they wanted. She planned to just go ahead and do what she wanted anyway. Let them have their male rituals if it made them feel better.

As if he knew what she was thinking, Joshua released her hand and slung his arm over her shoulder, pulling her closer. She winced at the pressure. Her poor body was protesting all the abuse. Joshua pulled his arm back and swore. "We've got to get you back to the compound." She could see the worry in his eyes, so she patted his chest to try to reassure him.

Someone cleared his throat. "We need to get moving."

She peeked around Joshua and found all four of his brothers still standing there waiting. Straightening her shoulders, she strode toward the men. Stopping just in front of them, she extended her hand toward the largest. "I'm Alex Riley. Pleased to meet you."

The corners of his mouth kicked up, but that didn't make him appear any less scary. His large hand engulfed hers. "Isaiah Striker." His eyes were as dark as Joshua's, maybe even darker as they stared down at her. She had a feeling he was trying to see straight to her very soul and that he was succeeding. She wanted to look away, but was ensnared in his gaze. Eventually, he seemed to find whatever it was he was searching for, released her hand and stepped away. Leaving her there with the other three, he strode toward Joshua and her father.

Alex turned back to the remaining brothers. They were all formidable men, but not in the same league as their older brothers. One of the men stepped forward. This one had medium brown hair and chocolate brown eyes that held a hint of mischief. He stuck out his hand. "Micah Striker." She shook his hand and blinked furiously when another man almost identical to him stepped up beside them.

"Levi Striker." He elbowed his brother out of the way and took her hand in his.

The last brother stepped forward. His hair was a deep, rich black and his eyes were somber as he gripped her hand. Unlike his brothers, he brought her hand to his lips and placed a tender kiss on the back of her hand. "Simon Striker." His voice had an almost musical quality about it. She found herself smiling at him.

"Thank you for making Joshua happy." He gave her hand a squeeze before he released it.

"I'm glad to meet you all." She glanced around the forest floor and then averted her eyes from the bodies. "I just wish it could be under better circumstances."

"We've got to get moving." Joshua walked over to stand beside her and she leaned into his side, just wanting to touch him. "There's trouble back at the compound. I'm not sure what we're going to find when we get there. Luther said there'd been a change in leadership. I don't think we're going to find Ian alive."

Her father swore and turned away. The man might not be real to her, but he was her uncle and her father's brother. Her heart ached for him. It would be horrible to come home after all these years just to find his brother dead.

She watched as her father stared off into the distance, wishing she knew what to do to comfort him. The last few days had brought brutality and death into her life, but it had also brought love and hope. So many mixed emotions swirled around inside Alex. Her father seemed so alone, so removed from the rest of them. She wished he had someone to share his life with, especially now that she'd found Joshua.

Joshua released a long, steady sigh. "I hate to break this up, but we need to leave. There are probably others scouring the woods and we're still about a two- or three-hour hike from the compound."

Isaiah nodded. "I'll go on and scout ahead. Not all of the men of the Wolf Creek pack are stupid enough to follow Luther and his ilk. I'm willing to bet that many of them don't even know what's happened. I expect the Carlos family didn't exactly challenge Ian in the traditional manner. Knowing them, they probably attacked Ian when he wasn't expecting it."

"I'd say you're right about that." Tension flowed from Joshua in waves. "Go."

Isaiah inclined his head and began to strip off his clothing. When he was naked, he shifted and loped off into the woods. Simon came forward and gathered his brother's clothing.

Levi and Micah went around the clearing, gathering all the weapons. When they were done the group headed out in the direction that Isaiah had gone.

James' blood began to boil as the reality of his brother's death washed over him. He would have his vengeance. Somehow. His gaze landed on Alex and a sense of peace enveloped him. Her presence alone was enough to bring him some comfort. This was why he was here. His daughter would be safe, no matter what the cost to himself. He owed her that much.

As he continued to watch her, Alex reached out and twined her fingers with Joshua's, following him into the woods. She was limping slightly and he could see blood had seeped through his shirt in several places. Joshua's back looked much worse, but he ignored it as he leaned down to listen to whatever Alex was saying to him.

They might not be officially bonded, but James could see the connection was there. Alex glanced back over her shoulder then and smiled at him. His little girl was gone forever, replaced by a woman any man would be proud of.

No, his daughter no longer needed him, but his pack did.

It felt strange to be returning home after all these years. But it felt good. The time had come for James LeVeau Riley to reclaim his lost life.

Chapter Twenty-Two

Joshua kept all his senses sharp, constantly searching the wind for the stench of bounty hunters and rogue werewolves. From what he'd learned, they not only had to deal with enemies from without, but traitors from within the pack as well.

Alex stirred beside him, drawing his attention. "How are you feeling?" He didn't like the fact they'd been unable to do anything about her injuries. He wanted her home where he could take care of her.

"Shouldn't that be my line?" She rubbed her hand gently over his injured arm. "I can't begin to imagine how you're feeling right now. To have your own people betray you like that." Alex sighed and shook her head. "I know you've got to be hurt and angry. I know you feel as if you failed Ian and want to avenge him somehow."

Once again he was reminded of just how lucky he was to have found this special woman. She understood him better than anyone else ever had. "I did fail him. We all did. We are the Striker family, the protectors of the pack. We never should have left him unguarded in the compound."

That's what burned in his gut worst of all. He and his family had always been responsible for the safety of the pack and the alpha couple.

"It's not your fault."

"Then whose is it?" he countered angrily. "It is our responsibility. *My* responsibility."

"You have to let it go, Joshua." Her fingers tightened around his. "You were doing what Ian asked you to do, what your alpha commanded you to do. You were fulfilling your duty to him and the pack." Alex scowled at him. "We've had this discussion before. You're not omnipotent."

He sighed and rubbed the back of his neck, trying to ease some of the tension that rested there. The gashes on his arms, back and chest pained him, but it was the ache in his heart that hurt the most.

"Give it time." Her voice was low and soft, a balm to his battered soul.

He knew Alex was right, but that didn't make it any easier. All any of them could do was go forward and face whatever lay on the path ahead of them. They were almost at the compound.

Alex stumbled and he caught her easily in his arms. She had to be close to collapsing, but she never uttered a complaint. Her face was chalky, her lips pale. Dark circles ringed beneath her eyes and the bruise on her face was a sickly yellow and black. He knew her body was battered and bruised as well and that her arms and feet needed tending.

He pulled her to a halt, picked her up and placed her on a tree that had fallen across the path. "Rest." She didn't like his order and made to stand. "We need to wait for Isaiah. It won't do for us to go into this blind. We're less than an hour away."

"Oh." She settled back on the log and sighed. "I guess that makes sense."

Joshua fought back a grin as he watched her. "Glad you think so," he added wryly.

The others came up alongside them with James in the lead. "How much longer until Isaiah gets back?"

"Not long." Joshua knew his brother would be back as quickly as possible.

The words were barely out of his mouth when Isaiah appeared from between two trees. He didn't waste any time, shifting back to his human form immediately. He launched straight into his news. "Ian and Patrice are dead." The news was as stark and blunt as his voice. "Luther and his brothers took them unawares. They didn't make it."

Joshua flicked his gaze toward James. The older man stood there, still as a statue, and absorbed the blow. His brother and sister-in-law were both gone.

"What about the others involved in this betrayal?" Joshua turned his attention back to Isaiah.

"Some of the younger pups of the Brody family are waiting at the compound." An unholy smile lit Isaiah's face as he took his clothing from Simon and pulled on his jeans. "Seems they want to challenge you, brother. They think they can defeat the Striker."

Joshua swallowed back his anger. So much loss. So much death, and all of it unnecessary. No wonder their kind was dying out. They couldn't stop this incessant fighting amongst themselves. He felt Alex's hand at the base of his spine. The heat from her palm, the contact between them, soothed him. "They are welcome to try."

He felt Alex's fingers jerk against his skin, but she said nothing, made no protest. She'd faced nothing but violence since she entered his world. He honestly was afraid she wouldn't want to stay with him in Wolf Creek. And who would blame her? Certainly not him. At this point, he wasn't sure he wanted to stay any longer. He was tired. Tired of all the fighting and death. And what was it all for?

Alex leaned into his side, her softness nestling against his hard body and he swallowed back the surge of emotion that threatened to overwhelm him.

This is what he fought for. For the chance to have a few moments of peace. To protect a special woman like Alex. For a chance to rebuild their society.

He wanted to howl, to change into his wolf form and run free through the woods with Alex by his side. He wanted to curl up after a long hard day with Alex in his big bed and spend all night making love to her. He wanted to fall asleep with her curled in his arms and wake in the morning with her still there.

And he would have it too. Determination fired him again, pushing away his fatigue. "What about the elders of the family. Donovan Brody isn't a stupid man." The Brody loyalty had never been in doubt until this moment and Joshua found it disconcerting. Donovan was not only a good friend, but also a man whose opinion he respected.

Isaiah smirked. "You might not get a chance to meet the younger Brodys. When I left, Donovan was headed for the compound with blood in his eyes."

"Damn it. That's my job. They challenged me." He knew his friend would handle the problem, but he would pay a terrible cost. It wasn't easy to have to kill a member of your own family, even if it was an extended member. "Which Brodys are involved?"

"His younger brother's children." Joshua knew they were all young males, ranging from the ages of twenty to thirty-five. Old enough to know better and young enough to be stupid. "It has to be the influence of the boys' maternal uncle. Their father is mated to a Carlos, isn't he?

Isaiah nodded.

It all made sense to Joshua. All those young men thinking they could destroy the fabric of the werewolf society and take over. What they didn't yet realize was the very survival of their race depended on that same society and the rules that were in place to protect it.

"We have to get going." James prowled forward. "The deaths of Ian and Patrice must be avenged. Then we will deal with the Brodys." He didn't wait for the rest of them, but moved off on his own.

The rest of them followed quickly. They knew the pain James was feeling. They'd all experienced it at one time or another. It was never easy to lose family.

Alex trudged forward. Each step was bloody painful. She wanted to ask if they were almost at the Wolf Creek compound but couldn't muster the energy. It had to be close.

She was so intent on just staying on her feet that she didn't realize Joshua had stopped until she plowed into his back. She grabbed onto his waist for support and managed to stay on her feet.

She could see the worry in his eyes when he gathered her close to him. "I'm okay." She patted his chest, loving the hard feel of it beneath her palm. She could tell he wasn't convinced, but there was nothing either of them could do about it right now so there was no point in talking about it.

"I wanted to show you something."

She heard it then, a loud rushing sound just beyond the

trees. She was shocked she hadn't heard it before now. Stepping beside him, she let him lead her off their original path. The trees seemed to part suddenly and her breath caught in her throat.

About thirty feet in height, the rock wall reached to the sky. Cascading over it was a shower of water, wild and fierce. Plants of all sorts grew along the banks of the river. The lush green was peppered with a splash of red and white as some flowers and berries flourished. A fine spray of mist shimmered along the top of the pool that formed at the base of the falls. It was completely untamed and absolutely breathtaking.

Joshua's arms came around her from behind. His chest was nestled up to her back and she leaned against him, careful not to put much of her weight against his injured chest, but wanting—no needing—the contact with him. His fingers slid beneath the fabric of her shirt and rested lightly on her stomach. "This is part of Wolf Creek," he whispered in her ear and she understood why he didn't speak aloud. There was something about this place that seemed almost magical and certainly awe inspiring.

"It's beautiful." Her words were totally inadequate to express what she truly felt, but she sensed he understood what she was trying to say.

His lips skimmed the curve of her ear. "When this is all done, I'll bring you back here and we'll swim in the pool."

"Really?" She tilted her head back against his shoulder. Reaching down, he brushed a lock of hair off her cheek as he skimmed his finger along her jaw.

"Absolutely." His lips curved upward. "I think it's something we'd both enjoy."

His smile was filled with such promise she forgot all about her aches and pains, forgot all about his injuries. When his head dipped toward her, she leaned upward to meet him. His tongue skimmed along her bottom lip and she gasped. Heat flooded her body, pooling low in her groin. A gnawing restlessness grew within her, goading her onward. She wanted this man, wanted his hardness within her. Thrusting. Claiming.

Joshua pulled back, his eyes closed as he sucked in a deep breath. "Not now." His eyes opened and the heat in them almost singed her flesh. "But soon."

It was a promise she planned to make him keep. "Soon," she echoed, returning his vow. He growled low in his throat as he took her hand and tugged her away from the majestic falls and back on their trail.

They hurried their pace until they'd caught up with the others. His brothers looked at them, but didn't say anything. Her father glanced her way and smiled, but it was a sad smile that didn't quite reach his eyes.

The tension mounted as they moved closer to their home. They stopped and waited several times as three of the men slid soundlessly into the brush only to reemerge a short while later with their fists clenched and their faces set in anger.

Finally, the entire group came to a halt behind a stand of rocks. From here, Alex could see a ten-foot-tall wooden fence that surrounded a group of houses. The large gate in the front was open as if in invitation. This had to be the compound.

Levi and Micah stepped forward. "There were two scouts in the woods, but we left them alone." Levi shook his head. "Honestly, one of them is barely twenty. The Brodys managed to coax two of the young Tallant pups into joining them."

Joshua shook his head at the foolishness of youth. "We'll catch them later and leave them to their uncle." He knew Grady Tallant very well and his nephews would rue the day they'd ever got involved in this mess. The Tallant family was much like the Striker family and prided themselves on their loyalty to the pack.

James stepped forward. "It's time to end this." He glanced behind them. "I don't trust them not to bring in more hunters. This might be our territory, but with so many traitors in our midst it would be easy for them to slip through. They might even take the opportunity to attack our women and children."

Joshua noticed how easily James used the word "our" and not "your". It seemed his pack loyalty was there full force. But he was no longer their alpha. "You're absolutely right. That would be a major coup for them and something our young hotheads wouldn't consider."

He turned to his brothers. "I'm going in to face the Brodys.

Protect Alex." He ignored the outraged feminine gasp and focused on the protesting men. "It is my right as Striker. It is me they are challenging."

"No." Isaiah said no more than that, but that one word said it all.

James pinned him with a steely glare. "I owe them for my brother and his mate."

Alex turned to Joshua. "If you think I'm going to let you go in there alone, you've got another thing coming." It seemed it didn't pay to ignore a woman. Alex was currently trying to drill a hole in his stomach with her finger. He caught her hand to keep her from poking further at him. Her gray eyes were the color of a winter squall with all the fury that it brought.

Joshua wanted to laugh. Most of his life he'd felt alone, distant even from his brothers. His job had demanded it. Or so he'd believed. It was the way his father had done things, but Joshua was beginning to believe his father had been wrong. There was strength in family, in sharing the burden. Not that he'd allow any of them to put themselves in danger, especially Alex, but it was nice to not feel so alone.

"Are you smiling?" Alex poked him with her other hand. "Honest to God, Joshua Striker, if you're smiling I'm going to pop you one." She curled her fingers into a fist.

He rubbed his hand over his jaw, covering his mouth in the process. "No, I'm not laughing."

"You are." She yanked her hand out of his and took a step back. "Men!" She threw up her hands and turned away, but he caught her and hauled her back into his arms.

Ignoring the fact they had an audience, he leaned down, letting his long hair drape over his face to muffle the words he whispered in her ear. "If I'm smiling it's because you make me happy, Alex." She stilled and sighed. He knew she didn't truly understand, but now was not the time to explain.

He released Alex and faced the rest of the group. "I go in first. If you're determined to come, watch out for one another." They knew he meant for them to watch out for Alex, but he wasn't stupid enough to make that kind of mistake twice and say it out loud. All the men nodded. They understood.

"Here, take this." James reached around to the small of his

back and withdrew a handgun, handing it to his daughter. "There are six silver bullets." Alex nodded as she took the weapon and checked it before stuffing it into the waistband of her jeans.

Joshua felt better knowing Alex wasn't completely unarmed, even though he had no intention of letting her anywhere near the fighting. His brothers and her father would protect her while he met the challengers.

Putting all thoughts from his mind except those of the coming confrontation, he strode down the path, following the familiar trail toward home. This time he didn't notice the trees or hear the songs of the birds. All his senses were trained on the gate in front of him. He could already smell two men just inside and knew there were more. Their fear tainted the air and burned his nostrils.

They should be afraid after what they'd done. They'd murdered the alpha of the pack and his mate. *Treason.* The only possible fate for them was death. He was their court, their judge and their executioner, and he'd come to pass sentence on them.

He strode through the gates like he owned the place, which he did. This was his home and they had dared to invade it. One of the young men hurtled himself at Joshua, but he met only thin air. Joshua whirled with blinding speed, caught the man around the neck and twisted. A sickening snap filled the silence. Joshua let the body drop and moved on.

"Luther and his brothers are dead." Stopping, he turned in a circle, sighting or smelling five other werewolves. "The hunters are dead as well. Come forward and face your punishment like men or I will hunt you down like the dogs you are." It was the ultimate insult to call a werewolf a dog and Joshua knew he'd get some reaction. These men had already proved themselves to be hotheads.

Sure enough, two more of them surged forward, both of them shifting into wolves on the run. Joshua stood with his arms folded across his chest, his legs spread wide and waited. He waited until the last possible second and then moved. Catching one of the wolves in midair, he flung it into the other one. They tumbled to the ground, quickly regained their feet and began to growl.

Three shots rang out in quick succession. Everyone froze as a cry tore through the air. The wolves in front of him turned tail and ran. Werewolves did not use manmade weapons during a fight. It was considered dishonorable. They met a challenger with their bare hands or in their wolf form.

Stupid! These werewolves had already shown they were without honor. He had been too angry to think properly. That was an error in judgment that might cost him his life. But more importantly, he'd put Alex's safety at risk.

"That's one who won't give you any more trouble," Alex said.

He should have known. Turning, he faced Alex, who stood with her legs braced apart and the gun her father had given her at her side. She'd already proved to be more than capable of defending herself and him.

"We don't use manmade weapons on one another during a challenge." If she was going to be his mate he had to teach her their laws.

She snorted. "Tell that to the guy with the rifle on the roof."

His gaze shot to the rooflines of the house and sure enough on the top of Ian's home a man was slumped over, his body hanging half off the roof, a rifle dangling from his fingers. "My apologizes."

"Accepted," she snapped. "Can we just finish this?"

"With pleasure." He stalked forward with his brothers by his side, sensing that the rest of the betrayers were making a break for the back gate. Joshua broke into a run. There was no way he could let them escape.

Frightened howls and vicious growls ripped through the air. Joshua and his brothers came to a screeching halt and watched the carnage unfold in front of them. Donovan Brody and the rest of his clan had arrived and they were making short work of their kinsmen. They showed no mercy. It was over in mere minutes.

Bodies of men and wolves alike littered the ground, their blood seeping into the dirt. Joshua tilted back his head and roared at the sheer sickening loss of it. He'd never understand what could cause a man to turn his back on his own kind, on his family, and betray their trust. But just because he didn't understand it, didn't mean he didn't feel the sorrow at their passing. They were all much too young to die.

Donovan shifted from wolf to human and strode toward him, seemingly totally unconcerned by his nudity or by the bloody gashes on his chest. He stopped when he was in front of Joshua. His pale blue eyes, so unusual for a werewolf, were as cold as ice. "My clan offers an apology to the Wolf Creek pack. We understand if you do not wish us to remain among you."

It was the ultimate shame for a clan to be banished from its pack and Joshua knew just what it had cost his friend to utter those words. He shook his head. "That I cannot do."

Donovan's head jerked as if he'd been hit and Joshua knew his friend had misinterpreted his words to mean that he would not accept the apology.

He held out his hand. "There is no need for an apology. I hold the Brody family in no way responsible for the act of a few angry young men. The loyalty of the Brody clan is never in doubt and the Wolf Creek pack counts itself lucky to have you." The words were formal but necessary to mend the breach between them. With Ian dead, Joshua, in his position as Striker, was acting head of the pack until a competition could be held to select the new alpha.

Donovan took Joshua's hand, smearing it with the blood of his slain family members. Joshua yanked the other man into his arms and gave his friend a quick, hard hug. The two of them separated and stepped back. Emotions were running high and the scent of blood, sweat and anger wafted in the air around them.

"We need to call a meeting of the pack. Here. Now." There had been too much discord. They needed a leader and the matter of Alex had to be settled. Her scent was growing stronger by the minute. Several of the Brody men were staring at her. The heat and change were almost upon her. There wasn't time to waste.

Donovan's eyes flicked to Alex and then back to Joshua. "I will send out runners."

Nodding, he turned his back on his friend, gathered Alex to his side and led her away. He snapped out orders to his brothers as he went, secure in the knowledge that all would be done as he asked. All of this would be over in a matter of hours and then he could finally be alone with Alex.

Chapter Twenty-Three

Alex stood just beyond Joshua's front porch. Five other homes and various other buildings circled around a fifty-foot clearing. She assumed the large log home belonged to the alpha of the pack. The rest of the homes were compact but cozy and blended in with the surrounding landscape.

She was feeling slightly better, but longed for about twelve hours of uninterrupted sleep. God, she was tired. But at least she was clean. After watching the brutal deaths in the yard, she'd been only too ready to follow Joshua as he'd led her away. The other men were all watching her in a way that made her both uncomfortable and aroused.

Now that the immediate danger had passed, her body was once again reminding her that she wasn't totally human. Her skin was tight and confining. Her breasts ached and her nipples were tight buds that brushed against her bra, sending a blast of heat rocketing down between her thighs. The folds of her sex were sensitive and she was consumed with an almost overwhelming need to touch herself. Her panties were damp, a stark reminder of her constant arousal.

Her feet were encased in a pair of soft slippers that Joshua had dug up from somewhere. She suspected they had belonged to his mother. He'd also given her one of his shirts to wear. It was an older shirt with a well-worn, often-washed softness about it. The material was a pearly gray that matched her eyes. Her jeans needed a good washing, but she wouldn't be wearing them for long. After this meeting, she was going to go find a bed, crawl into it and sleep for about twelve hours straight.

Raising her hand to the back of her neck, she rubbed. She

still felt battered and bruised, but the hot bath had helped loosen up her stiff muscles. The long scratches on her arms and the furrow from the gunshot had all been properly cleansed. Joshua had taken the time to rub a healing ointment on it himself. She'd allowed him to do so, knowing instinctively he wouldn't be satisfied unless he took care of it himself.

But turnabout was fair play. He hadn't been too pleased, but he'd sat and allowed her to tend to his injuries as well, all the while complaining it was unnecessary. As a werewolf, he would heal much faster than a normal human would. Still, she needed to take care of him in some small way.

Then he'd planted a rough kiss on her lips, told her to stay out of trouble, and stalked off to talk to some of the men who had arrived. *Stay out of trouble.* None of this was her fault to begin with. Trouble just seemed to follow Joshua around. She'd wandered outside to look around but was starting to get rather uncomfortable with all the covert stares she was receiving from the groups of men and women who were gathering.

She felt very alone and uncertain and she didn't like the sensation. All these other people knew one another. She was the odd man out, or rather odd woman out. It was because of her those other werewolves had mutinied and died. Alex didn't think her transition to life here was going to be easy.

She was contemplating retreating back to the covered porch of Joshua's home when she heard footsteps coming up behind her. She glanced over her shoulder, hoping it was Joshua, but had to swallow her disappointment when it wasn't. What was wrong with her? She'd never been the type to need a man around before and she sure as heck wasn't going to start now. Taking a deep breath, she let it out slowly and went to meet her father.

"How are you?" He stood back and ran his eyes over her body, his fingers tracing the bruise that still bloomed on the side of her face.

"I'm okay. How about you?"

One corner of his mouth kicked upward. "I'm fine." He drew her into his arms and she rested her head against his solid chest. "I'm sorry this has been so hard on you." He rubbed his hand over her back, soothing her frayed nerves.

"I know you are." The last thing she wanted was for him to feel guilty. He'd done everything he could possibly do to protect her and, no matter what, he was still the best father a girl could have. But she was also looking at him a bit differently these days. "So what will happen now?"

He released her and stepped back. "That depends." Wrapping his arm around her shoulders, he guided her toward the side of the clearing. The bodies of the traitorous wolves had been carried away while she'd been getting cleaned up and, except for the blood staining the ground, there was no sign there had ever been a fight.

She dug her heels into the ground, bringing them both to a stop. He was evading her question. More than once she'd noticed the way he looked at the forest around him. There was sorrow and longing and so many more emotions mixed together in his face. Alex knew this homecoming was hard on her father, but it was what he needed. She sensed he was more at home here than he'd ever been in Chicago. The wildness of the forest and mountains suited him.

She stared up into his golden brown eyes, wanting him to know that she understood what he was feeling. "If these past few days have taught me anything, it's that life is short. Don't be afraid to go after what you want."

His face was sober, his hands gentle as he cupped her face. "You're all grown up, aren't you?"

She smiled at him. "Yeah, I am. You did a heck of a job with me."

He gave a short bark of laughter. "I guess I did." His expression once again became serious. "Are you going to follow your own advice? Are you going to fight for what you want?" He stared past her and she followed his gaze. Joshua was standing across the yard, his stance seemingly relaxed, but his eyes tracked her every move. "It won't be simple, you know. He won't be an easy man to live with."

Now that was an understatement if she'd ever heard one. "I know."

The wryness in her tone made him chuckle. "I see you know what you're getting into."

"I do," she whispered softly.

Her father nodded. "So be it. Stay by my side until the time comes."

Before she could get him to answer her question about what was going to happen, Joshua stepped to the center of the circle. All the people who had come gathered around. When everyone fell silent, Joshua began to speak. "Our pack has come under attack from the outside and from within." There were shouts and general mumbling, but he raised his hand for silence again. "Our leader and his mate have been brutally slain by people they trusted. Justice has been carried out and those men are no more."

The tension was thick enough to cut with a knife and Alex stood like the rest, waiting for Joshua to continue. He was a natural-born leader—an imposing figure with his tall, muscular build and his dark, piercing eyes. It wasn't so much the way he looked, she decided, but more the way he carried himself with complete confidence and composure.

"We all mourn their loss." Men nodded, while many of the women wiped tears from their eyes. Alex hadn't known these people, but even she felt their loss.

"But we must have a new leader," Joshua continued. "The pack cannot be left vulnerable."

Several men stepped forward, placing themselves in the ring with Joshua. Alex watched, wishing she knew what would happen next. Joshua nodded at each man in turn. She recognized one of them as Donovan Brody, the werewolf who'd had to slay his own kinsmen.

"We will challenge you for leadership." She didn't know the man who spoke, but he was tall and hugely built, not like the lean, muscular builds of most of the others.

Joshua shook his head. "I am not challenging for the leadership." The crowd sucked in a collective breath. Voices were raised in protest. Even the two men standing across from him appeared stunned.

"If you're not running for pack alpha, then who is?" An older man across from her shouted.

Her father stirred beside her and took a step forward. "I am." All heads turned toward him. Alex could see the wonder and disbelief on some faces.

"You abandoned that post years ago," the older man countered.

Her father nodded. "Yes, I did. I was young, I was angry and I was lost. I am none of those things now." His eyes swept over the challengers. "It is still my right as a member of this pack to challenge for leadership."

Alex stared at her father, amazed he would do such a thing. But then, he'd always been a protector, she realized. And now that their home and neighborhood were lost to him, he needed someone or something new to focus all those protective instincts on. When she thought about it, she couldn't think of anyone better for the position, except maybe Joshua.

"What say you, Striker?" Donovan Brody took an aggressive step forward.

Joshua looked toward James. "The Striker family has always supported the LeVeau family. That has not changed."

"You're only supporting him because you want the woman." Another man strode angrily into the circle.

Joshua shrugged, but didn't deny the accusation. "That is a separate issue, Gavin, and will be dealt with after this one is settled." The other man glared at him, but took a step back.

Alex's stomach was churning. What would happen if her father wasn't accepted as leader? What if he had to fight? What if he were killed? Her breathing was getting shallower, so she forced herself to breathe deeply. She had no idea what a challenge entailed, but it couldn't be good. These were a brutal people.

Her thoughts brought her up short. She might not know what would happen, but her father did. These were his people. God, she was so confused.

Her hands were clamped into fists at her sides as she watched the drama unfold. A part of her wanted to run to be with her father, but her instincts told her that that would be a mistake.

"Don't worry." The words were a mere whisper beside her. She flicked her gaze to her side for a moment and was surprised to see Joshua's younger brother, Simon, standing next to her. "Everything will be fine."

"How do you know?" Her words sounded angry and

belligerent even to her own ears, but he seemed to take no offense.

"I don't really know your father, but I remember how things were when he was leader of the pack. I was just a young man when he left. But I do know the legends of James LeVeau. He's not the sort of man who would start something he couldn't finish."

Alex forced her fingers to unclench. Simon was right. She had to trust her father. "Thank you," she whispered back to him. Simon nodded and they both watched as several men stepped back until only four remained in the circle—Joshua, her father, Donovan Brody and one other man.

The crowd was growing restless as the younger men stared at her father. He stared back at them, waiting patiently.

"What will it be?" Joshua queried both men. "Do you fight or do you accept James LeVeau Riley as alpha?"

The larger of the two men, the one that was unknown to her, nodded at her father. "I will accept James LeVeau. My father always spoke very highly of you."

Her father nodded back at the man. "Grady."

Donovan shook his head. "I will challenge."

Joshua nodded. "So be it."

Alex bit her lip to keep from crying out as both men stripped off their shirts, tossing them aside. She could feel the growing excitement in the crowd as they began to circle one another. They were both exceptional specimens of manhood, but only one of them was her father. She tried to swallow but her throat was too dry. She twisted her hands in the tails of the shirt, unable to pull her eyes away from the scene unfolding before her.

Donovan lunged first. Her father easily sidestepped him and waited while the younger man gathered himself once again. She wanted to yell at her father. He seemed so relaxed and unconcerned. Then she saw his eyes. His body might be relaxed, but his eyes told another tale. There was death in those eyes. The other man would back down or her father would kill him.

Oh, God. What was happening to her world?

Alex stifled a scream as Donovan attacked again. James

met his lunge this time and the two of them grappled, neither able to gain the upper hand. Dust flew around them as people began to chant in a language she didn't understand.

The fight ended so quickly that Alex couldn't believe it. In an astonishing display of fighting prowess and strength, her father flipped the younger man, tossing him to the ground. He then jumped on Donovan's back, hooking his strong forearm around his opponent's neck and arching it back. One twist and the other man would be dead. As it was, Donovan seemed to be having a difficult time breathing.

"Yield," her father growled out from between clenched teeth.

At first, she wasn't sure the younger man would yield. Her skin went clammy and her stomach lurched. Finally, after what seemed like an eternity, Donovan's head gave a small jerk. Her father released him and Donovan fell facedown in the dirt, gasping for air. Her father stood beside him, watching and waiting. And when Donovan rolled over onto his back, James LeVeau offered him his hand.

Once Donovan had regained his feet, he nodded at her father and took a step back. Joshua strode forward. "It has been decided. James LeVeau is once again alpha of the Wolf Creek pack."

Alex couldn't contain herself any longer. As cheers rang across the clearing, she raced forward and grabbed her father, hugging him tightly. "You could have been killed," she whispered.

Her father shook his head, gathering her close. "No, Alex. There was never any chance of that happening. Young Donovan wasn't really trying to beat me. This was more for show to satisfy the crowd."

Alex pulled back and glared first at her father and then Donovan Brody who was watching her with heat-filled eyes.

"Is that true?"

Donovan shrugged. "I want the man to be my future father-in-law, I'm not about to kill him am I?"

Alex took a step closer to her father. "I don't understand."

"Most everyone will easily accept your father as alpha." Donovan's tone was gentle. "He was one of the best leaders in the history of the pack. But the tradition of leadership challenge has to be upheld." Moving forward, he stroked his finger across her cheek. "The real challenge is for the right to claim you as mate."

Her gaze jerked to Joshua who was standing there with his arms crossed casually across his chest. "Did you know this?" He inclined his head toward her. "So everyone here knew that except me?" Anger coursed through her veins, firing her blood. "It was only stupid, uninformed me who wasn't aware that I'm supposed to provide the main event in today's entertainment."

"Now, Alex."

She whirled around and scowled at her father. "Don't you 'now, Alex', me. Somebody should have told me. Somebody should have asked me because the way I'm feeling right now, I'm not in the mood to accept anyone for mate. Ever!"

She started to stalk off, but Joshua wrapped his hand around her upper arm, stopping her. "It must be done. That is tradition."

Her eyes narrowed. "Tradition?" Her voice was soft, but she could see the worry clouding Joshua's face. Good, he should be worried. Donovan chuckled and she turned on him. "You find this amusing?"

"I find you magnificent and worthy to be my mate."

"Well good for you. I, on the other hand, don't find you very worthy at the moment."

"Alex," her father cautioned.

But she was beyond caution. The anger and fear of the past days coalesced in this one moment. She jerked out of Joshua's hold and stepped out from between the men. "Who else here thinks to challenge for the right to bed me?"

"Alex?" She could hear the anger in Joshua's voice as he pulled her around to face him.

"That's what this is about, isn't it? It isn't about the fact that I didn't know until a few days ago that I was a werewolf, or at least a half-breed. It isn't about the fact that the only life I've ever known is gone." The crowd had gone silent. Once again she tugged away from Joshua and faced them. Strangers all, they watched her.

She saw anger on some faces and shock on others. A few

245

wore expressions of understanding and sympathy, which had tears pricking at the backs of her eyes. She sucked in a breath. She would not let them see her as weak.

"None of you really want me. You don't know me." Several men protested and stepped forward, including the one her father had called Grady. "You want me because of some biological reaction that I can't control. You want me because I'm in heat." Her face burned as she spoke the words, but she wouldn't back down. Not now.

"See what diluting the blood lines will do. Disrespectful half-breed." An older man and woman stepped forward and spit on the ground at Alex's feet.

Joshua was by her side in a second. "That is my future mate you disrespect, Miles Jenson."

Jenson just laughed. "She is weak and will breed weak pups that will probably have to be put down."

Joshua was as still as a stone, but Alex could feel the winds of fury raging through him. He glanced over at her father, who had come to stand on her other side. Some silent communication seemed to pass between them and her father nodded. Joshua turned back to the angry couple. "If you do not wish to live among such tainted bloodlines, you are free to leave."

The older woman paled. "You would banish us?" Shock was evident in Jenson's voice. He pointed a trembling finger at her. "She is the one who is disrespectful to our ways."

"She doesn't know our ways," Joshua pointed out. "Three days ago, she had no idea who and what she truly was."

"Her father should have told her." The man was totally indignant.

"I hoped to spare her this." Her father finally spoke. He surveyed the crowd before him. "I knew many of you would hate her, despise her for her human blood. I didn't even know if she would be werewolf or human, so I waited. Because I knew that just as many of you would want to claim her as a mate. Women of our kind are not so plentiful any longer that a strong, healthy, beautiful one can be overlooked. Even if she is a half-breed."

Her father turned back to her and smiled. "So I raised her

as best I could. Alone. And she is a strong woman. The kind of mate any man would be proud to call his own." Her heart ached at the emotion in her father's voice. She wanted to reach out to him, but knew she had to let this scene play out. She knew instinctively both their futures were on the line.

"If you find that kind of woman offensive, then you are welcome to leave." Her father stared at the couple, who seemed to shrink beneath his gaze, and then he swept his eyes over everyone gathered. "And that goes for anyone else who thinks the same. I am alpha here now and she is my blood. Accept her or leave."

Alex held her breath. There were rumblings, but no one made any move to leave. Miles Jenson stepped forward and bowed his head low in submission. "My apology." Alex thought he might choke on it, for it certainly wasn't sincere, but her father graciously accepted it. She made a mental note to keep an eye on this man and his entire family. There would be more trouble from that corner for sure.

Joshua stepped forward. "That leaves the business of the challenge for Alex unresolved." He ignored her gasp of outrage. "She is mine." His voice was hard and brooked no disagreement. "Any who wish to challenge, do so now."

"Don't I have any say in this?" She faced him, standing so close that the tips of her slippers were touching his boots.

"No."

"No?" She poked him in the chest. "I don't think so. Mine is the only voice that matters."

Whirling around, she faced the crowd once again. "Before you all beat yourselves to a pulp, you'd best know one thing. I'll accept who I want to accept and no one else. Anyone who thinks they can claim me better be prepared to get a knife in the ribs."

"What a woman," Grady whispered almost soundlessly as he stepped forward.

"And who do you choose?" Brady Donovan's face was inscrutable, but she thought she caught a glimpse of some softness in his eyes. She could easily have fallen for him if she'd never met Joshua. But she had met Joshua and there was no accounting for taste when it came to love.

Turning, she glared at the man who had captured her heart. Joshua was overbearing, infuriating and sexy as hell. The thought of any other man touching her left her feeling cold. She gave him her back again and sensed his growing frustration. "I will have no one but Joshua Striker." There, let him think about that.

His large hands came down on her shoulders, turning her to face him. "The challenge must be met," he gritted out from between clenched teeth.

Alex had finally reached the limit of her patience and endurance. The adrenaline rush that had carried her through the challenge with her father had petered out. The anger that had sustained her was gone, leaving exhaustion in its wake. She swayed on her feet.

"You do whatever you have to do. In the meantime, I'm going to bed." Ignoring all the stares, she walked toward Joshua's home. "I'll be waiting," she called back over her shoulder. "If anyone other than Joshua gets in bed with me, they should be prepared to be castrated."

The men all shuddered as they watched her leave. Joshua was torn between laughter and going after her, throwing her over his shoulder and dragging her off to bed. The only reason he didn't do either was because, like it or not, the issue of the challenge had to be settled.

He watched the sway of her hips and then growled when he realized that half the men there were watching it too. He'd seen the exhaustion in her face and wanted to go and gather her into his arms and hold her while she slept. He wanted to pamper her, see to her needs and then...then he wanted to make her his.

Donovan and Grady watched until Alex let herself inside the front door of Joshua's home. They both grinned when the door slammed shut behind her. "Now that is a woman worth challenging for." Grady nodded his head in agreement with Donovan.

Joshua began to strip off his shirt. "Which one of you wishes to challenge first?" A heavy hand on his arm stopped him and he lowered his shirt back down.

Donovan was staring at him, a smile playing at the corners

of his mouth. "I said she was worth fighting for, not that I wanted to be turned into a eunuch when I beat your sorry ass."

Grady chuckled. "I like my parts right where they are, thank you very much."

Joshua was astounded. He knew neither man was afraid to challenge him, nor were they afraid of claiming Alex. What they were doing was showing their respect for her and for him in front of the entire pack.

"You've got balls to take on that one, Joshua." Isaiah slapped him on the back. "But I think she's exactly what you need."

James came to stand before him and all the men fell silent. "You accept her choice?"

They all nodded. James smiled and turned to Joshua. "She is unconventional and unused to our ways, but she will make you one hell of a mate."

"I know." Joshua had waited long enough. He strode toward his home, ignoring the catcalls and advice being hurtled at him from all quarters. "Isaiah, you're in charge for the next few days." Laughter and hooting followed his words. "We'll have the formal ceremony then."

He lengthened his stride, all of his thoughts on finally claiming the woman who was his.

Chapter Twenty-Four

Alex came awake in stages. It took her a second to remember where she was and, when she did, she wished she was still asleep. Yesterday's scene replayed in her head. God, had she really stalked off and left Joshua and the rest of them standing there with their mouths hanging open?

Burying her face in her pillow, she tried to block the memory. Yes, she had. It had been worth the embarrassment just to see that.

She had no idea what had happened after she'd made herself scarce. True to her word, she'd stripped down to Joshua's shirt and climbed into bed. She remembered stirring when someone had climbed in beside her, but since it was Joshua, she'd drifted right back to sleep. If he'd come with the notion of bedding her last night, he'd gotten a surprise. She'd been too exhausted to stay awake.

Now she really had to go to the bathroom and there was a muscled arm thrown around her waist. Joshua had gathered her close to him when he'd settled next to her and hadn't loosened his grip the entire night.

Carefully, she inched over to the edge of the bed, which actually wasn't that far away. Joshua was sprawled across most of the king-sized mattress. Although, she supposed she couldn't complain. It was his bed after all.

His fingers curled around her waist. "Where are you going?" he mumbled.

"Bathroom," she whispered, hoping he wouldn't really wake up. He loosened his grip and she slid out of bed. The wood floor was cool against the soles of her feet and her toes curled as she stood there looking down at him. If she was staying they'd need to get an area rug or two.

Standing beside the bed, she stared down at Joshua. Most people appeared different when they were asleep—softer, more vulnerable. But not Joshua. Even in sleep there was no softening in his rough-hewn face. If anything all the harsh angles and planes were even more prominent. His shaggy black hair appeared even darker, cushioned against the white pillowcase. The plain white sheet had slipped down to his waist, exposing the long muscular lines of his back. She was pleased to note the wounds on his back were already healing and would probably be gone within another day or two.

Trying not to make any noise, she padded to the bathroom. When she'd taken care of her most pressing needs, she faced herself in the mirror. Her short hair was tousled, but she looked better than she had in a while. It was amazing what a good night's sleep could do to restore a person. Her face was still pale, except for where colorful bruises marred her skin. Shadows still smudged the skin beneath her eyes, but overall she thought she looked better than she had yesterday.

Her skin began to tingle as she stood there. It had been doing that on and off all night, frequently waking her, but she'd been so exhausted, she'd managed to ignore it and fall back to sleep.

Alex unbuttoned the fastenings at the top of the shirt and shoved the material to one side, letting it slide down her arm. The furrow left by the bullet was still raw and tender, but it was healing. The long scratches from the wolf's claws would probably leave scars as well, but they too were beginning to heal.

She slid a few more buttons free and stared at her chest. Bruises were visible from where her seatbelt had restrained her. Her face was still colorful, but considering what she'd been through, she wasn't feeling too bad. Nothing a week or two of rest and food wouldn't cure. Even her feet were doing better. The salve Joshua put on her wounds after her bath had worked wonders. Like the rest of her, they were still battered but on the mend.

Alex started to button the shirt again, but her hands

stilled. Her skin began to itch wherever the fabric touched her body. Sliding the shirt down her arms, she let it slip off her body where it pooled around her feet. Her skin was hypersensitive and she moaned when she touched it. Heat began to seep through her like a living, breathing entity. Her breathing had quickened and she began to perspire.

She buried her face in her hands. What was wrong with her? Maybe she'd picked up an infection or something running around the woods?

Her womb spasmed and liquid seeped from her core. She raised her head to stare at the woman in the mirror. For a split second, she saw the face of a wolf semi-imposed over her face. Then she knew.

She was in heat.

This time there would be no reprieve. Once she took this step forward her life would be changed forever. There would be no going back.

Her breasts ached and she cupped them to try to ease the riot of sensations rocketing through her. It didn't help. If anything it made things worse. Her nipples were diamond hard against her palms. She shifted her hands and that slight pressure on her nipples had her groaning. Liquid trickled down the inside of her thigh.

Stumbling out of the bathroom, she made her way back to the bed. Joshua was wide awake, reclining against the pillows as if he'd been waiting for her. The sheet was pooled around his waist but did nothing to hide his erection, which had tented the fabric. His wide, tanned chest was exposed and Alex growled low in her chest.

Joshua smiled and opened his arms.

She didn't need a second invitation. She knelt on the end of the bed and crawled up his legs until she was sitting on his stomach. He wasn't the best looking man she'd ever seen, but there was something about him that drew her. She never tired of looking at him and knew she never would. He was sexy as all get out.

And he was hers.

Placing her hands flat on his chest, she stroked his skin. Muscles rippled beneath her fingers as she slid them over the magnificent expanse. She loved the crisp mat of hair that spread from nipple to nipple, the way the band of hair narrowed as it bisected his stomach and headed toward his groin.

He groaned as her fingers brushed his nipples. "Are you certain this is what you want?"

Poor Joshua. She could feel his erection pressing hard against her bottom, but still he was honorable to the last. It was one of the reasons she loved him.

In answer, she leaned forward until her breasts brushed against his chest. Oh, that felt lovely. Better than lovely. Then she placed her lips against his, showing him what she wanted.

His mouth was firm and warm as it pressed against hers. She flicked her tongue over his lips as they parted, inviting her inward. And she went. Unable to resist his lure, she stroked her tongue into his mouth, groaning when he sucked on it. He rested his hands lightly on her hips, his fingers gliding up and down her sides until she thought she'd scream in frustration.

Her sex was hot and wet and screaming for release. She spread her legs wide and rubbed herself against the hard muscles of his stomach, seeking relief from the constant ache. The movement caused her breasts to skim across his chest and the crisp hair stimulated them further.

She had to pull her mouth from his when breathing became more difficult. "Joshua?" There was a tinge of fear in her voice. She didn't quite know what to ask for. Didn't know what, if anything, could ease the clawing need within her.

He captured her breasts in his hands, his thumbs stroking her distended nipples. "It's all perfectly natural, Alex. Just go with it. Feel it. Allow yourself to sink into the heat."

She felt his words like a stroke against her skin and arched her back so that her breasts were brought into closer contact with his hands. "It hurts," she moaned as her vagina contracted again.

Joshua sat up in bed and lowered his head to her breasts. He flicked one and then the other with his tongue before settling his mouth over one and suckling. Alex threaded her fingers through his hair and held him close. God, that felt incredible. She felt the deep sucking motion between her thighs as if he were touching her there as well. Her hips moved of their own volition, undulating against the hard planes of his stomach.

She was close. So close. Release was just a caress, a touch, away. Her entire body tightened. Poised. Waiting.

He stroked his hands down her sides and inserted one of them between her legs. One touch. That's all it took. His finger brushed her clitoris and she exploded. Tipping her head back, she cried out as heat surged through her. Her body convulsed as pleasure washed over her. She could feel his lips at her breast, his hand between her thighs as a gush of warm liquid flooded onto his belly.

When it was over, she slumped against Joshua and he wrapped his arms around her. She felt warm and content as she nuzzled her face against his neck. He always smelled so good, kind of outdoorsy mixed with a musky male heat. She snuggled closer and the heat that had subsided began to build again.

She groaned. "I thought it would stop."

He nipped at her neck, making her gasp even as she tilted her head to one side to give him better access. "The only way to make it stop is if I take you. You need my cock inside you, filling you."

His graphic words had her in a state of full-blown arousal as quick as that. "Then do it." She pushed the sheet down and tried to take him into her, but he stopped her. She growled at him. And then was appalled at herself.

Joshua gripped her in his arms and rolled until she was beneath him. Planting her feet on the bed, she arched against him, practically purring with delight as his hard length stroked over the swollen folds of her sex.

Joshua laughed and smiled. She momentarily forgot all about sex in the presence of his happiness. It shone from his eyes, making him appear younger. He leaned down and kissed her nose, her cheeks, her forehead and her mouth. Soft kisses, biting kisses, hard kisses. She wanted them all and he gave them to her.

His tongue trailed a wet path between her breasts and he playfully lapped at her nipples. She shifted restlessly beneath him, but he trapped her against the mattress using his much larger and stronger body to subdue her movements.

"Joshua, do something." She was so close to coming again.

"I need to claim you in the traditional way of our people." He lazily sucked on her nipple, released it and then blew gently across it. He pressed his hips harder against her sex and she squirmed, trying to get his erection closer to where she needed it most.

Alex's skin was coated in a light sheen of sweat. Overwhelming need pulsed beneath her skin. At this point she didn't care what he did as long as he was inside her. "Anything," she panted.

He sat back on his knees, his sex jutting out in front of him. Long and proud, it bobbed toward her. A blue vein pulsed with need and as she watched a bead of pearly white fluid seeped from the tip. She licked her lips, wanting to taste him.

His mouth was set and a drop of sweat slid down his temple. "On your hands and knees."

She knew then what he wanted. How he planned to take her. And the idea of him claiming her in that manner sent a fresh wave of liquid heat rushing through her. She undulated in front of him, unable to move until the latest wave had crested and receded. But Joshua was finished waiting. He lifted her and flipped her onto her stomach.

Alex laughed at his unrestrained enthusiasm and then groaned as he pulled her up onto her hands and knees. She braced her hands on the bed and lowered her forehead to the pillow.

"Spread your legs." It was more growl than command and she widened her stance, letting her knees slide over the sheets until she was fully exposed to him.

His fingers molded the globes of her behind, kneading that tender flesh as he leaned closer. "You are so beautiful. So pink and wet and ready. And it's all for me, isn't it, Alex?"

"Yes," she groaned, gripping the sheet so forcefully with her fingers she was surprised the fabric didn't rip. Blood rushed to her head, making it impossible to hear anything but their harsh breathing and the sound of her pounding heart. The ripe smell of sex and need permeated the air, along with the faintest scent of something spicy that sent her arousal spiraling even higher.

"What is that smell?"

"You. Me. Us," he whispered, punctuating each word with a kiss down her spine. His fingers stroked over her swollen folds, dipping into her slit and retreating again. She pushed her bottom toward him, encouraging him to do it again. His fingers continued to circle her sex. She could feel liquid arousal sliding out of her.

"That's it," he crooned. "Your scent is intoxicating. It's telling me that your body is not only ready, but also willing to accept mine. And you are ready to accept me, aren't you, Alex? Once you become mine, I will never let you go." He withdrew his fingers and blew gently over her wet flesh making her vagina clench unbearably hard.

"Yes." At this point she'd say anything, do anything to get him to finally fuck her. She needed him inside her. The heat and the aching need were becoming unbearable.

"I'll take you whenever I want, wherever I want and you'll never deny me, will you?"

"Never." She gave him the words she knew he needed. She didn't begrudge them to him, knowing instinctively that after what had happened, he needed to assert his claim in every way possible. His wolf nature demanded it.

His fingers dug into her hips as he pulled her back toward him. She sucked in a deep breath and began to pant as he pressed the thick head of his penis just inside her opening. "More," she managed to gasp out between breaths.

"I claim you as my mate. Now and forever." Joshua surged forward, not stopping until he was buried to the hilt within her.

She felt the slightest twinge of pain and then there was only heat. She tilted her head back and cried out at the pleasure of being filled by him.

"I can't wait," he gritted out.

"Then don't," she gasped.

He slid his hands upward and beneath her until he was cupping her breasts in his hands. Holding her steady, he shifted his hips, pulling them back until only the tip of his cock was still within her. He pumped forward, slamming back into her.

Her inner muscles softened to accept him, even as they

rippled and clenched around him. It was amazing. There were almost too many sensations for her to take in at once. Her body was burning from the inside out.

Joshua continued to hammer into her body, but it still wasn't enough. She needed more. Catching the mating rhythm, she began to slam her bottom back to meet his thrust. The slap of their flesh as it met added to their joining, heightening Alex's pleasure.

Her lungs felt like they might burst as Joshua drove into her again and again. The smell of sex and spices grew thicker and her heart continued to pound harder and harder. She couldn't take much more. Every cell in her body was screaming with tension.

Joshua slid one hand down between her thighs and stroked the bundle of nerves at the apex. She came the moment he touched her. Her inner muscles clamped down hard on Joshua's shaft and he yelled with pleasure. Unbelievably, she felt him growing larger within her. He filled her so completely that the sensation was uncomfortable, bordering on painful. She tried to pull away, but was unable to dislodge him. His cock was locked inside her.

"Alex," he growled. He was still growing within her. She could feel the head of his cock reaching impossibly deep. Heat flooded her as he came. Joshua tilted back his head and howled as he emptied himself into her womb.

Shivers raced through her body and she came again. This time the convulsions were so hard she almost dislodged him from behind her. He gripped her hard and pumped his hips in short, hard jabs.

She lost all track of time, but finally she collapsed down onto the mattress, shaken and spent by the intensity of their joining. Joshua came down on top of her, still locked inside her. He shifted slightly to the side so that all his weight wasn't on her. His face was buried in her neck and his heart pounded against her back as he gasped for breath.

She wasn't in much better shape. All her various aches and pains which had been forgotten in the heat of passion were now making themselves known again. She shifted, trying to get more comfortable.

Joshua groaned and levered himself up on his forearms. He kissed her nape and all the way down the curve of her spine as he eased up onto his knees. They both groaned when he pulled his softening erection from her.

He fell back against the pillows and drew her into his arms. His lips were soft on her forehead as he brushed his fingers over her cheek. "Don't cry, my love."

She hadn't realized she was crying. She wiped her eyes, feeling emotional and stupid. "I'm sorry. I don't know what's wrong with me."

"It was the intensity and the beauty of our joining." He peppered her face with soft kisses before cradling her back against his shoulder. "That and hormones. There is nothing wrong with you." His voice, though soft, had an edge to it. "You are perfect."

She laughed as she nuzzled his neck. "I'll remind you that you said that when I'm doing something that gets on your nerves."

He stilled and then he chuckled. "You are mine now." There was a wealth of satisfaction and emotion in those four words.

"And you are mine."

His arms tightened around her.

"I love you," she whispered against his chest.

He shifted until she was lying on her back with him looming above her. His hand trembled as he pushed a lock of hair off her face. "The words, I love you, do not begin to express what you mean to me." His eyes seemed to get even darker as she watched him. "You are everything to me. The air I breathe. My reason for living. You brought joy to a life of duty and responsibility. There is nothing I would not do to make you happy."

"Oh, Joshua."

He shook himself and gave her a lopsided grin. "And I may never say those words again as long as we live."

She laughed, knowing that was what he'd intended. "It doesn't matter if you never say them again. I know what you feel here." She placed her palm over his heart.

Joshua slid his hand over her heart and smiled when he felt the heavy thud. "I claim you as my mate, Alexandra Riley

Striker. Mine to keep until the day I die."

"I claim you as well, Joshua Striker. Mine to keep until the day I die."

As a tear slid from her eye, he leaned over and kissed her. Even though she was exhausted, the familiar heat began to slide through her body. "Again?"

He shifted so that she was beneath him once again. She could feel the heavy weight of his erection against her hip.

"Again," he whispered as he traced the curve of her ear. "And again. And again."

Alex parted her lips and sighed. His tongue stroked over them and she decided her body wasn't quite that tired after all.

Chapter Twenty-Five

Joshua sighed with contentment as Alex snuggled closer to him. He'd lost count of how many times he'd made love to her. She completed him. Their joining had changed him in ways he couldn't even comprehend yet. Certainly their life together would be a challenge. He grinned at the thought. Even when she was an old lady, she'd be keeping him and their children in line.

His hand slid over her belly. His children. Just the thought of her thick and ripe with child made him want to howl. It was still too early for that to happen. Female werewolves rarely ever conceived their first time. Nature gave them a few years to mature before they reached their peak fertile years. Still, the thought of it was overwhelming. He managed to contain himself, but just barely. He wanted the entire world to know that she was his.

He couldn't wait until she made her first change. Her fur would be soft and various shades of brown. She was going to be a beautiful she-wolf and he couldn't wait to take her on her first run through the forest. Perhaps he'd even take her back to the falls. She'd like that.

Closing his eyes, he sighed again. He'd have to feed her when she woke again. She hadn't eaten before she went to bed last night and she needed to keep up her strength.

She stirred beside him, her eyes fluttering open. "Hi." Her gaze was shy and her cheeks turned a beguiling shade of pink.

"Good morning." Joshua felt his cock stir yet again and barely stifled a groan. Alex was too sore after last night. Plus, if they didn't show themselves soon, he had a feeling his soon-to-be father-in-law would be pounding on the front door.

Alex absently began to tease his chest with her short fingernails. Joshua closed his eyes and arched into her touch. Her hand moved lower, bumping against his erection. His eyes flew open and he swore when she wrapped her fingers around him. "It's too soon. You're sore."

She batted her eyelashes playfully. "Not that sore."

He growled and rolled out of bed, dragging her with him. Alex squealed and then laughed as he tossed her over his shoulder and carried her into the bathroom. She reached down and pinched his butt. Joshua was so surprised he almost dropped her.

Alex grabbed onto his flanks and gave a yell before dissolving into laughter again.

"Think that's funny, do you?" he grumbled as he turned on the taps in the shower. She didn't answer, but he could hear her snickering under her breath. Two could play this game. Sliding his hand up her thighs, he palmed one sweet cheek of her ass.

She stilled. "Joshua." He could hear the nervous excitement in her voice.

"What?" he innocently asked as he caressed the other cheek before sliding his fingers into the crease of her behind. "You don't like me touching your gorgeous butt?" He freed his fingers and gave her a smart smack on her butt. She jumped and began to squirm so he did it again.

"Let me down you big bully," she grouched.

Joshua laughed and swung her around, planting a hard, quick kiss on her lips. Alex wrapped her legs around his waist and her arms around his neck. He could see the pleasure in her eyes even as she groused. "You owe me for that."

"Do I now?" He stepped beneath the spray with her still in his arms.

"Uh huh." She nodded as she leaned down and grabbed the bar of soap and started to rub it over his shoulders.

All laughter fled as he stood there, absorbing her love and care as she washed him. Not since he was a very small child had anyone done anything like this for him. Oblivious to the emotions bubbling within him, Alex put the soap back on the ledge and ran her fingers through his hair. "I love your hair. Did I tell you that?" He shook his head, unable to speak past the lump in his throat. "Well, I do. It's so thick and gorgeous."

His cock was as hard as steel. He wanted Alex. Badly. The way she was touching him made him want to tip back his head and howl with pleasure. He needed to claim her. Again.

"Joshua." She stilled as if suddenly sensing his change of mood. "What's wrong?"

"I need you," he ground out from between his clenched teeth. He was hanging on by a thread. Alex was warm and wet in his arms, her sweet scent drifting up to his nostrils. She was as aroused as he was.

Clasping his face in her hands, she leaned down until their noses were touching. "Then take me."

He turned and lifted her higher as he pressed her back against the wall. She cried out and arched her back as it hit the cool tile. Joshua took advantage of her out-thrust breasts and lapped at one firm, juicy nipple.

Alex slid her fingers into his hair and fisted in it, holding him to her as he opened his mouth and took her inside. She tightened her legs around his waist as he suckled her.

"More," she urged, gasping as he transferred his attention to her other breast. She squirmed, trying to get the head of his cock inside her. "Joshua."

His name came out of her much like a wail. God, she'd never needed anything like she needed Joshua inside her. Now. After last night, she figured it would be quite some time before she'd feel this kind of arousal again.

All it had taken was one look.

His mood had changed swiftly from one of teasing to lustful in a heartbeat. Alex didn't care that she was slightly sore after a night of intense lovemaking. His need awoke hers, stoking the flames within, making the heat burn in her veins.

She wiggled, trying to get closer to him. His erection was bumping against her sex, teasing her with each touch. Her folds were slick and swollen with need. Joshua tongued her turgid nipple and sucked it into his mouth. Heat flashed from her breast to her core.

Unable to stand it any longer, she tugged at his head. He released her nipple with a loud, wet pop. His eyes were the same color as rich, thick coffee as he leaned in closer, using his lower body to pin her against the wall. Water beat down on them, the bulk of it deflected by his broad back.

Keeping his gaze locked with hers, he reached between her legs and spread the folds of her sex wide. "You're always hot and wet." She could hear the pleasure in his voice.

She jerked when he slid one finger inside her. As much as she wanted him, there was no escaping the fact her sheath was swollen and tender after last night. He pulled his hand away from her and dropped his head on her shoulder. "Alex," he began, but she stopped him.

"I want you." Her nails dug into his thick shoulders as she levered herself over the tip of his shaft.

"Are you sure?" He raised his head and searched her face.

"Yes."

He flexed his hips then, slowly burying his erection in her one inch at a time. He went slowly, giving her inner muscles a chance to relax and accept him. By the time he was seated to the hilt, she was panting hard and shivering. His cock filled her. His body surrounded her.

She could smell him on her skin, that unique scent of soap and musk and man. Her nose twitched as she caught the scent of something new. It was a deeper, richer smell, one that reached down inside her and excited her most primitive self. Wolf. Alex knew she was scenting his wolf and wondered if he could do the same with her.

"I need to fuck you." His voice was low, guttural, as he sucked air into his lungs.

"Do it." She used her grip on his flanks to lift herself up an inch before dropping back down.

Joshua's control snapped. Grasping her ass in his hands, he began to thrust. Every time he pulled almost all the way out of her, Alex struggled to keep him locked inside her. When he thrust back in, she sighed with relief. They belonged together.

The pace quickened, their bodies moving in perfect synchronicity. All the hair on her nape stood on end. Her limbs felt heavy, yet energy thrummed through her. She was close.

Could feel her orgasm gathering low in her belly.

As he continued to thrust, Joshua leaned down and nipped at the base of her neck. Alex screamed with pleasure. Her inner muscles contracted and liquid flooded her core. Her orgasm washed over her. Joshua jerked. Throwing back his head, he yelled her name as he came within her.

She wrapped her arms more securely around him, never wanting to let him go.

They stayed locked in each other's arms until the water pouring down on them turned cool. She shivered. Joshua swore and slowly released her until she was standing on her own two feet. She leaned against the tiled wall for support as he adjusted the water temperature.

"I didn't mean to do that." He looked so aggravated she laughed.

He just stared at her and slowly a smile crossed his face.

"I'm not complaining," she informed him. Reaching around him, she grabbed a washcloth and started scrubbing. "Well, I might complain about the cold shower, but not about what happened before that."

Joshua gave a quick bark of laughter before grabbing the soap and making sure that every part of her was clean.

Later that night, Alex stood on the edge of the woods and shivered. The moon was almost full and the night was cool. Joshua stood behind her, his hands on her bare shoulders. "Take your time. There's no rush."

Easy for him to say.

She was standing here as naked as the day she was born with nothing but his bare body protecting her from the view of the others. Everyone was waiting for her to make her first change.

Their official joining ceremony had passed by in a blur. Ritual words had been said and vows exchanged. Alex wished she could remember exactly what it was she'd agreed to, but she'd been too nervous to pay much attention. She inwardly shrugged. What was done was done. She'd find out the details later. Surrounded by all the members of the pack, it had been all she could do to keep from turning and running.

She loved Joshua. Of that she had no doubt. But the ceremony was the final nail in the coffin of her old life. There really was no going back. She was now a member of the Wolf Creek pack. Some people welcomed her with open arms, while just as many were suspicious or downright hostile.

She shivered again. And within a few moments, she'd be changed forever.

That is if she could manage the transformation.

Joshua had explained it all to her earlier this morning after they'd finished their shower. Over breakfast, he'd told her it was perfectly natural and he had every faith in her that she could do it. She wasn't so certain. She'd overheard several men and women speculating on whether or not a half-breed could actually go through the change and take wolf form.

"It's all right, Alex." Joshua's voice was low as he whispered in her ear. "If it doesn't happen now, we'll try again another time. Don't put so much pressure on yourself."

"I want to do this, but I'm not sure I can." There. She'd said it. Voiced her fear out loud. "Part of me wants it to happen, but part of me is scared."

He wrapped his arms around her and gave her a quick squeeze of reassurance. She felt surrounded by his love and acceptance.

"That's perfectly understandable. You've been through so much in the past few days. If you need more time, we'll wait."

"Really?" The last thing she wanted to do was to disappoint or shame him in front of the other members of the pack.

"Really."

Joshua sounded certain, but she could hear the muttering starting behind her. The crowd was getting restless.

"Tell me again what I'm supposed to do."

Joshua sighed so hard her hair fluttered. "Alex, don't try so hard. Just relax, close your eyes and feel your wolf. She's there. Right beneath the surface of your skin. You've felt her before. She's familiar to you."

Closing her eyes, she let Joshua's voice and words seep into her soul. He was right. She had felt her wolf within her.

Now that she knew what it was, she realized she'd been feeling that other presence inside her for quite some time now. She'd even briefly glimpsed her wolf in the bathroom mirror before Joshua had claimed her.

"I want to share the night and the woods with you. Show you all the wonders that exist in the world of the wolf. It's not all bad, my love."

Alex could hear the aching in Joshua's voice. She wanted to share that with him too. Taking a deep breath, she let it out slowly and let her mind drift. The wolf was there in her mind's eye. Alex studied her. She was smaller than Joshua's wolf, but that was to be expected. Her fur was thick and lush, a rainbow of browns from mahogany to tawny brown and every shade in between. But it was the eyes that caught her attention. The eyes were very familiar to her. They were the same pale, silvery gray eyes she'd seen in the mirror since she was a child.

The wolf was her and she was the wolf. She got it now. They weren't separate beings at all, but two sides of the same coin.

As if acceptance was all that was needed, Alex felt something beginning to ripple beneath her skin. Joshua loosened his hold on her.

"Let it happen," he whispered before stepping back.

Alex reached out to the wolf within her, embracing her totally. The wolf surged forward, wanting to be released from its human form. She fell to her hands and knees and arched her back. Bones cracked and reformed. Fur covered her limbs. Her face contorted, her jaw lengthening. Her vision changed, growing sharper. Smells assaulted her from all around. Strength rippled through her muscles.

She took a step and stumbled. A low growl came from within her. She blinked, all of a sudden realizing that she was no longer human. She was wolf. It felt strange. Yet she was still herself. The primal urges of the wolf were there, but she was still able to think and reason.

My love.

Alex spun around and came face-to-face or rather muzzle-to-muzzle with the familiar, large black wolf. Joshua. She'd heard him in her mind.

Are you all right?

She could hear the concern even though no words had been spoken aloud. Concentrating on him, she nodded. *I'm fine.*

Then run, little wolf. Stretch your legs and run.

Alex gave a happy yip and padded toward the forest. She didn't have to look behind her to know Joshua was with her. She could sense his presence. He kept pace as she picked up speed.

Other wolves ran alongside them. Some of them passed her, disappearing into the forest, while a small, select group ran with them for almost an hour. She recognized most of them and knew Joshua's brothers and her father were with them, protecting her and sharing in her first run as a wolf.

Alex had never experienced anything like this in her life. Everything seemed more somehow—brighter, more vibrant— just more. She felt totally alive and at one with her surroundings. She knew where every creature of the forest was for at least half a mile, from birds to squirrels to a lone black bear. The smell of the rich, dark earth filled her nostrils. She could see easily even though it was nighttime.

She didn't want it to end, but Joshua started to herd her back toward the compound, nipping at her when she dared to try to veer away from him. She snapped back, but he didn't look impressed. Instead, he growled at her. Not willing to push her luck, she reluctantly turned back.

Don't worry, little wolf. There will be more times to run.

Can anyone else hear us?

No. The only mental communication is between mated pairs.

That was a relief to Alex. She didn't want to have to worry about other people being able to hear her thoughts. *Can you hear me all the time?* She wasn't sure she liked that idea.

Joshua's laughter rang in her ears. *No. We have to concentrate to hear or send a thought.*

That's a relief.

The compound came into sight and Alex was suddenly glad. As much as she'd enjoyed the experience, she was ready to become human again. Stopping on the edge of the forest, she closed her eyes and embraced her human form. She felt her wolf protest, but sent out waves of assurance that the wolf would have many more times to run in the future. Her bones began to shift and reform once again. Alex was surprised that it didn't hurt. Not really. It was disorienting for a moment, but then it was over.

Alex slumped on the soft forest floor, smelling the pine trees and feeling the moss beneath her. Strong arms picked her up from the ground. Joshua. She'd know his touch anywhere.

"Thank you." His husky voice was filled with unspoken emotion. "Thank you for accepting me and joining your life with mine."

Alex touched his face. It still amazed her how much this man had come to mean to her in such a short time. She loved him. He was a part of her life now. Forever. "Thank you for sharing your life with me."

His arms tightened around her as his mouth came down on hers. Their lips melded, their breath mingled, as Joshua carried her across the compound to their home.

In the distance, a lone wolf began to howl. It was quickly joined by another wolf. Then another. Until finally a whole chorus of wolves sang to them. Alex's heart began to pound. She understood what they were saying. They were singing to her, welcoming her into the pack.

Joshua paused outside their door and they both stood and listened until the last howl faded. Then he carried her inside and kicked the door shut behind him.

Epilogue

James LeVeau Riley stood with his hands on his hips and looked upward. Stars peppered the night sky, illuminating the dark woods beyond the compound. He watched as Joshua carried his daughter back to their home and shut the world outside.

Alex had achieved her wolf form and was now completely a werewolf. She would grow into her newfound powers in the weeks ahead with her mate by her side. Pride filled him. She was a woman any man would be proud to call daughter.

Joshua had claimed his daughter in the tradition of their people. It was done. He wasn't sure how he felt about it. On one hand, he was glad to have her settled. On the other hand, his little girl was gone and a grown woman remained. Their relationship would be different from now on.

It was good for both of them. He was looking forward to his first lone run with Alex. She was a beautiful wolf and that wasn't just parental pride talking. The joining ceremony today had given the entire community something to celebrate. Unfortunately the burial of his brother and sister-in-law would be next.

He sensed a kindred soul in the darkness. He wasn't alone, but no one approached him. A sense of loneliness washed over him as he thought about his wife, Leda. Even after all these years he missed her. Missed the feeling of togetherness, of solidarity, of belonging that came with loving and mating with someone.

His daughter had that now, and for that, he was eternally grateful. Turning, he headed toward his brother's house, now his home once again. There was much work to be done. There were still bounty hunters who wanted them dead. And James wasn't convinced all the traitors had been sniffed out of the pack. They'd need to be extra vigilant. The women and children had to be protected at all costs.

Isaiah watched James LeVeau walk away. He was grateful to the older man for challenging for the position as alpha. If not for him, Joshua would have certainly challenged, especially with possession of Alex at stake. That would have left Isaiah in the position of having to accept the duty of Striker or handing it off to one of his younger brothers, who were nowhere near ready to handle the responsibility.

Just thinking about it made his skin itch. The walls of the compound seemed to close in as they always did. His father had never understood him. No one in his family seemed to understand he needed to be free in order to survive.

Or maybe they did.

Joshua had taken over the position of Striker instead of Isaiah as if he'd been born to it. And not once had his younger brother ever criticized him for stepping aside and not accepting the responsibility. That was good, especially now with everything that had happened. Things would be tense for a while, but they would survive. It was what they did.

His new sister-in-law would help ease Joshua's burden and for that Isaiah was grateful, because as soon as things calmed down he was leaving for a while. He didn't know where he was going, only that he needed to get away by himself. The violence was growing within him and if he didn't get away, he was afraid it might actually hurt someone in his family.

He turned away, ripping off his clothing as he went. He needed to run free and untethered. Shifting as he ran, he disappeared into the thick forest, his clothing left lying in the dirt.

About the Author

To learn more about N.J. Walters, please visit www.njwalters.com. Send an email to N.J. Walters at njwalters22@yahoo.ca or join her Yahoo! group to join in the fun with other readers as well as N.J. http://groups.yahoo.com/group/awakeningdesires

GREAT
CHEAP
FUN

Discover eBooks!

THE FASTEST WAY TO GET THE HOTTEST NAMES

Get your favorite authors on your favorite reader, long before they're
out in print! Ebooks from Samhain go wherever you go, and work with
whatever you carry—Palm, PDF, Mobi, and more.

samhain
publishing ltd

WWW.SAMHAINPUBLISHING.COM